FINAL WHISTLE

By the same author in the
Lincolnshire Murder Mystery Series

Dead Spit
Seaside Snatch
Once Bitten
Dead Jealous
Or Not To Be
Twelve Days
Sacrificial Lamb
In Plain Sight
Tissue of Lies

You can contact the author by e-mail at:
carysmithwriter@yahoo.co.uk

AN INGA LARSSON NOVEL

FINAL WHISTLE

Cary Smith

FINAL WHISTLE

Copyright © 2019 Cary Smith

All rights reserved, including the right to reproduce this book, or portions thereof in any form. No part of this text may be reproduced, transmitted, downloaded, decompiled, reverse engineered, or stored, in any form or introduced into any information storage and retrieval system, in any form or by any means, whether electronic or mechanical without the express written permission of the author.

This is a work of fiction. Names and characters are the product of the author's imagination and any resemblance to actual persons, living or dead, is entirely coincidental.

The views expressed in this work are solely those of the author and do not necessarily reflect the views of the publisher, and the publisher hereby disclaims any responsibility for them.

ISBN: 978-0-244-82099-2

PublishNation
www.publishnation.co.uk

The problem with doing nothing is
not knowing when you are finished.
— *Nelson De Mille*

1

November 2018

Sharing a breakfast table with a man is not something I was at all used to at the time. To calculate the number of occasions in my life would in my case, never be a matter of counting the fingers on two or more hands and add a few toes if not an abacus, as some would need to. If I'm being perfectly honest and colouring up as I say this, the thumbs on both hands would be about the right figure. Tall lanky creep Jeremy Dale and now dear Edward are the pair who spring to mind.

Eating breakfast together I'm talking about!

With the Dale swine I should certainly have known better than to have anything to do with him, let alone share a breakfast table. Wasn't even a decent breakfast as it happens; white of the sunny side up a solitary egg was all runny, there was no black pudding and the bacon was too salty.

'Shhh,' I chided the moment I spied Edward enter my breakfast kitchen in his light grey suit and bright white shirt. 'They've just been saying there's been what sounds like a murder.'

This was in fact only the third time he had stayed over for a couple of nights in case you are wondering. In one of the spare rooms I might add before too many of you get on your high horse and start to judge.

'Is that right?' he sighed and slipped onto a wooden chair with his back against the wall across the table from where I was stood.

'Up in Washingborough of all places apparently,' I said and realized he probably had no idea where the village was. 'Just outside Lincoln. You'd never think it would you?'

'Please don't get all supercilious Jacqueline, about where's the right place for a murder. Just be media speculation and quite possibly nothing of the sort when it turns out. Chances are these days it'll just be another stabbing. Gone are the days when they had real life reporters on the ground with pencil and pad. Nowadays most of it is just asinine ideas they pick up from these troll people on Twitter.'

'There's some lovely properties up there, not the sort of thing you expect to be honest.'

'I would,' he responded. 'Got more to lose.' Edward picked up a slice of wholemeal toast from the metal rack, flipped it over to see it was well done on both sides and slipped it onto his plate. 'More money than sense quite often seems to me. Any other news?'

'Something about putting a load of money into ambulance service improvements for the elderly and a cash machine has been ripped from the wall in North Somercoates.'

'All hold the front page stuff then,' was his sarcasm.

'And I think they said a new marina is about to approved for Cherry Willingham.'

'That as exciting as it gets around here?' he asked with a snigger. 'Might I suggest we have more important things to discuss than tittle tattle about a suspicious death which'll probably turn out to be nothing of the sort when it comes to it, or about nicking a cash machine?'

'You and your horses.'

'No Jacqueline. You and your horse,' said Edward as he spread marmalade straight onto his toast. Something I had noticed about him the first time he'd stayed over. Coating his morning toast in a whole range of different preserves, but always without butter or spread which once upon a time was margarine. Another thing, he never puts salt and pepper on his food. The salt issue I can understand, but a spot of pepper in the right place is all part of the process of seasoning our food surely. I've cut down on gravy in the past decade as sauces have taken over, but Edward is ahead of me and has none at all. Not wishing he says to spoil the individual tastes of the food. I only have a little these days with roast meat but not with anything else.

'I'm sorry, but I'm still thinking about it,' was me being a tease.

Edward glanced at his watch. 'You'd better get a move on. The French won't hold their horses - to coin a phrase,' he thought was more amusing than I did.

'It's a lot of money...' I continued the ploy and then had to wait for him to empty his mouth.

'To be made remember. Horses breed and when they breed they're worth money, a lot of money. Plus a few quid here and there they might win for you in the meantime. It really is a win, win situation. To be honest the racing is just a front to keep joe public amused while all the business is going on in the background.'

'I know there's money to be made in breeding,' I said as I placed a mug on the spare mat at my place setting. 'So you keep reminding me.'

'It's what I do. I invest in horses for people and remember money makes the world go around.' This handsome man was back to his toast.

'I'm not sure I want my world to go around,' I said as I plopped down onto my chair opposite Edward and rested my arms on the table.

'Leave it high and dry in a bank with their piddly little interest rates, for other people to use and make money from. Why should it be crooked bankers who make money off your back, why not you? Why shouldn't you be the one to make money or is it a five letter dirty word? It's a strong sound investment.'

'To be honest, it's probably because I don't really have a desperate need for it,' was me really being too honest.

'Everybody needs money,' he chortled.

'For what for example?'

'For whatever you want,' he tossed back. 'A new bigger house, a world cruise - you name it. A wise investment in the morning and you could be heading for outer space in one of Branson's spaceships.'

'I get sick in a pedalo and anyway Oakdenne House is my family home. The lady's not for moving.'

'Are you really saying you're quite willing to let me go to the sales in the morning, buy horses for a lot of people with bulging wallets and more money than sense and you're going to leave yours to go mouldy in some bank somewhere?'

'P'raps just one.'

'One horse? And then we'll see how it goes?' the questions were all over his face as well as verbal.

'Would you mind?' I asked softly and just placed my warm hand on his. He was such a good man.

'If it's what you want. There'll be other sales.'

'But not as big as this one.'

'True of course,' he told me and took the last bite of his toast. I'd seen lime and coconut marmalade in a farm shop, but I'd not tried it. Edward certainly seemed to enjoy the taste. 'Breakfast?' he queried with a slight wave of his hand now free of toast.

I shrugged. 'Feel a bit off this morning.' It was the parting and probably because all this was so new to me I always felt like this. There was no way I was going to admit it to anyone, least of all Edward, but it has always been the loneliness I hate. The hours I've spent in the big house over the years all alone with never a word from anyone. Except Molly my cleaner of course and those who want something from me. At least the rest of my day would be free once Edward had headed off to the Eurotunnel. Yes I'd be on my own, but on my own without any commitments, any demands on my time or willingness to help. Chance to slip into town I'd decided, have a coffee, do a spot of people watching, maybe have a sneaky cake.

'You are all right?' he asked and then drank his coffee.

'I'll be fine.'

'Much on today?' he enquired.

'Need to pop into town.' Truth was I had no real need to go anywhere, but if I stayed in the chances were the phone would ring, someone would almost demand my help and I'd feel obliged as you do. I have never been the sort of person who can just ignore the rings and let it run to answerphone. Chances are I'd be persuaded to do someone a favour and then when it was all done and dusted they'd be at home with their families, their husbands and the kids, but what about me? Too late to do anything, too late to go anywhere, just me and my Kindle or a spot of television.

'Do you feel better now?' I asked. 'You were certainly stressed when you arrived.'

'Just what I needed after the week I'd had. Quiet couple of days, good company, lovely food and a drop of fine wine. Perfect.'

'I'm pleased.'

Edward looked at his watch, took another good drink of coffee and was on his feet. 'Time and tide,' and I just sat there and watched him just saunter off through the latched door to take him up the back stairs.

It was all too ridiculous for words. Edward had no idea at all just how lonely I was at times, but then how would he? It was not something I'd ever admitted to anyone, least of all him. To land him with my troubles wouldn't be at all fair. He was a very busy successful man, but above all he was kind and thoughtful which I was very grateful for. The moment he arrived in Normandy I knew he'd give me a call. He might be miles away, abroad quite often but I always knew he was there if I needed him. Always a cheery word and above all somebody I knew I could trust at last.

Not like the others who might phone. Chances are it'd be somebody from the drop-in group for lonely people the council set up with a grant from somewhere or other. How ridiculous. Get the desperately lonely like I am at times, to help the lonely and then leave me on my own.

More than a few times at the end of the day all those so-called lonely people just saunter away and leave me stood there forsaken with the keys in my hand. Nobody ever asks how I am, do I have company for the evening? Just dump me at the end of the day when they'd wrung out the best I can offer to leave me empty and alone. The irony got to me the most, the way they just assumed.

Come the worst part of the day, especially in mid-winter and I am always the one crying out for somebody, anybody just another voice, a bit of company.

I heard Edward bustling about upstairs and knew exactly what was going on. He'd be carrying his holdall down the stairs, out the front door and tossing it onto the back seat the way he always did. Same procedure as the previous couple of times he'd stayed over, so I was used to the ritual by now. He'd scamper back upstairs next for one last look around and pop into the en suite. Then I'd hear him flush the loo, before he'd come back down and in no time at all I knew I'd be on my own again.

'Sure you've got everything?' had become part of the goodbye procedure. I was still seated when he reached me to wrap his strong arms around me, pull me in close and kiss me fully on the lips. When as he moved away he tossed his car keys in the air and caught them one handed in a nonchalant gesture. Such a well groomed man with those dark eyebrows and just a tiny whisper of grey above his ears.

'You're buying one horse. Am I right?'

'I've upped the anti a bit,' I admitted with a cheeky grin. 'If I'm doing this, might as well do it properly.'

'D'you know I thought for a moment there...' He shook his head from side to side and smiled down to me. 'Up to what?' he asked as he took hold of my hand.

'Forty,' I replied, slipped the folded cheque from the top pocket in my blouse and handed it to him.

'Pounds?'

'You said make it Euros.'

'What?' he said.

'Joke.'

He shook his head, exhaled and I sensed just a hint of pleasure in his look as he opened it and peered at the cheque. 'I might even manage to get one with all four legs,' he bent down and kissed my cheek and for a moment I just wallowed in the smell of the man. 'Anything else?' he asked as he moved away again. I so wanted to tell him not to go. He really didn't have to, in fact he didn't have to work; I most certainly had more than enough for the pair of us to live a good life. Nothing over-the-top and ultra-luxurious in the way of yachts and private jets, but we could most certainly have a good life together.

'I'm fine,' I said when the truth was I was anything but. 'Off you get.'

The moment the front door closed, and the letterbox responded with a tinny clank I was journeying towards one of my bad heads. I really should have talked to Edward, should have explained how I'd not been wholly truthful about my situation.

Next time I told myself as I stood up and started to clear away what little there was on the kitchen table. Next time I really would come clean, I promised myself.

2

I make no apologies for ruffling a few feathers as I tell my side of the story, and hope you are prepared for the way I am. Too sanguine and honest for my own good I think, would be most people's opinion.

This tale most certainly will be warts and all because it is exactly how you'll find me and I make no excuses. I'm quite sure the modern thought police and other outraged sensitive souls will find fault with my intelligent yet less than politically correct terminology. If that is the case I'm afraid you'll have to like it or lump it. If this book is not your kettle of fish at all, you can always hand it in to a charity shop or chuck it in the recycle bin.

I realize some of you will regard me as being somewhat antediluvian in my outlook, but so be it, that's just the way I am.

For instance, I am forever coming across alarmingly ridiculous suggestions from dotty snowflake pressure groups suggesting nonsense such as not allowing schools to call female pupils 'girls', but are quite happy for the lads to be addressed as 'boys'. How bizarre and politically driven is such utter baloney?

Don't get me started on schools, or we'll be here for ages. To my mind going back to the basic rules of schooling are long overdue. Turn up on time in the correct uniform for all ages. No phones in school, sit up straight, face the teacher and be silent in class are just the basics. Alas too many parents these days have just given into their kids demands for all this perpetual self-expression nonsense. Demanding they choose what to wear, what to eat, how not to behave, what car the family will buy, and as a result inevitably end up being almost unemployable.

Ah well, not my problem.

So, where was I? Oh yes, you are being given the opportunity to read this right now, because I thought I'd tell my side of the story rather than wait for events to create a big hoo-ha in the scurrilous media's once it all comes to court. We all know what they're like, just grab hold of it and get it all round their necks. Do their very best shouting and screaming to make something out of nothing and make a bee line for the angle which happens to suit them and their skewed political leanings best.

I can see the headlines now with more than a hint of sexual innuendo heading my way next year all of which is likely to haunt me for ages and is something I know I most likely will have to face head on and deal with.

One way for me to deal with the malicious nonsense will be to steer clear of newspapers, and as I don't get involved in all the stupidity that is social media I could very well survive.

Media of course were once the main providers of chip paper but the PC brigade stopped it all for some ridiculous reason no doubt. We all get shouted at all the time about the environment, then they do something daft like cut down more trees to make chip paper. The mind boggles, well at least mine does and one day I'm quite sure it'll turn into scrambled egg with all the utter garbage in the world today.

Chocolate is good for you, then it's not, then dark chocolate is. Don't dare eat nuts or pile on the pounds. then somebody makes money with a nut diet. You couldn't make it up! Broccoli will help your heart, and then it will make you fat. Statins Save Lives says one headline, then a red top thunders *Statins Kill Hundreds*. Seems to me like an endless round of people making claims they cannot possibly justify combined with the media desperate to stop the slump in their sales. I ignore all such nonsense these days, after I came across the idea potatoes can be harmful when I was surfing the web.

And another thing while I'm in the mood, where on earth did the 'noughties' phrase come from. We've had seventeen-hundreds, eighteen-hundreds, nineteen-hundreds all of which have always been absolutely fine, yet instead of twenty-hundreds we get totally bemused by the stupidity of noughties which is constantly confused with naughties.

I'm told it's all part of the hook-up culture, the incessant need to 'hook-up' to those the young consider to be like-minded. I reckon what they mean is bonkers.

All to do with maturity of course. Apparently a fifteen year old today is far less mature and worldly wise than say I was at the same age. Reason they give is all to do with their lack of life experiences, so if you're looking for an excuse for your teenage child, there's one for you.

Enough now. Time for you to buckle up and please remember on this journey together don't bother to have a grumble later on because you have been duly warned.

I'd love to be able to add atmosphere with descriptions of a gusty gale blowing in from the east, with big black billowy clouds hanging on the breeze to dry. Or perhaps write a monologue about the torrential rain wreaking havoc and the threat of snow drifts amongst all the intrigue.

Sorry. None of that. It was just a very average sort of dry Lincolnshire autumn day and not very much to report at all.

Anyway, before long on the Thursday after my Edward had left I was back to *BBC Radio Lincolnshire* waiting for the news to come round again and get up to speed on what had been going on up in Washingborough.

Loneliness is not something I have been attracted to as others are. I have read more than once of people who much prefer solitude and their own company and have no desire to join in, take part, or talk to complete strangers in a crowded room. To me it had always been a case of being found wanting. Wanting to mix, wanting to blend in, join in and yet for most of my life the very people I was supposed to coalesce with had always let me down badly.

I knew of course it went all the way back to Roger Styles and the day forever emblazoned on my heart when I had been totally devastated, just tossed aside by him like an old rag doll for no reason he has ever been willing to explain.

I've been called Jacs for a long time by the way. It all goes back to my boarding school days, when nicknames were used more often than some of the ones the girls were baptised with.

One of those schools unfortunately where people with popular names such as Brown, Smith and Jones were given a number. "Come here Jones 8," you'd hear. "This homework is as bad as I've read Brown 5." The use of the word homework was sadly ridiculous, it was a boarding school and we lived in the dorm. I was lucky there was only one lanky girl there lumbered with the Epton-Howe moniker.

As an aside do you know there are more than 200 girls in America with the name Abcde. Seriously. In France they allocate a letter of the alphabet each year you must use as the first letter of the name of a dog born that year. In a year or two it'll be Q.

Anyway, where was I? Ah yes. Jacs was something mummy could not abide of course and would not hear of it being spoken in the house. It was always *'Jacqueline dear'* this *'Now then, Jacqueline'* and *'Jacqueline my pet'*. Never *'duck'* of course the yokels around here tend to use for some reason.

Daddy of course being daddy called me *the Daughter* and sometimes I do wonder if it might be because he couldn't remember my name. The way he always introduced me to people and how he spoke to me. "Let me introduce the daughter" he would say in company and at home, when he was there, it was "now then daughter" more often than not.

Enough of me prattling on for now. Time to get back to Thursday morning in November after Edward had left to head for France.

It was all rather too silly for words once he had driven away down my drive heading south west. Something from my upbringing told me once the washing-up was done and all evidence of him having had breakfast was long gone to just have another quick scour round before I spotted Molly West my cleaner parading up the path. Smooth down the duvet on his bed and plump up the pillows; she'd never know.

'Morning Miss Jacqueline,' she said when she walked in through the scullery door.

'Good morning Molly. Hope you don't mind dear, got one of my heads, think I'll just sit quiet if you don't mind.'

'Anything I can get for you Miss Jacqueline?'

'I'll be fine. Be in the Morning Room, you just carry on and I'll see you Saturday,' and I took the morning paper with me and a fresh coffee I'd just brewed and found a comfortable chair.

That's another thing. Newspapers. Picked one up in the coffee house the other day. Like us on Facebook it said and Follow us on Twitter. Is that really the extent of their ambition nowadays? Seems to me the world no longer has any substance with everybody desperate to be chased by the same bunch of twerps.

Making myself scarce was just an excuse of course. Couldn't be doing with Molly's chit-chat, about what she'd been up to all week with her dreadful kids, where they'd been and with who and when. Always something new it seemed, had to have the latest fad, as if as a family they couldn't possibly let the current fashion pass them by. Not so much of a problem – I can always switch off, it was the aftermath which always worried me. The inevitable nosey questions about what I'd been doing which in this case I'd find a tad difficult without mentioning darling Edward.

I knew one thing for sure, I would never have the same issues with Derek when he arrived. My trusted gardener always keeps himself very much to himself out in the grounds and at that time of year he had plenty to do with leaves falling. The only issue I've ever had with Derek is his reluctance to even step foot inside the house for some reason, almost as if it wasn't his place to do so. He probably did miss the squire if the truth be known, somebody he could touch his forelock to. Too long in the forces probably and he'd got so used to using number rank and name, and found the increasingly equal real world somewhat difficult to cope with as some frequently do. Most conversations took place in and around his potting shed and the two greenhouses.

I am sadly the last remaining Epton-Howe from a line stretching back through the Epton lineage to when the place I call home was a settlement for dwellers called simply Spald. Time and circumstance – and the Great War in particular, had taken its toll and now I'm the sole survivor. The last remaining Epton from a long line of Lincolnshire folk.

Daddy Arthur's two much older brothers had both been killed in the Second World War, and Mummy's younger sister died tragically at the age of four in what was always described euphemistically as a farming incident.

Always possible somewhere the other end of the county or further down in say Rutland and beyond miles away there are other Eptons, Howes or Epton-Howes with a slender link to my dynasty, but none I have ever heard of. Certainly none I have uncovered of any consequence when working on my family tree. There were certainly some odd-ball characters in my past I'd really rather folk knew nothing about, but certainly none likely to lay claim to anything of mine come my inevitable demise.

As it happens *Radio Lincolnshire* only repeated what I'd heard earlier about the police launching a murder investigation along with some gubbins about a shop being defaced with graffiti.

Something I've often wondered, why is graffiti always made up with fat letters?

Just a thought.

3

Detective Inspector Inga Larsson trundled her big black chair with the squeaky wheel from behind her desk out into the MIT Incident Room and parked it. Uninteresting and unread emails were the bane of her life and today had been no exception.

Aimless banter was periodically slipped between lengthy bouts of head down absolute concentration as if it was the light relief their minds demanded.

How it is with any unexplained death. Trained and experienced detectives acting like beavering acolytes. As it was that day with many sat working the phones on incoming and outgoing often to ragamuffins desperate for their five minutes of fame they can brag about to so-called Friends on line. People with actions to achieve, ideas to check, all crammed into forty eight hours with those first couple of days flying by in no time.

The muted murmur humming around the room faded as Inga returned to her desk for her work tablet and her mug of coffee. By then all of her main team had got the message, and in fact her second in command Detective Sergeant Jacques Goodwin was on his feet stood by the first of the three white boards.

'Welcome to those on loan from PHU and all points west,' she began as she scanned her core team and these add-ons. 'Thanks to any who have had to change shifts to accommodate our exacting requirements.' Inga could see some had an earnestness about them, others were there purely because they'd been told to by DCI Stevens who was no doubt happy to get rid of them for a day or two. She allowed the look she gave every one of them to settle amongst her audience before she looked up at Goodwin.

When she met his sympathetic gaze he decided his boss was comfortably settled enough to point at a photo of the body of a white male in the mortuary.

'Here we have twenty-eight-year-old IC1 male Graeme Alistair Coetzer of South African extraction a couple of generations back, found by his mother on the floor of their bungalow in Washingborough. The only son, in fact only child of Amber Coetzer the widowed wife of Gordon Coetzer who was killed in a building site accident four years ago. According to the doc it could well be some form of poisoning, the primary reason we've been called in.' Jake as he prefers to be called, looked at Inga and she nodded. 'Looked like a heart attack but then there were other elements she was not happy with.' Jake tapped a photograph of an attractive woman with his index finger. 'This is the mother Amber who was away from Monday morning until late Wednesday afternoon, and initial suggestion from the doc is her son Graeme Coetzer died sometime on the Monday evening. Bonfire night. She left home early on Monday morning for a couple of days away in Gateshead she apparently won in a competition.' Jake folded his arms. 'It is not physically possible for Amber Coetzer to have killed her son early in the morning then caught the train at Newark to Newcastle.'

'Why impossible?' Inga asked from her chair.

'The son was at work that day.' Jake responded. 'Sandy MacLachlan's been looking into this Graeme Coetzer. We have door-to-door going on right now and we've talked to Amber Coetzer but only briefly.'

'Don't see it,' said Inga shaking her head. 'Nothing's put on with this one, she really is in a dreadful state to be honest. Lost her husband few years back, now her son. All she's been left with is the compensation money she finally got earlier this year, but what good is it to her now?' She sipped her coffee. 'To be honest I've only spoken to one relative to gather what we know so far. She's in no fit state to talk about anything, and from what I can gather she has no idea at all. Just went off on this trip and was joined up there by her sister who lives in Anwick north of Newcastle.'

'This trip boss,' said Raza Latif. 'This the one she won in a competition?' the Detective Sergeant asked. Raza was the sort of policeman who left his job at the door each day. Whoever his friends are, they're not coppers not part of an in-crowd and as a result Inga always felt he takes time to get back up to speed. Always playing catch up.

'Free trip to Metro Centre in Gateshead with overnight stays at the Holiday Inn,' Inga smiled. 'Probably not your cup of tea.' To be honest it wasn't hers either. Inga was never one for shopping for shopping's sake. Not something she did on a regular basis and certainly not with a couple of girlfriends in tow as others tend to for some reason.

'Who did she win it with?' swarthy Raza asked.

'Some magazine alledgedly. According to the people we've spoken to Amber's one of these women who does competitions all the time. Wins all sorts apparently, so it wouldn't have come as a big surprise.'

'People would have known she'd be away then?'

'Immediate family, neighbours probably. Just some of the things door-to-door hope to establish with a bit of luck. I've spoken to the immediate next door neighbours and a couple of her pals who were at the friend down the road who is putting Coetzer up for a few days while CSI go through her place with their fine tooth comb.'

'Mystery man?' said Jake when there was a lull.

'Yes please,' said Inga as she tapped her tablet.

'Amber Coetzer had a man friend. Problem is that's about all we know so far,' and looked at Inga for guidance.

'At some point,' she said when she lifted her head. 'We'll have to go back and talk to this Amber about him, but from what we can gather he's a bit of a mystery man. Comes and goes, nobody's really seen him, turns up late goes early, all a bit odd. Woman I spoke to says he's never been there when she's called round, but apart from her and the woman next door there's nobody who calls on a regular basis. If she's anything like us, we don't see my neighbours from one week's end to the next. Some of this is supposition I guess.'

'What you suggesting?' Jake queried.

'I'm not sure he's her fancy man or anything like it, probably there a great deal less than people imagine.' She peered back down at her tablet. 'One who would know of course is no longer with us.'

'Any news from our roving Scotsman yet?' Jake asked.

'Not so far. He and Ruth have gone to pull in friends and anything else they get a handle on. Mention of Sandy reminds me. Who may I ask is going to step up to the mark with DS Scoley away?' Inga asked as she looked at the incomers. 'We currently have

DS Scoley on a specialist course', she explained. 'Up with Police Scotland. Doing cyber-crime and cyber threats all part of her information communications technology she's been interested in for a while.'

'Up at the Police Scotland college at, er...Tulliallan,' Jake struggled to add.

'Where coincidentally Sandy MacLachlan did his training.'

4

Hello there. This is Jacs if you remember, back telling my side of the story.

It was ridiculous really and I knew it, yet like so much in my life I had never done anything about it. There are three or four of these coffee house places I frequent, but with all this bitting and bobbing about I have never really settled for any of them on a regular basis. Couple of nice ones in town, then one or two out at Springfields shopping outlet. For some reason I seem never to have taken the time to savour the range of coffees in any of them or got to know the staff.

There are of course some places to avoid who serve little more than slops in the name of coffee frequented by the almost human detritus of society.

But then being invited out for coffee is not something which happens to me very often I'm sorry to say.

I'm not like daddy Arthur in so many ways. When I do get invited I often allow the other party to choose where. With him there'd have been no messing about. "Meet in Coffee Insitu at ten," he'd tell whoever it was for example. With him you knew not to argue, not dare to suggest you try somewhere else. Arthur Epton-Howe was not for having any of it. No siree.

Of course this so-called coffee culture is nothing of the sort. Why do the younger generation have a desire to claim ownership of so much of modern society?

I know people who in their late teens visited coffee houses more than fifty years ago on a regular basis. We of course have the youth of today wearing clothes they think are new, modern and in their words, happening. Truth is of course fashion is like a roundabout in the park. Every decade or so the same thing tediously comes round again and again. Some of the fashions I see today I wore way back last century such as jeans with holes ripped in them. Then true to form the grunge types brought them back in the nineties, now this GenX shower think they're being innovative. Not.

I notice friends of mine, or to be more accurate people I know, have increasingly begun calling folk they come across by name. The girl who serves them at the chemist or the one on the checkout at the supermarket. I have never done it, never take any notice whatsoever of what it says on their badges. In fact I really have no idea why they wear them, what does it matter if the silly girl is called Chevvy or Mercedes? They are usually a burden they are stuck with for life.

What we all delight in at aged twenty is really not quite the in-thing or fashionable when you're thirty two or forty two as in my case. Boyz II Men I had enjoyed immensely in my teens are now hardly setting the world of downloads alight currently, and are not being lined up for Glastonbury, as far as I am aware. More than once I have imagined how ludicrous I would now look with a *Boyz* tattoo on my left buttock.

That's another thing. Glastonbury. Why on earth do we have to suffer such irrelevance on our television screens for a weekend? To my mind such a tedious festival is all about savouring the experience. Enjoying the cloying mud again, guzzling dubious booze, smoking weed and most of all encountering the lousy sanitation arrangements. It has nothing whatsoever to do with good music or you supping a few cans, chomping a pizza slumped on your sofa in a onesie fashionable a decade ago.

I glanced at my watch but as I really had no idea where Edward would be at what time it was a pointless exercise.

He was heading for France that much I did know. He'd not told me the time of his Eurotunnel train from Folkestone and then again I'd not asked. Knew of course how he had to go home first to sort his mail, drop off his weekend bag, pick up another he'd said he'd already packed for the trip. It was certainly a busy life.

Yearling racehorse sales were what he was heading for in Deauville I'd tried to look up of course on my iPad in bed. He'd said the name of it all, but I'd forgotten. I have never driven abroad which surely is part and parcel of not being adventurous enough in my life. Perhaps next time he was off on one of these trips Edward would take me with him and by then I'll know him a bit better and perhaps he'd let me drive. Some of the way at least.

Once he reached France according to what I had looked up it was not a great stretch to this Deauville. French racehorse yearling sales and my first nibble at owning a racehorse.

That day with Edward heading for France I was there in the café enjoying my own company for a while and had treated myself to an Almond Biscotti to dip in my Americano. I certainly know how to live don't you think?

Had managed somehow to avoid all the zombie phubbies who glued to their phones bump into you in the street with such annoying frequency.

It was the lovely man in my life who came to my rescue, just when I had allowed myself to become enveloped in thoughts of what might have been with Roger, still working on the family farm. Thoughts of Edward being a bloodstock buyer for the rich and famous gave me a real boost. I'm sure you'll agree it was much more exciting than just being a farmer.

How ridiculous. After all this time I still keep track of what the swine Roger is doing these days. Still farming a huge acreage so I understand and had apparently taken over most of the operation from his father some years back. Somewhere down the line they'd got into the flower business and pumpkins apparently by the lorry load or so I had been told.

Probably because already I was in a mood of anticipation mixed with a hint of once more being on my own, almost before my people watching session had begun I was in need of international rescue.

When it turned up it was not Jeff Tracy just plain old Felicity Gilmour as it happened.

'Hello Jacqueline, mind if I…?' she offered as she just slid her tray onto my table and plonked herself down.

'Please do,' I said to the tall woman looking like a poorly stuffed sausage. Sort who is never out of the hairdressers and most certainly would never allow herself to be seen without full make-up and as ever was very much dressed far too young. Her figure was probably down to too many hours with her 'ladies who lunch' friends I would not want to endure. Know for absolute sure I will never be cast in the thin scraggy role of a waif, but am not in need of a decent corset like her.

'On your own?'

'I am now.'

Gilmour lifted her tall latte glass from the tray, then the saucer and her receipt and then pushed the tray onto an empty table nearby. She then messed about folding the receipt to slip into her handbag. Why would she need a receipt for a measly couple of quid I wondered; then remembered the television personality I'd sat behind on a plane once who had insisted on a VAT receipt for a cup of coffee. There's tight and there's tight I mused. She'd be better off going without a few cappuccinos and putting the money towards a firm control corselette to stop her stomach doing a good impression of the South Downs.

'How are things with you, dear?'

I really do hate it, when people refer to me as "dear". That aside, things were generally quite good. Had actually been much better of course for the two days Edward had been at the house. Something else I need to do, next time Edward visits. Bring him into Spalding, join the coffee culture with a man on my arm and with any luck perhaps I'll spot Roger the Dodger and his tubby little wife.

'Just having a break. Edward's on his way to France as we speak.' Do you like the way I just slipped it in?

'Do I know him?' podgy Gilmour asked nosily.

'I shouldn't think so,' was a ridiculous thing for me to say. None of my friends had met Edward McCafferty. 'He buys and sells bloodstock.'

'Really? How interesting,' she said but I seriously doubted if the woman really found it so, or even understood. Actually it was interesting. What Edward did was not the run of the mill sort of career you come across every day.

'Heading for Deauville today on his way to buy a few yearlings,' I said as if I really knew what I was talking about. It was just snippets of information I had gleaned from him to be honest, but she wasn't to know.

'Be all sheiks and Arabs and people of that sort no doubt,' she said scornfully and if spitting on the floor was still in vogue I'm quite sure she would have done so.

'So I understand.' Yes it probably was and I was sorely tempted but decided against revealing all just yet.

Gilmour of course had to start talking about Brexit, so I just let her drone on.

As far as I'm concerned we appear to just be drifting aimlessly towards this break from Europe. Those from the far right who claim to be and far left who'd like to be running the country, are in fact too busy feuding with other bullies in their own parties to even pause a moment to look at our NHS, schools, prisons and care homes.

Then out of nowhere this Fliss woman produced her phone.

'Just thought of something, won't be a moment,' and she was there tapping and prodding her phone. 'So short of memory that's the trouble,' she said as if I was in the slightest bit interested. 'I've got a thousand photos on here, but I'm loath to delete them.' She looked up at me, probably for sympathy she was never going to get. 'Photos define who you are, don't you think?' I didn't respond, I was speechless and in the end this rude woman gave up whatever it was she was trying to do. Be one of those app things no doubt. Look up a recipe, call an astrophysisist for advice or fly to Mars in an hour. I know not which.

At the club for the lonely I help out at once or sometimes twice a week if I'm pushed, the people there simply put up with this Fliss Gilmour and others of her ilk.

She was the dibby woman who had at one time at the club suggested they serve Earl Grey tea. My betting is, should you visit her, silly Fliss would be the sort to offer you a choice of fancy teas: Camomile, Assam, Blue Lady or Matcha. If however you were to choose coffee instead what's the betting she'd secretly make you a cup from a jar of Lidl's finest? All pretentious twaddle.

In in environment so dependent upon volunteers they were never going to complain, but there was certainly a better atmosphere when she was not about. 'Children all well?' I tried to get the woman off subject.

'Most certainly,' she assured me. 'Damien's still up at Durham of course and Amanda seems set to become a data scientist. Already doing a good amount of on-the-ground trend hunting as part of her internship.' Another subject I wished to God I'd not gone down. She sounded a right one. You know the type, plodding along the street wearing huge ridiculous earphones. Be no good to man or beast I thought as I glanced about and saw what looked like a very pleasant woman chatting away quite happily to a friend. Why don't I know women like her? Why am I always stuck with...'Of course with our Chloe now into double digits we'll need to start looking at what's best for her, and to be honest she's becoming more confident in her clutch moments which is such a good thing, but you know what they're like at that age and no doubt her inner monologue will change. Terribly modern of course and future-facing which is a real bonus to my mind. Think its best if you keep girls away from red brick, most people I know are pretty much over them. What think you?' I realized I was sat there with my mouth open picturing this awful child arriving at university on a Brampton folding bicycle she used as her middle class badge of honour.

'I agree.' What sheer stupidity this woman uttered. She is the best illustration of a superficial woman I know. From the dyed bouffant coiffure to the tarts heels.

'Never at all sure what sort of people she'd have to mix with and you just can't be too careful in this day and age. What say you?'

'Of course,' I struggled to utter when I really wanted to give her a mouth full, and not for the first time.

Me and young people? More than anything else like, I just wish they'd learn to talk properly, innit.

'Would you mind awfully?' said this dreadful Gilmour suddenly. 'Just spotted an old friend,' and she was on her feet. She moved so close I was fearful for a moment a hug was imminent. 'See you at the club next time you're there,' and I almost just said the groovy "whatevs" I'd heard tarty giggly girls come out with and with two short journeys she transferred herself to join another female at a table against the far wall. Blonde hair tied into pigtails then wrapped around her head.

In a matter of seconds I was back on my own. Loneliness once again had joined as my only friend, but in this case it was the better of two evils.

I always wonder how seemingly intelligent people get sucked in by all this nonsense.

Anyway, where was I? Of yes, a middle-aged couple I did not know took two seats at my table within a few minutes, and as people tend to do in Britain they just talked to each other about people and places I knew nothing at all about.

Oh how I wished I was on my way to France with my good man. I imagined the weather would be so much better than the overcast dullness I could see was still outside.

Talking of the weather, heard a forecaster saying the weather looks better than the get go. What on earth does that mean for goodness sake? Brolly weather or time to get the sandals out?

My thoughts returned to a lovely hotel, lingering over beautiful French food and a bottle of their superb wine and a good man. What could be better? Certainly not a coffee and these two chattering on about the caravan they'd booked in Mevagissey. Mr and Mrs Beige – where do people like them buy their clothes? – were just chattering on and I'd watched as he poured four sachets of sugar into his cappuccino which just sat on the froth.

Fliss Gilmour was still by the far wall no doubt bragging to her friend. I remembered how she tends to get all snooty about television. Some time back there had been one of those very good murder mystery police dramas on TV for a few weeks we discussed at the drop-in club. You know the sort, lasts six weeks or so and particularly good when done by the BBC.

We were all discussing the dramatic finale but typically Gilmour claimed not to watch scheduled programmes, because and I'll always remember this, she said "it's so over". You've got to laugh haven't you?

Wonder what people hope to gain by coming out with such ostentatious garbage. Could be of course people such as her are simply repeating something they've been impressed by. I'm certainly not and my mother would just say she was showing off.

To be honest I want to know why they shoe-horn women into programmes on a token feminism basis. When the audience laughs because it is obvious they feel duty bound I absolutely cringe. To my mind it is so sad how we as a gender have to be force-fed other women for no legitimate reason.

Knew a woman at one time who reckoned she only ate ostrich eggs and even claimed to have eaten one produced by an emu. I checked on Google when I got home. They're the size of a dozen standard eggs, and take 90 minutes to cook. You'd need a bloody big egg cup!

Something I really enjoy to be honest, people watching. I'm quite happy in my own company to a degree and I know some of you will always have a need to meet up with your girlfriends. I can sit with a decent coffee (or two) for ages just taking on board other people's odd quirks and habits.

That very day was a case in point. I was fascinated sat there with the Beige couple to observe this man at the next table drink an espresso coffee with his spoon still in the cup the whole time. I hope none of you are going to tell me how it's the done thing and it's awfully on-trend along the Kings Road!

Apologies for going off tangent, but I do have to say I'm not at all the sort who goes through life giving people marks out of ten for hair, clothes and shoes. Have to admit though I've seen one or two who would struggle to attain a combined total of three.

The silly pretentious Gilmour woman is the sort according to others at the drop-in who are into this sort of thing, who apparently is forever on social media, spouting about herself. *Cocktails tonight again...in VIP Lounge at East Midlands...just enjoying a glass or two of Prosecco...Avacado on toast for brunch.* She probably thinks people are influenced by the likes of her. How very sad. From what I've been given to understand the stuff they call Prosecco was once called Babycham. Certainly what a wine connoisseur of my acquaintance reckons. Having tried neither myself I'm not one to judge.

While I'm on the subject, may I ask if anybody knows what a hipster coffee is? Read somewhere deconstructed coffee is the same thing, but I'm still none the wiser.

When these coffee shops first started to mushroom in towns and cities I did wonder why. Now I thoroughly enjoy my time in them. The coffee for the most part is good and far better of course than in large stores, but it is the people watching I gain most satisfaction from.

There was a young woman who by her look I suppose must have been influenced by selfies and social media. I cannot for the life of me understand why people like her make themselves look so odd by doing ridiculous things to their faces. They finish up expressionless with those bizarre plucked or false eyebrows, lifeless eyes and puffed up lips.

Coffee, an Americano if you remember, once finished I set off for a stroll along Hall Place and called at a butchers. Probably because I felt pleased with myself I bought a good portion of chicken, bacon and leek casserole I'll have with new potatoes and a dozen pork and apple sausages, my favourite, I can always use.

All good stuff but not quite up to the standard my old butcher used to come up with, but alas like so many they closed down a couple of years back. At least it will save me a job.

5

News from DCs Sandy MacLachlan and Ruth Buchan when they arrived back with information on Graeme Coetzer, provided some sliver of optimism.

Inga Larsson was pleased Ruth seemed more confident these days but she had a long way to go to run alongside Nicky Scoley who'd had going on for a couple of years' experience down in deepest Cambridge.

The pair had been back to talk to neighbours and discovered Graeme was well liked but apart from employment based events such as people leaving or celebrating something in particular they understood he didn't really mix. Behind this disinclination to socialize was his reluctance to do so anywhere he knew where they would not serve his favourite real ale.

Graeme Coetzer was too into his all-consuming hobbies and it was his obsessive behaviour which kept him apart from those he worked closely with apparently. They all knew about the death of his father of course and although she had never discussed it, through the local media they were all aware of the compensation his mother had recently been awarded.

One little snippet two young women they bumped into pushing babies in prams offered was Graeme's concern regarding a Lucas Penney, who they understood he was not greatly enamoured with. The team had managed to gather from the local grapevine how he was a fairly new friend of Amber who always seemed to be at the bungalow when Graeme was away supporting Manchester United. Not just supporting, this man lived and breathed the club and the players and everything about them every bit as much as he loved his real ale.

He was the sort Sandy and Ruth discovered who had an expensive season ticket to Old Trafford and one old fella they chatted to reckoned Graeme attended every home game for season after season and followed them through thick and thin and recently had even taken to travelling abroad to matches all over Europe since his mother got her money.

When not doing so, they reckoned he just sat at home with a bottle of Wobble Gob or one of Black Widow or both and supped while watching old DVDs of Man United past glory days.

Two women Ruth had homed in on who knew Amber, felt the negative reaction to the bloke who visited was a natural response by Graeme. They felt he could sense this intruder was likely to be somebody who just might be trying to replace his father, the man who had introduced his son to the world of the Red Devils. At his age he had no need of a step-dad.

The two women suggested if this mystery chap supported another team he would not be made welcome in the Coetzer household by the son, so obsessed was he. Were it Newcastle, Arsenal or Manchester City they could very well be at loggerheads frequently and a perfectly good reason why they understood they never appeared to be in the bungalow at the same time.

DC Ruth Buchan and DS Raza Latif had reaffirmed how Graeme Coetzer had worked on the Monday and was then due to drive across to Manchester on the Tuesday to link up with other travelling fans and fly out to Turin for the Champions League.

'Where they filmed *The Italian Job*,' Sandy popped in.

'What are you on about?' Inga asked.

'Turin where the football was, is where they filmed the Minis roaring through the streets.'

'As I was saying,' Ruth went on. 'He was due to fl to Turin on the morning of the match. He'd booked a room at the Premier Inn for the Tuesday night.'

'Who were they playing?'

'Juventus,' Sandy confirmed. 'They're based in Turin, and out of interest Man U won.'

'I know they're fanatical some of these people but supporting the wrong team is hardly a good reason to kill somebody,' Inga suggested as she listened to their report. 'Otherwise we'd be piling them up in the streets in some places, especially where they have two teams in one town.'

'There's a lot of folk out there don't like Man United,' said Ruth.

'You suggesting this was football based, not necessarily this Lucas Penney but just someone this Coetzer lad upset?'

'Have we got the eTeam looking into his activities online?'

'Of course. They've got both phone and laptop, both of which have Man United screensavers as you can imagine.'

'And what's the betting it'll all be football orientated?'

'Or football hooligan websites,' Raza just popped in.

'But it might just lead us to a contratemps with a West Brom fan or somebody.' Inga sniggered. 'Having a go at say a Leeds supporter on line about the merits of one player against another is one thing, but then jumping in your car and heading down the A1 from his flee infested bedsit to Washingborough to have it out with him is a bit of a long shot.'

'Just a minute,' from Inga Larsson quietened everybody down. 'Think you'll need to explain all this to this ignorant Swede who doesn't support any football team. Just because you support one team, why on earth would you hate another?'

'Tribal,' said Sandy. 'One reason I've got no time for it, all too tribal, as if it's more important than the beautiful game.'

'Arsenal hate Spurs, Man City hate Man United, Newcastle hate Sunderland with a vengeance.'

'But why?' Inga persisted.

'Religion. Yous get a lot of it up my way,' Sandy advised. 'Rangers and Celtic is Protestant against Catholic,' he added. 'Back in history some others were similar.'

'I didn't really like Roger Federer, but I don't hate him, I'd never do him any harm, not scream and swear at him.'

'Can be racist too.'

'Some of the football loons,' Jake Goodwin joined in, 'actually put the matches their team plays against a local rival above all others. Don't care who they get beaten by, how bad their team plays as long as they beat the ones they hate from fifty miles down the road.'

'It's only football for goodness sake,' Inga sighed. 'Enough now,' highlighted her exasperation. 'Let's get on, I still can't fathom it all. Are you two following up this Lucas Penney or are there other leads you picked up from neighbours taking priority?' she wanted to know.

'Not a lot else to pick up on,' said Sandy. 'When somebody's as obsessed with things as this guy appears to have been, it seems it left little room for anything else in his life.' He smiled. 'And before you ask, no woman.'

'In fact it was suggested there never has been a woman - married to the club was one suggestion I got,' said Ruth Buchan. 'Two women I spoke to said he was a nice guy, but could be better if it wasn't for the football and the ale.'

'Because they don't like Man U? We back to all that?'

'No. Because his whole life revolves around them and his ale, got no time for a woman or anything else or so it seems.'

'Probably couldn't afford one to be honest,' said Raza. 'If he was going here there and everywhere. Season ticket for Old Trafford'll cost you a pretty penny for starters then add on a couple or three bottles a night, and he runs a car so he can get to matches. I know some women do put up with it all, but they've got to be pretty rare.'

'And stupid.'

'Car?' said Inga.

'Tech lads have got it,' Jake assured her.

'Got to be football hasn't it?' said Inga almost to herself looking up at the pair stood there in front of her desk. 'This is football orientated, this is inter-club rivalry and he's said the wrong thing to the wrong person or bragged as they do. Might be an idea to have a word with the eTeam to see if they're checking for him being a texting and tweeting troll.'

'Do we know exactly how yet?' Sandy queried, as he made a note of the request.

'Not had any forensics through yet, but they're still talking poison.'

'Oh ma'am,' said Sandy and chuckled as he did so. 'Football supporters poisoning each other?' She smirked her response. 'Racist abuse, homophobic frequently, a good smack in the mouth maybe, but poison? Seriously?'

'What else have we got?' she then interjected. 'C'mon Sandy you tell me.'

'Early days, early days.'

'You're probably right,' Jake said but knew he was being stereotypical. The macho tribal warfare knows no bounds when it comes to the beautiful game. As far as he was concerned the sport gave up the right to the description some many decades back.

By the end of the day, there were three very distinct groupings on the white boards.

One was Graeme Coetzer and his Manchester United fanaticism heading for Manchester the day after he died with no known enemies to date. Apart of course from supporters of every other football team in the land.

Board two listed his mother Amber away for two days, loss of her husband, the compensation and her love for entering competitions. It was almost as if mother and son both had obsessions. More than one contribution had mentioned about her supermarket buying as being controlled by what products had prize promotions, such was her all consuming passion.

Then there was a short third list headed 'Lucas Penney' with very little against his name. In fact nothing but his name.

6

Hello there all of you, Jacs here. How are you doing? Time I think for me to get on with my tale.

When my neighbour's son suggested I would find one of these tablet computer things useful I must admit I had been very reluctant. In fact, to be honest I waited getting on for a couple of months from the first suggestion to actually walking timidly into an Apple store. Now I wouldn't be without it, I was truly a convert like most people it seems.

I had read but did not fully understand all about what they described as indicators on the subject of horses. Such as early foaling sales, 2-year-old careers of the dams and even about sires' aptitude at producing early-performing horses.

I assumed it meant more to Edward than it did to me and I guessed it was all second nature to him.

Whiling away my time during the summer I'd dip in and out of the latest Test Match score which was much more to my liking. A day at Trent Bridge in the sunshine was most certainly more my cup of tea.

What you're brought up with and by whom, there is no doubt has a real effect long term. Usually positive of course, but on some occasions it can brew negativity. Perhaps Edward's father had been a bookie or even a gambler and was where he got it from. He'd certainly not been a jockey, not if Edward's present stature was anything to go by. He was never the progeny of someone knee high to nothing very much.

Daddy Arthur had been a great cricket fan. Had all his favourites, stacks of Wisdens and autobiographies he'd read from cover to cover more than once and enjoyed nothing more than a quiet Sunday in his battered sun hat spent in a deckchair beside the boundary watching his local Leatherhunters play. Played quite a bit in his youth, and had attended Test Matches at all the major grounds in the country at one time or another and a fair number abroad. Had no time for football had Arthur Epton-Howe and in fact despised any sport where those partaking didn't play entirely by the rules; something he was an old school stickler for. Cricket in the summer and Rugby over the winter and he was quite happy. Pleased to be able to get in a Baa-Baas match at Twickers or the Ashes Test at Lords. To him such experiences and money was what life was all about.

Were he still alive he would never appreciate what football has to offer nowadays. In particular the unsporting behaviour of feigning injury, sliding on their knees nonsense, spitting, shirt tugging, diving, insulting referees and all the other doltish nonsense in the name of sport we saw in bucketloads at the World Cup in Russia.

As for this football's coming home business, what utter rot that is. If football is going home it has to go home to Scotland where it was invented. Not to England who took a while to catch on.

I'm convinced this added-on time nonsense at the end of matches will very soon end in tears. So obviously open to abuse and corruption, my guess is it'll be the next big sport scandal to grab the headlines when some referee admits to being paid mega bucks to just play on until his paymasters score.

Whilst I'm on the subject. One thing I've never understood is why football fans include themselves in the exploits of their favourite team. "We played well today" they say as they arrive home when the most they've contributed is an hour in the pub, screaming obscenities during a 1-1 draw and a further four pints.

I have to admit now how when the phone finally chirped I fought hard to stay as calm as my pent-up nerves would allow.

'Hello there my sweet,' greeted me almost before I'd finished announcing my number and I really was all of a fluster.

'How are you? Safe journey?' I asked with my hand actually shaking.

'Pretty good actually.'

'Hotel to your liking?' I managed to squeeze in.

'Very much so, one I've used before actually, but to be honest one hotel is very much like another.' I went to speak but he beat me to it. 'I've been thinking, we were silly weren't we? You should have come with me. After the sales I'll have to be here for a few days making all the transport arrangements as you know. We could have made the most of a few days here in the sunshine together.'

'You're making me very jealous.'

'Next time then, we'll make it a date. Have these sales more than once a year, so next time we'll come together and we can make use of the French passion for wining and dining.'

'Thanks for that. I've got a casserole with new potatoes!' was what I rushed out but the invitation was running amok up and down my body.

'Oh I'm sorry, I didn't mean...'

'Don't worry, you enjoy yourself and if you get the chance have a look around for nice restaurants we can visit together next time.' I hadn't felt so excited for a very long time.

'I most certainly will. You keeping busy?'

'Went into town for a coffee this morning and got my lonely folks club tomorrow to keep me occupied.'

'I'd better be off,' Edward said. 'Somebody wants a word with me. I'll be in touch about the same time tomorrow when I've finished the first day. You never know I might have a horse for you by then.'

'Make it a good one, and not too much vino tonight, do you hear?'

'Yes madam,' he chuckled. 'Keep smiling, speak to you soon.'

'Love you,' I said without thinking.

The moment the call ended I remembered the latest on the murder in Washingborough. How according to local radio it might well be somebody's son and apparently according to their reporter his mother was helping Police with their enquiries. Wished I knew somebody other than the chunky Rene woman I could phone about it. Always so sad don't you think? When a relationship becomes so intolerable a mother has to kill her child.

Trouble is, with cases such as this I know it will be months and months before you get to hear about the nitty gritty. By then you've almost forgotten what it was all about in the first place. Read somewhere those Crown Prosecution people are given six months to piece their case together. Is all that time really necessary I wonder, or are they working to rule so to speak? Use all the allocated time whether needed or not.

A casserole never tasted so good, so thrilled was I with life and I knew I would go to the club in the morning in a top notch mood. Normally with my evening meal I would make a small pot of Earl Grey tea for one. Luckily I remembered there was still part of a bottle of red in the pantry we'd had left over from our last meal together.

I know Edward would always choose his wine very carefully. These days too many people it seems to me just grab any bottle of plonk providing it's cheap, when it really is the last thing you should ever do. If you are eating beef for example, plucking one at random and you can so easily finish up with an understated and more importantly underpowered red. Edward I know is no wine buff but certainly more of a connoisseur than to spoil his meal with a bad choice.

I just sat there with my glass of Sainsbury's finest in my hand and my empty plate pushed to one side and wondered where Edward was enjoying his evening meal. Be waiter service no doubt and I wondered if he knew much French, or whether he'd just have to point to the menu and hope. Get out his phrase book and look up the words for chicken or beef and hope against hope the delicacy they serve up is not buttered green beans, fondant potato and onion jus surmounted by topside of the winner of the 3.40 at Longchamps.

For some reason a great deal of fuss is always made about French food. When in truth it really is no better than ours. What I do give them credit for is the way French parents do not allow their offspring to run riot in restaurants. The eateries incidentally do not provide 'Kids Menus' which over here amounts to nothing more adventurous or appetizing than a burger, chips and beans.

In France they just have sensible smaller portions of what their parents are eating.

All alone in my kitchen, sat at the table covered with the green and white gingham cloth I chuckled to myself at the thought and became emotional thinking about how next time the sales came around I could introduce my Edward to the finer arts of French fine dining. Then I came down to earth with envious thoughts of him supping a Bordeaux Chateau Grimand, you know the one with just a hint of truffle and a smoky finish. The rat.

Life all of a sudden had something at the end of the tunnel, we may be apart right now but I was convinced we seriously had a future together and my life at last was destined for good times ahead, and my sad past was of no consequence any longer.

7

Almost from the crack of dawn next day life really seemed worth living. First thing I'd spoken to young Brandon Wishaw who lived in the 'Granny Annexe' or to give the proper title Oak Cottage.

My name for it, but it was indeed an accurate description for the cottage. When grandmother had reached the stage where she could barely cope on her own, daddy Arthur had built a bungalow for her in the grounds of Oakdenne House, sold her big seafront home in Worthing and no doubt pocketed the proceeds.

How daddy was I'm afraid. His ambition in life apart from blatantly accumulating as much lucre as he could by fair means or foul, was to be a ruthless toff with a desperate need to cozy up to the landed gentry and Tory party bigwigs. A man born of centuries of privilege who reeked of upper middle-class snobbery and disdain for the working man.

Since grandmother's demise and the subsequent death of both of my parents I had rented out Oak Cottage. My mother had always been concerned about 'strangers' living on our land albeit a hundred yards away almost tucked behind the orchard. Just leaving a perfectly fine home sitting there empty was scandalous in my eyes, particularly in this day and age when more and more people find it difficult to search out a decent place to live. If I had anything to do with it, leaving habitable property empty would be made a punishable offence.

Of course I had been very careful about choosing a tenant, and my use of one of these private detective people as well as an Estate Agent had probably been regarded as rather over the top at the time but proved its worth. The Wishaw's were a fine family. Robert, his wife Prudence and their good son Brandon.

It was the lad in fact who had encouraged me to take on board all the good things about modern technology, and had been a surprisingly astute and patient tutor and in times of trouble a handy problem solver to call on. In return I had also been a willing guinea pig in little experiments he carried out as an aside to his day job.

Brandon was certainly into all this modern technology stuff, but by no stretch of the imagination could he be regarded as nerdy. Well, at least not in my eyes.

True he worked as a software program developer – the non-geek understanding of what he did which even I can comprehend.

I never have fully understood what he was trying to develop but knew it was something to do with all round sight and sound sensors and not just visual, all loaded if necessary onto one of those drone things. The ability for a sensor to see not only what was in the lens field of vision but also behind the camera. It was all a bit too complicated a concept, when he started on about artificial intelligence aspects. Too three sixty degree body sourcing with variable wireless webcam and ultimate fifth generation invisible infra-red and night vision big brother for me by a long chalk. All fitted into something not much bigger than a tennis ball.

By the way this is not me suddenly being all techy, this is me quoting him and I've probably got it all arse about face anyway.

MVV he called it. Multi View Vision he says with an ANPR adeptness way beyond the capability of the police.

I was aware of and fascinated by him testing the unique sensory perception abstraction aspect of his device with his bike on several occasions. Loath to ask too many questions for fear of feeling really foolish at the answers.

I had seen him first thing on my way to the drop-in, and it was probably my good mood which had resulted in us having a lengthy chat about life in general and how his latest experiments were working out without going into too much technological detail.

Probably because I was thinking about my day ahead with those suffering from within the horrible world of loneliness I have frequently dipped in and out of, which had given me the idea.

'As you know I sometimes help out with a group who try to spice up the lives of lonely people,' I said to him without ever having mentioned to him or anybody else how sometimes I felt myself to be one of the forsaken. 'Been thinking Brandon, it's easy to say and not so easy to achieve when people suggest they should get out more. You can be lonely in a crowded room. Wondered about tablets.'

'For what?' he said as if I was referring to a pill for arthritis.

'For them to communicate with one another when they're not at the drop-in and obviously with family and friends,' was my reasoning. 'If they've got any friends of course,' was quite unnecessary, but I'd said it and it was right.

'They could certainly do that. With Skype they could talk to anybody, anywhere as well.'

'But they don't all have someone like you they can call on, someone with your patience shown to a fuddy-duddy like me. Do you know if there are people who would demonstrate to a group like ours? Show them how easy it all is.' I put my hand up. 'Without it all being a hard sell or making them look completely gormless.'

'I don't, but I can certainly make enquiries.' He put a hand on my shoulder. 'Leave it with me.'

'Thank you son.' How I wish it were true, how I'd give anything to have a son like Brandon. 'Appreciate it. You might even find a few more guinea pigs.'

I really am a great admirer of the way in which the Wishaw's have brought up their son. They had obviously offered clear guidance when needed but in the end had allowed Brandon to work things out for himself. Other parents I am sorry to say simply interfere too much, are far too pushy and are forever putting their needs first. Taking their children out of school to go on silly holidays and forever mixing them with adult company. No wonder so many are hopelessly confused, popping pills and drunk a great deal of the time.

Why for instance are today's mollycoddled children so overprotected by their parents? Having them driven or bussed to school which those without children have to pay for. What are they in fear of I wonder? Certainly not exhaust fumes to damage their lungs. Paedophiles hiding behind every tree maybe, when they are exposed to far far worse on the internet they are encouraged towards by the same obese parents. It's a fact how most children spend less time outdoors than prisoners.

I wince when I see children endlessly staring at screens and worry about their lonely futures.

Some things make me so angry. Anyway, where was I? Oh yes, Brandon.

What a great start to a lovely day it had been chatting to Brandon with a touch of blue sky on a November day. Made life appear so much better when I arrived at the lonely club and there was no sign of dreadful Fliss Gilmour. Remember her? The one with demeanour bordering on smug was not there nor were one or two other pompous women I can't stand the sight of.

Communication is my watchword as far as the lonely are concerned. I do my level best to chat to each and every one who attends. Some of the women don't see anybody from one week to the next; maybe the postman if they happen to be looking out of the window at the time. Of course these days my tubby jolly postman in his shorts is not as frequent a visitor as he once was and when he does bother the junk he has heads straight for the recycle bin.

It was of course down to folk like me and the other kindly helpers to find a subject to chat to the women about. I say women, because menfolk are not very often seen and I wonder why it is. Do they not get lonely in the same way as women? Or perhaps they are just loath to admit they are. Supposed to be so reliant, when they are often nothing of the sort, and walking into a room full of women I can imagine would be too daunting for some.

We had arranged for a woman to attend who was into this card making business. Not sure any of our women would actually take it up in the way this fussy woman had, but even I found it quite interesting and took a note of the woman's details. Having a stock of her one-off unique cards I thought would be a nice idea to keep at home to send to people, rather than the bog standard dull expensive pink ones you find in the shops.

It was a good session in that it gave those attending something different to talk about, and if it gave just one of them a new interest it would be good news.

It was six o'clock almost on the dot our time, when my phone rang and I knew it was THE call. My man.

I was buzzing not just with thoughts of him, but with the day I'd had. Edward told me he had done good business but as yet had not found quite the right horse for me. I had told him if I was doing this I wanted a grey but he'd said it was not really the main criteria he would use when selecting a yearling and had made some remark about donkeys often being a similar colour. I let Edward talk about everything he had been up to – my chit-chat about the card-making at the drop-in for the desperate was not quite the bright and cheery news he wanted, so I kept the goings on to myself. Most of it was women's talk anyway and guessed of little interest to an international horse trader like Edward McCafferty.

I just managed to squeeze in a query about the food and immediately became a tad jealous, but knew not only was he enjoying good French food and wine but at the same time he was carrying out a good food guide for the pair of us for the future. Perhaps he could read a menu after all.

All in all it had been another good day and I was pleased with myself as you can imagine.

8

Had to be done. There was no getting away from it, a visit to Amber Coetzer was on the agenda; one aspect of her role in life DI Inga Larsson did not care for one little bit.

All the platitudes and sympathy she'd have to spew out for somebody she did not know, who in more than one case she'd dealt with had actually turned out to be the culprit.

Inga was never cut out to be a bereavement counsellor and at times found it somewhat difficult to find the right words. Such expertise may be able to offer the necessary support during such difficult times, but it was something she lacked.

Did somebody overcome with grief when their whole world has been turned upside down really need a nosey copper poking her oar in?

Do what you can if there is no alternative but Inga knew there were others better placed than her.

CSI were still at the bungalow and anyway she understood Amber Coetzer was apparently suggesting to Family Liaison how she had no intention of ever returning to the family home she had shared with her late husband and with her now dead son. Memories from both mixed together would most probably be far too much for most people to take.

DI Inga Larsson and DC Ruth Buchan her new regular escort on such missions had usefully some time back completed a spell with Family Liaison before she joined MIT. Not Inga's scene at all but not necessarily her fault. While others were undertaking Family Liaison training she'd have been up to her ears in the joys of rape-crisis management.

They headed for an address two or three roads away from the Cotzer bungalow in Washingborough at the far end of a cul-de-sac to be greeted at the front door by a Myra Gaunt, and what a soppy woman she turned out to be. Pleasant enough, but softly spoken and terribly twee, who wouldn't say boo to a goose. She did however offer them tea which turned out to offer false hope as it was not far removed from dish water. Weak and willing? Willing it most certainly was not.

Word coming back from Family Liaison was this Coetzer woman had accepted her son's death. None of the time delay you would normally get waiting for a death to kick in. Was it Inga wondered because she'd been through a sudden death before with her husband? Is it easier somehow second time around she wondered?

This Amber looked tired and grey, in fact she appeared worn out, but it was really nothing more than Inga would expect under the circumstances. She looked a mere shadow of the woman they had pictured on the white board back at Lincoln Central. She appeared to be a very attractive woman in her late forties with deep brown hair and an excellent slim figure for her age.

Once all the laid down procedures along with the tea and sympathy were out of the way, Inga decided it was time to see what they could discover about the woman, her son and this Penney character.

'I'm sorry we had to move you out to let the CSI...'

'No way!'

'I was saying,' Inga insisted. 'We need to let the scientists do their work...'

'Makes no bloody diff'rence. Not going back there.'

What a great start was Inga's attempt to ease the dark haired woman into the questioning phase. Hair looked dyed. Change of tack: 'We understand Amber, you won a competition for a couple of days at Metro. Can you remember who was running it?'

'In a magazine musta been, but to be honest I enter so many I can never remember exactly. Do two or three a day, sometimes more.' Inga had already noticed she had two magazines on her lap. 'Prizes just turn up all the time.'

'And this prize was a trip to Metro?'

'Yes.'

'And what did it amount to exactly?'

The room did not have a good vibe, but then it did not have a good look either. A musky smell and dated, sort of place TV location people are on the look-out for all the time.

'Free train tickets and a hotel room. Holiday Inn it was at the Metro Centre.'

'Was it run by Metro do you know, this competition?'

'Don't think so,' she said and shook her head at the same time.

'Was there anybody there to greet you?' experienced Ruth asked. 'Somebody you had to register with maybe? Somebody to say hello Amber, well done you.'

'No.'

'So, what form did the prize take then?' DI Inga Larsson just looked at the dark brown haired woman without make-up. 'What did you have to hand in at the station, some sort of voucher was it?'

'Tickets.'

'Train tickets?' Ruth checked and Amber nodded. 'And the Hotel?'

'All I had was a letter, just said report to Reception all arrangements have been made.'

'And they were?'

'Yes. Handed the letter to a woman at Reception, gave me my room key and explained everything as they do.'

'So, at no time did you come into contact with anybody from the people who organised the competition?'

'Not that I know of.'

'The letter,' said Ruth. 'Who was it from exactly?'

With Ruth Buchan taking over and asking the questions Inga was able to just glance around. The carpet could have done with a good clean and this woman was never a customer at Ikea for sure. It was all very dour and drab, a mixture of different browns and wishy-washy fabrics. Whole thing needed lightening with dashes of colour and the muslin curtains were most certainly all wrong. Needed a makeover and no mistake.

'One of those internet things.'

'How do you mean?'

'The www dot coms thingybobs they have these days.'

'Can you remember who?' received a shake of the head. 'Do you still have the letter?' How long had the dreadful striped wallpaper been there Inga wondered as she scanned the room. She guessed since 1974 give or take a year or two.

Amber pouted and shook her head again. 'Hotel kept it.'

'Was winning something of that order unusual? Have you won anything similar before?'

'Not a hotel stay.' This was hard work, but under the circumstances it was about what they would expect from somebody suffering the trauma of the loss of a loved one and in her case of another loved one. Never going to be full of the joys of spring, willing and able to help in any way she can. It was one of the elements Inga could not abide, the futility of it so often. It was the fact she knew how people in Amber's position so often hold the key to their moving on with the case. They know things nobody else does.

'Can we talk about Mr Penney?' Inga posed gently but there was no reaction. The DI looked at Amber with clear, steady eyes which clearly said I'll not move away before I have your answer. She paused. 'Mr Penney?'

'If you like.'

'What can you tell us about him?' For once Amber looked at this Myra Gaunt for guidance which was not forthcoming.

'How do you mean?'

'How did you meet, where do you know him from?'

'Worked with my Gordon many moons ago, lass.'

'Do you know where it was?' Amber Coetzer just pouted. 'Where did Gordon work?'

'All over.' They were back to the sheer graft.

'And you've known this Mr Penney how long?'

'Not very long,' and just as Inga was wondering where to go next, Amber went on. 'It was Gordon knew him, he'd heard about the accident, all in the papers it were. Got in touch asked if he could do anything to help. Just a really nice gesture, good man and I could see why he and Gordon got on so well.'

'How old was your Gordon if you don't mind me asking?'

'Fifty five, when he died.'

'Would this Penney be about the same age?' Inga really wanted to know to start building a picture.

'I should imagine so if they worked together,' made no sense at all. She worked with men more than a dozen years older than her and Ruth was a few years younger.

'But you don't know exactly how old he was?'

'No,' she said shaking her head. 'Why would I?'

'And how long has he been visiting?'

'Six months or more probably. Last time was about three weeks since.' Inga had a follow-up but it could wait.

'Did Graeme get on with him?'

Amber chuckled. 'As well as he would with any Man City supporter,' she smiled for the first time. 'Should have warned him really, should have said Graeme was staunch United.' She released a breath down her nose and grimaced. 'Been to all but three home matches this century,' she said. 'And then it were when he had those palpatations.'

Psychological profiling courses she had attended were of little use sat there looking at Coetzer. Nothing from those boring lectures would come to mind right there and then. Was this woman really just pretending, acting out her grief and distress or was this all for real?

'They didn't get on, this Lucas and your Graeme, am I right?'

'Wouldn't say that, but supporting diff'rent teams it was clear they'd not be great buddies. Can't happen can it?'

Ruth just didn't follow this train of thinking at all. Never had done. It was all this unnecessary ridiculously tribal nonsense which frequently gives the game such a bad name. Never having had a brother she had just not ever been into all this footie business.

'Did they fall out?' Ruth asked.

'No,' she responded with a chuckle. 'Decided in the end it'd be best if Lucas popped round when Graeme was away. He was always suspicious of him, but all be part of the team rivalry no doubt. Got this idea in his head about Lucas being after me money.' It was time for the lightbulb on top of Inga's head to flash warning signs. 'Couldn't get all the time could Lucas, so it were usually when Graeme were off somewhere with United.'

'And why couldn't he get?'

'Has his own business Lucas does and knew where to invest for best returns. Done me real proud so far.'

'You've given him money?' This was the first they'd heard of it.

'Yes bit by bit. Gets good returns and no mistake.'

Inga turned to look at the wishy washy Myra sat there hands pushed down between her knees. 'Any chance of another cuppa?' she asked. 'I'm sure Amber could do with one.' Truth was Amber had not touched hers but Inga needed to get the woman away for a few moments at least. She looked at Ruth and winked. 'Give Myra a hand please, there's a girl.' She waited while the cups and saucers were collected up and the pair of them had left the long lounge and Ruth had quietly closed the door.

'Can I ask Amber? How much are we talking money-wise?'

'Altogether?' Inga nodded. 'Probably about...let me see, be twelve thousand pounds I think now.'

'You've given to Lucas?' Inga was aware the amount she'd received in compensation had amounted to just over one hundred and seventeen thousand.

'To invest, not given it to him,' sounded very indignant. 'Doing well Lucas says, now things are a tad

better with interest rates. Don't understand it all myself, Gordon used to deal with all the money and stuff.'

'You just gave him twelve thousand.'

'No,' she said and chuckled. 'Made it in three thousand lots each time, makes it easier, then the people at the bank don't ask too many questions. You'd think it was their money the way they poke their noses in.' Inga wanted to tell the dozy woman there was a very good reason for it. To stop fools like her being conned.

'How did you pay him?'

'Remember Gordon saying more than once when he put money in the bank, women behind the counter always got something to say, used to take the mickey out of them something chronic.'

'This by cheque?' Inga persisted.

'The money?' Inga wanted to scream at her, *of course the bloody money!*

'Yes,' was blunt.

'Cash. Lucas said it was easier his way, don't have to wait for it to clear, can take ages with cheques he said, need to get it into the special account as quick as you can and get the best interest.'

'And you've got details of the account?'

Amber shook her head, and pouted again. 'No sorry me duck. Lucas is dealing with it all.'

'How do you know your money's doing well?'

'Lucas said,' she shot back as if it was obvious.

Inga pulled a notebook from her bag, she handed to Amber Coetzer with a pen and asked her to write down the details of all her husband's places of work, and in particular where he worked with this Lucas Penney. As it turned out her memory was very sketchy over where he had worked and when, but they'd have to work with what they'd got.

'Is he pretty much local this Lucas Penney?'

'Oh dear me, no. Comes from just north of Hull up Beverley way.'

'Is it where your husband knew him from?'

'Grimsby he said. Said it's where he and Gordon first worked together.'

'Sorry to bring this up,' it was time for the crucial follow-up. 'When was it your Gordon had his accident?'

'25th June 2014,' would be etched in her memory.

'And this Lucas has been visiting since when?'

'Be about…just after…about Easter time it'd be.'

'Talk to me about Graeme and his football,' was a clever Inga switch of subject now she had the news she wanted.

'What d'you want to know?'

'Has he ever been involved in any of the hooliganism?'

'No, of course not,' was adamant.

Inga already knew the answer. There was nothing on the Police National Computer (PNC) about Graeme Coetzer at all and according to DS Raza Latif was not even a sniff about him on the National Criminal Intelligence Service database who list all known hooligans.

'I take it he has a season ticket.'

'Of course.'

'How long has he had one do you know?'

'Since he was a kid and Gordon bought him one.' Inga already knew from information the club had provided along with Graeme's booking to travel to Turin.

Inga Larsson didn't want the tea of course, just a way of getting nosey Myra out of the road while she talked money. Just the sort who leave mawkish flower tributes still in cellophane at roadside shrines for people she doesn't know.

The pair of them had to suffer more of the dreadful excuse for a cup of tea before they left most of it and headed off to find something decent to drink.

In the car the Detective Inspector was more than a little annoyed. 'Are you seriously telling me this stupid woman actually gave some passing stranger a load of cash?'

'Seems like it,' Ruth confirmed.

'How many warnings do people like her ignore? Bet if we phoned up and asked for her pin number she'd give it.'

'Probably because we seem like figures of authority.'

Back in the Incident Room still bristling Inga Larsson had a job for DC Kenny Ford who had been attached to them from PHU again. Going bald in his mid-thirties but shaved his head to hurry up the process.

The boss had already tasked him with tracing Gordon Coetzer's employers and trying to establish where he might have worked with a Lucas Penney. He had started of course with the construction firm where sadly Gordon had met his death. To their credit they were as helpful as they could possibly be and promised to e-mail him details of Gordon's work period and said they would hunt down any records they had on a Lucas Penney.

Now Inga wanted Kenny to confirm from the information he had at his disposal the date of Gordon Coetzer's accident and the date the compensation had been paid out. June 2014 was just as she had expected for the accident as was January 2018.

9

Hello. Some of the stuff you've been reading I knew nothing about of course. I was simply carrying on with life, totally unaware of what was just around the corner.

My Edward phoned again next evening of course just as he had promised. This delightful man enthused about the grey stallion he had bought me and promised when the opportunity arose to take a photograph and email it to my laptop.

Don't tell anybody will you? But to be honest I was glad it would be him dealing with it all. I've never sent an attachment to anybody and to be honest have no idea how I would go about such a thing. At least I know should the situation arise young Brandon next door will come to my rescue.

Edward was by then dealing with the movement and transportation of the five horses he had bought for clients, would then make his way back to the UK with them and head for Lambourn and the various yards where they were all to be stabled.

Be about another week he'd said before he would be in Newmarket and could then get up to see me, but he'd keep in touch as much as he could.

The moment he rang off I remembered again about the murder I'd forgotten to mention. I had so wanted to tell Edward about the dead man in Washingborough as it turned out was a Manchester United supporter and according to *Radio Lincolnshire,* the Police were looking into a football connection.

Never mind I thought to myself, I'll just have to remember to tell him next time he phones.

Wish somebody would investigate why TV commentators have over recent years become so dreadful. Why they need to utter such pointless tedious gibberish and shout and scream?

Did they learn nothing from the genre's past masters? Often wonder what a complete balls some of they would make of "...crowd are on the pitch, they think it's all over – it is now!"

Was never going to be a case of me getting one over on my Edward but he had been very sceptical and I knew I would delight in informing him it really was murder up there in the village. What did concern me was they never mentioned the mother any more. Was she still helping with enquiries, been thrown in the slammer awaiting trial or given a date to return and just packed off back home?

Felt a concern for her I truly did. If she had killed her son she'd not get my sympathy but I still couldn't help but think about her. How her life had changed in an instant for ever, and wondered how on earth she would be dealing with the prospect of life in a manky prison cell. Maybe for ever with no going back. No chance to say sorry pet, do everything she could to make things better as mothers do.

Made me shudder just thinking about it I can tell you. Wondered how I would cope should anything like it befall me.

Edward had said another week, and I knew he'd be busy dealing with those horses but I was still disappointed when he didn't phone next day. Was it really too much to ask? Not as if he had to find a phone box in France and have the right Euros to drop in the slot or whatever they do over there.

Have to admit it now. It was a bit of a glum Jacs cooking for the homeless, but they are always a cheery lot regardless of the position they find themselves in so I shouldn't really grumble. It was also something worthwhile to keep my mind occupied and their circumstances are always a great deal worse than mine have ever been or likely to be. In truth I was just a bit disgruntled that's all. I knew every one of them I was feeding given half a chance, would swap their life for mine at the drop of a hat.

Guess the poor woman up in Washingborough, very much still on my mind, would swap her new life for mine without a second thought.

I won't lie to you, but after three days of silence I did begin to worry about my Edward. On the fourth day of nothing I had phoned his mobile out of concern for his safety as by then I'd have expected him to be back in the UK and at the very least would have just given me a heads up about his situation.

Just a sound on the phone, a long tone was ominous.

I must have delved into the scurrilous emails on my laptop five or six times a day since I'd last spoken with him. Edward had promised a picture of my grey horse. Nothing.

Guess by now you're thinking I'm behaving like a young blushing schoolgirl over this man.

Nothing from Edward. Certainly not an email with an attachment I might not know how to deal with but there was plenty of course from people trying to sell me things I would never ever buy or want me to sign up to some daft scheme. Young people have a name for such nonsense but I can't for the life of me remember it.

Sorry but I really don't want to go to a Next Sale or buy Edward a shirt from Cotton Traders and quite frankly I don't give a toss right at this moment if my latest bank statement is now available on line. Please Amazon, not today. I know 99p is a good price, but I've got two books on my Kindle I've not got round to reading yet. I can't handle any more at present! I'm sorry but I'm really not in the mood.

Going to the lonely club next day was not the wisest decision I have ever made in my dull little life. It was one thing feeling lonely from time to time but it was quite another to be in complete unhappiness surrounded by other sufferers at a drop-in. I simply had no get-up-and-go, no enthusiasm to help those around me. I was nowhere near close to the state I had been when mummy died, which had been the last big trauma in my life, but I was very concerned for my Edward's safety.

The sad passing of mummy had been some time coming, and had been quite obviously a reaction to daddy Arthur's sudden death. Miriam Epton-Howe had not expected his heart attack and was provided with no opportunity to say goodbye to her Arthur; the aspect I know had hurt mummy the most.

I knew how she had for the most part been brushed aside by daddy during their marriage and had always played a minor support role in his life, and now the same had happened at the time of his demise.

A lingering death was surely not what Miriam would had wanted for the one man in her life, but it was the complete opposite which caused lasting hurt. It was how I would prefer to end my days, here one minute gone the next. Best way I've always thought for the person concerned. No pain, no agony, no incapacity, no lingering slip sliding into the inevitable. Not so good I appreciate for those left behind, those who had waited too long to say what needed to be said, even if it were only a few choice words of love and affection.

In really quiet moments of reflection and contemplation I can almost feel mummy's hand in mine even now. Those last few months as she slowly slipped away from me were for the most part blissfully quiet affairs, and we would sit side by side like an old couple on the sofa hand in hand. It was as if mummy knew her days were numbered and was desperate to retain contact with the one thing which had been a constant in her life for decades. Someone to be there with her at the end because quite honestly there was nobody else.

Had daddy Arthur still been alive it was obvious mummy could never have relied on him for comfort and companionship. I frequently wondered in those last few months and still do so now, how she had felt about being virtually abandoned.

It was almost as if mummy had played out her designated role in life and now she had just been left to drift away into oblivion.

She was always concerned with respectability and would so often say "We're a respectable family" which was ridiculous statement with her husband chasing floozies probably every day of their married life, and the people she was saying it to probably knew exactly what he was up to and who with.

Even now I wonder if she was ever jealous of those other women daddy went with. Were they in receipt of the love and caring which in truth was rightfully hers? I doubt it very much as it is unlikely daddy truly cared for anyone other than Arthur Broderick Epton-Howe.

Had mummy in effect wasted her life and had I been partly responsible for what she should have enjoyed in her dotage? I had never been able to offer her grandchildren to love and hold dear because I was the one who could and should have provided but I'd been thrown aside by that shit Roger; and in some respects I had never stood up to my bombastic father. I'd just cow tow to his demands all based upon what was best for him and his damn money pot.

Talking of money pots of untold wealth, whenever I hear talk of or read revelations about law firms specialising in offshore fraud in tax havens my immediate thought is daddy Arthur. Using some shadowy network of offensive companies to launder money and avoid tax was probably an everyday occurrence to him.

Over the next week I was loath to admit it of course, but I did not eat well, not enough to keep a fly alive as my dear old mummy would say.

When I worked two whole days at the St Joseph's Sanctuary refuge preparing and cooking meals for the homeless and those in no state to tend to themselves I couldn't face sitting down and joining in at meal time as I normally did.

I suppose people would say if they were ever to know, how it was to my credit I had made sure the homeless crew had not missed out as a result of my private and personal problems. For long hours twice during the week my mind was never on the task in hand, and I lacked any form of enthusiasm for my work. In a matter of a few days I had gone from being on top of the world to now being down in the dumps and dare I admit it – lonely. Twice in a matter of a few months, absolutely in my element in Australia at the Commonwealths back in April, then home to the hum-drum dull and dreary life I lead, although I did take in the England v India Test at Trent Bridge.

As it turned out of course it was the only one England lost. Then I was up again on a high with getting to know Edward and meeting him back in early August initially and now this. A dramatic plummet back down to earth.

No matter how bad I felt inside I still knew my lot was a great deal better than those around me including the poor wretch up in Washingborough.

I guess it's quite possibly what you're thinking right now. Asking what on earth has this snobby woman got to moan about? Bet you're aching to tell me I need to try to eke out a living on the ruddy benefits pittance you get each month especially if you're on this Universal Credit nonsense. You're right, I'm sure I'd have something to moan about if I was stuck on it. All right for the likes of me I must admit never having been on zero hours with sky high rent for a place reeking in damp and mildew.

I admit I have the ability and where-with-all to savour the good things in life, own a huge great big home and land, a fortune in stocks and shares, a more than considerable property portfolio which I have to admit in some cases includes almost whole streets and to top it all a more than decent bed to sleep in each and every night.

Of course, by sheer good fortune I've never been part of this 'generation rent' they're calling folk these days, but had I been I'd have certainly done something about it.

Sorry, but the young of today spend far too much time and money on instant gratification instead of doing what their forebears did so well. Went without and saved hard for tomorrow and as a result are now able to enjoy the benefits we all admire.

Since mummy died I had given freely of my services to a number of different organisations and there are still two charity shops who know they can call on me at short notice should they be in dire need of a helping hand.

I'll be honest with you now, things had become very bad since I'd not heard from Edward. I became seriously downhearted when his phone still just responded to my attempts to call with a dull tone. At times I'll admit I just wished I too could be taken like daddy Arthur. Here one minute, gone the next, forgotten. After all, who in God's name would ever miss someone like me?

The loneliness had by then engulfed me in a way I am quite sure I had truly never ever experienced before. I felt as if I was being put through the very same life episodes as mummy had endured. An absent man.

Back home on my own, my good deed at St Joseph's completed once again, I was far too preoccupied with what I might have done wrong.

How had I got it all so wrong with Edward? The line of self-questioning brought me time and again round to one subject: Roger Styles.

What had I done seventeen years ago to make someone I was betrothed to go with another? Not only go with another as in be unfaithful, but plan to marry. Down the aisle they went while I had sat at home up in my bedroom crying my eyes out. The very same bedroom I had laid in and cried in again now. Back in 2001 I had certainly been in a dreadful state at one o'clock when I knew they would be stood side by side in the St Mary and St Nicholas parish church. Roger in a new suit no doubt and pretty little Brenda all in white. Pretty she was then, not the dumpy little thing she has turned into, I guess is me being bitter and twisted.

All happening in the very church where I thought Roger and I had planned to marry before the end of the year. I have tormented myself over the years with thoughts of confetti, the bridesmaids, the 3-tier cake, the honeymoon…

Mummy and Daddy didn't give a tinker's about the end of my love life as I recall. Although the subject was never mentioned I'm sure they were both hoping I'd choose someone more sophisticated and wealthy, a go-getter travelling the globe from exciting city to exciting city. Roger of course according to mummy was only a farmer boy.

Amazing how times change, but to my mind not necessarily for the better.

When Roger and I planned to marry we had been going out together a while, then got engaged after he'd asked daddy for my hand in marriage and we planned our wedding. Despite both our fathers being worth a few bob neither of them were of a mind to stump up for a house for us. This of course quite rightly was in order for us to understand the value of money. We planned to rent to start with then save until we had the deposit and obtain a mortgage. The way things were done and had been done for generations.

Talking about getting engaged. I understand some female wants engagement rings done away with,

because according to this silly bism it is anti-feminist. What preposterous nonsense. Becoming engaged to be married is all about love and commitment and has nothing to do with being somebody's chattel. I do worry what gets into some people these days and wonder if all this nonsense is the product of university life.

At least with a father like mine I simply had to learn fast. How I wish so many of today's young people could do with some aspects of a parent like him around.

So many of them these days have not learnt to think for themselves, can't seem to solve issues alone and certainly find adversity a real problem to deal with.

All down I'm afraid to the poor darlings being overindulged and financed stupidly by the harmful bank of mummy and daddy.

Problem now is, their parents and grandparents in particular who were exactly the opposite when they were growing up will not now give their challenging attitude a rest. They have an in-built need to continue to do the same for their so-called siblings leaving them bereft of capability in so many aspects of life.

Nowadays of course they all have to have it NOW. They meet over alcohol, have sex, move in next day, have kids with daft names, a giant flat screen television, an expensive phone each, some virtual reality gizmo, snort cocaine, buy a coffee machine and every mod-con you can imagine then moan like heck about how they can't raise enough for a deposit.

Excuse me! You've got it all arse about face.

Now I had lost another. Lightning had struck twice. Not lost Edward to another as far as I know, and on this occasion no talk of marriage had come into our relationship, but lost him I now considered I had. Why else had there been nothing? No phone calls and no email and certainly no attachment with the picture of my grey horse he'd bought at the sales in France for me.

If tragedy had somehow befallen him I would never know of course. Jacqueline Epton-Howe was never going to be the next-of-kin anyone would contact. If he was indeed dead, there would no doubt be others somewhere dealing with the brunt of the tragedy. All I could do was pray he was safe and well. Even if he no longer had any feelings for me I wished the good man no harm.

At three o'clock gone in the morning I was sat bolt upright in bed in the dark in tears again another seventeen years on, having spent hours trying to figure out what was the same about 2001 and now? What could I have possibly have done to frighten Roger away into the arms of another and what had I now idiotically repeated to simply ensure Edward had just disappeared from my radar?

We've all been through such nights and they really are no fun are they? Think it's the clock which annoys me more than anything. Why on bad really nights do the hands move so incredibly slowly?

10

By morning there were no firm conclusions, the relationships were so completely different. Varying ages and eras, contrasting people and places to some extent, personalities and circumstance. I'd not been a virgin when Roger told me it was all over back then and I'd had but one lover up to that point - him.

Was other men the issue?

Surely not. Had my life been littered with dozens of lovers, good and bad I can well imagine my reputation might be of concern for some men.

Edward could not have expected me to be as pure as the driven snow at my age, as white as the dress I was planning to wear. Couldn't possibly be, as the name of Roger Styles had never come up in conversation and as far as I know Edward would be completely unaware of the farmer boy and especially the Dale sod.

Why then had he never even hinted at sex? Had it been up to me? Was it modern protocol, should I have been bold and invited Edward into my room and ultimately into my bed? Surely it cannot be what he was waiting for. A black tie event. By Invitation Only.

Another sad day gone and being the soppy sod I am, I had counted each and every bad one. To be truthful I had actually put a cross on each day on my calendar. How sad am I? In the end when there had been absolutely no contact, no hint, no nothing, when the postman called I became excited. For all of the thirteen seconds it took me to scamper to the oak front door, only to discover it was my bank telling me about a change of their head office registered address. What a waste of money. Plus of course just more pitiful nonsense Royal Mail had been paid to deliver to all and sundry whether they were in need of it or not.

I had not been to the lonely club yet that week and when there was a knock on my front door before I'd even given thoughts of what to have for my evening meal a cursory glance, I knew to hold my tongue. Chances are it would be a nosey so-and-so asking after my welfare, which probably meant in truth they were short staffed for Friday.

'Hi,' said Brandon arms folded leant against the wall beside my front door. 'Got five minutes?' I had all the time in the world, but lacked interest and most certainly patience.

'Is it important?' I asked with an undertone of *I really don't have time for this, so if you'd be so kind...*

'Mum's a bit concerned about you.'

'I'm fine, honest I am.' Brandon didn't move a muscle. I just sighed and peered at him. 'Good days, bad days, we all get them.' The look on his face told me he'd not bought it, but would you have?

'And your friend?' His hand went up and I wondered if a pipe of peace would be next.

'Not about at the moment,' was the best I could do and swallowed hard.

'Is that right?' Brandon let his hand fall from the wall and he took a step forward. 'Mine's coffee with a dash of milk, what about you?' And before I could do or say anything this tall good looking lad had squeezed past me and was striding off down my hall.

By the time I had closed the door and my mouth, recovered from his audacity and reached the kitchen I was the one leaning against the doorpost. 'Tassimo or instant?'

A few minutes later there had been no further conversation apart from an instruction here and there before we were both seated in the Morning Room either side of my old coffee table.

'Now,' he started. 'What's this all about? Got to say mum's very concerned for you, said you've gone from your bubbly best to...' he lifted his hands.

'Isn't this the wrong way round?' I queried with the hint of a snigger. 'Shouldn't I be offering you words of advice, a shoulder to cry on and listening to a young man's testosterone fuelled troubles and woes?'

'There is a problem then.'

Admitting it all to myself had been hard enough, but coming out with all my innermost trials and tribulations to a young man...'Something we all go through,' I said in a vain attempt to slide around the subject. 'People come and go in our lives, something you'll get used to in time.' I couldn't could I? Talk openly and honestly with young Brandon?

'Excuse me for being disrespectful, but are we talking lovers tiff here...'

'Are we what?' was thrown out with my first chuckle in what seemed like ages.

'You fallen out with...whoever he was?'

'Edward. Edward McCafferty.' I simply couldn't could I? Talk to a lad young enough to be my son. Truth was, had I married Roger back then, someone just like young Brandon could very well be our son sat opposite me right then and there. What would you have done in my position? Just come out with it all to a lad from next door?

'Any chance of a reconciliation?' Brandon asked.

'Shouldn't imagine so, especially...' I really was so close.

'Go on.'

'All quiet on the western front, as they used to say apparently.'

'He hasn't been in touch? Is what you're saying?' Now I was struggling and daren't let the lad see how upset I was and almost in a desperate move I was on my feet into the kitchen and fussing about with opening a new packet of biscuits. 'Excuse me,' he said to nudge me out of the way. 'Let me do it.'

'Yes sir,' I responded, opened a cupboard, lifted down a biscuit barrel my mother'd had for years with Chinese characters and designs in gold and blue and returned to my seat in the Morning Room.

'He from around these parts?' Brandon asked when he appeared barrel in hand.

'No,' and immediately I knew such negativity was no answer. 'Based somewhere near Worcester, south of Birmingham, anyway.'

'You been showing him the sights?' Brandon asked. 'For what they're worth.' I'd had a list of things I'd hoped to show him.

'Afraid not. Edward never wanted to go gallivanting about when he visited and I could understand it. He spent so much of his time travelling up and down the country all he wanted was a bit of peace and quiet.'

'What did he do, this...Edward?'

'Horse trader.'

'Not meat surely,' he chuckled. 'I thought…'

'No,' stopped him. 'He buys and sells racehorses.'

'I was going to say,' said Brandon as he sipped his cappuccino. 'You into all that?'

'No,' I had to admit. What was the point in pretending? 'Don't know much about it at all to be honest. Love great sport but horse racing's never really appealed. Done the Derby and Grand National, but never Cheltenham.'

'This how you met?'

Now we were in the realms of don't go there. Now it was most certainly time to call a halt to this before I was completely engulfed in embarrassment. Already I felt as if we were like some old couple with this conversation running back and forth.

'How are your experiments coming along?' I tossed in. It's all very well you sitting there being all critical and clever with bundles of hindsight, but I had to do something. I was actually living this remember, not just reading about it like you are.

'Still a few wrinkles to iron out. Talking of which, dad mentioned he'd seen this Edward heading in from out Moulton Chapel way. Where d'you say he's from?'

'Worcester.'

'Mighty strange route in.'

He was right. 'Anything as yet on my idea of introducing tablets at the club?' fortunately came to mind. I just had to somehow move him away from Edward. Every time I thought about him things just got worse and now Brandon was adding fuel to the fire and I simply could never let this go down the lonely hearts route.

'Probably his sat nav. Do the daftest things at times.'

'As long as your cameras don't do silly things,' I offered and sipped my hot coffee.

'Not right is it?'

'What?' I slipped out with a breath with mug still in my hands.

'Coming that way?'

'Wha…what's it matter?'

'You sure you're all right?' he insisted. No I was not all right, but how on earth could I admit it to anyone as young as him? I closed my eyes. Who else was there? Nosey women at the club, people like Fliss Gilmour? Some of the people I feed at the hostel were really good people, just down on their luck. Could talk to one or two there I suppose, but most of them had more than enough problems of their own.

'And if I'm not?' was out before I'd given the matter any thought at all.

'Talk to me?'

'Have you eaten?'

It was now Brandon's turn to be confused by the chain of conversation, a look written all over his handsome young face.

'No, but...'

'Give your mum a call to explain and I'll knock us up something. Lasagne do?'

'Wait a minute,' he insisted, and for the first time there was a degree of annoyance in his voice as I got to my feet.

'I'll be honest with you I've not had a decent meal for days. So, how about we get ourselves organised with a bit of food, I'll find a bottle of plonk and we can have a chat?'

All this with Brandon was a massive step in my relationship with my neighbours, as until then I'd had little or no social interaction with Robert or Prudence Wishaw, and it had nothing to do with my being their landlord.

I just feel a sense of awkwardness and perhaps I am too polite to invite Pru over for a cup of tea. Why? Because I really would not want her to feel obliged to reciprocate and it then turn into some sort of regular event she'd then feel she should not dip out of for fear of upsetting her landlord. At the same time I had never wanted them to feel I considered myself too good. All the tawdry business I had left behind with my parents, all wrapped up in class and status nonsense. A dilemma, but this broadening of contact with Brandon was certainly a step in the right direction.

Lasagne appeared as if by magic. Truth was it was one I'd prepared earlier as they say, cooked that very morning in the ridiculous hope somehow my Edward might just turn up out of the blue to surprise me, which he had never done before. All it needed now was the beef and pork, pasta, Italian mozzarella and creamy béchamel warming through.

There never was a next time he would just turn up I have to advise you right now, so you fully understand my dilemma. Therefore I sadly have to report how it had been the last time I one Jacqueline Rosemary Miriam Epton-Howe ever heard from Edward McCafferty.

11

As I prepared the meal and set two places at the table in the dining room my mind ran through a whole host of scenarios of how I just might talk to Brandon about my problems. How should I approach the situation I now found myself in? How much should I tell a young man, what should I tell him and most important to what degree should I admit my fears?

Worst fear? The dreaded thought of bursting into tears right there in front of a young man sat at my dining table. The sheer ignominy would I knew just be too much.

As we sat across my dining table from each other I wondered why it is so few of the young people today know how to handle and use cutlery.

In Brandon's case of course he owes his manners and behaviour to his parents. Whereas so many mothers in this day and age are too obsessed with showing off their obesity to the world sat in a hot tub, taking selfies and downing another gin cocktail to educate their offspring.

Oh how I wished I was more like mummy in the way she had appeared to deal with relationships, almost at times as if they were happening to somebody else. Daddy Arthur had indeed been the sort of successful man anybody would be proud to have as their husband, provided they never knew the truth. The sort some call a proper man's man, a real hard core dyed-in-the-wool big bluff Tory who didn't care who knew it.

Some time back a goon had admitted he didn't eat ice cream because he was a man. To be honest with absolutely no feminine side to him daddy would have fitted the bill, had a very similar attitude to life. 'Women's work' was what he saw all domestic chores, and it is doubtful whether he had ever done the washing up and most certainly not the ironing.

Had no time for all these other folk, he usually referred to as 'lefties' and 'pinkos', but it was just his out of date way; take it or leave it would be his motto. He of course had an absolute ghastly galaxy of names he used for homosexuals and lesbians not to mention anybody less than pure white and English.

I simply cannot imagine how he would react to reports of young children claiming they are transsexual and all this supposed gender confusion business would have him hollering abuse from the rooftops. Just the thought of his reaction to such claims I'm sorry to say really make me chuckle.

In truth it was the way he had been brought up, and to some extent we all owe the way we are, the way in which we think, behave and engage with others, to our forebears to a degree.

Problem with Arthur Epton-Howe was he had been a philanderer and in fact at the end had died in some other woman's bed.

A Rosanne Scutt it was, what a dreadful woman she turned out to be when in anger I had decided to seek her out and looked into her background. Just one of three he was having on-off affairs with apparently, and mummy just didn't seem to care. Arthur was her husband and I guess Miriam knew no matter what, he'd come back to her. Except of course on the fateful night when he'd had a cardiac arrest in the awful woman's boudoir.

I was certainly pleased and to some extent relieved none of them were at his funeral I was aware of, but had the distinct feeling had they turned up mummy would most probably have been most courteous and thanked them for coming.

Arthur Epton-Howe's life was always one of big bucks, big business, but along with it were hideously offensive fun which very often was male exclusive, so it was little wonder mummy spent her life hidden away in Oakdenne House with her only daughter as her constant companion.

Daddy absolutely adored that aspect of life. Being the life and soul of the party was true delight to the big bombastic man.

Few years it has been now since mummy had joined him in the family plot in the cemetery. Years of regretting not being more forthright with my father by not insisting I had a proper career. It was all very well running the home in mummy's dotage, preparing meals, cooking a whole series of somewhat exotic and wholesome meals for daddy to then discover he had eaten out only when he returned home in the early hours. Being a lady of leisure like mummy was all very well, but where had it all left me now I was on my own? Doing good deeds like mummy? This lonely walk-in club was a prime example and how ironic is it now I ask? The vast majority of those suffering were in their position simply because their husband or wife in truth had moved on or had passed away.

My problem was I had never had a better half to start with.

When mummy passed away as her only daughter, only child in fact, I should have by then been happily married for a good number of years and produced grandchildren for her.

Think the way things turned out I was better off as an only child. Can you imagine me coping with a bichon frise of a little sister or should I be all PC and call it my sibling.

At times I almost feel ashamed as if I have failed as a human being. Get the feeling some people see me as not being a complete woman as I've not had a brood. I seem to have become a sort of social pariah – a woman without children is so often cruelly seen as someone to avoid, almost as if being unfruitfull is something you can catch.

Other women of course are the worst, and I find they bring up the subject of children quite deliberately with loaded questions. *'How old are yours now?'* or *'How many is it you've got did you say?'* When their best topic of conversation is about the need to rebuild their pelvic floors I'm out of there sharpish I can tell you.

There is more to life than having babies, but some of course are incapable of doing much else besides. Be what they refer to these days as a skill set I suppose. Providing bad sex, having scurrilous kids, but not up to achieving anything worthwhile after.

Had daddy had more sense and not been so stubborn about his preferred role for women in the world it would have been of considerable benefit. A staunch Conservative who had no time for Thatcher – a poshed-up housewife and a mere small town grocer's daughter in a man's world was how he would describe her on a good day.

They did however have one thing in common, neither he nor Maggie Roberts as he often called her, could stand men with beards. I cannot imagine what daddy would think in this day and age when so many have been browbeaten by their women desperate for them to be part of the latest pitiful happening.

Daddy was a serious wet shave man all his life and to his mind men with beards were always 'pinkos'. This absurdly was based on his perception of them being lukewarm communists wearing sandals all year round because boots are a right-wing concept.

At times I did wonder if he was even happy with women getting the vote at all, so rooted was he in old traditions. Convention and ritual introduced to him at public school no doubt. He'd have been more than happy with Rees-Mogg based purely on where he had been educated, but had not lived to see the twerp's unfortunate rise to prominence.

Nowadays there are many things I know would have annoyed the great man and I really cannot imagine what he would have thought of men and boys wearing earrings.

One of my constant nightmares these days is seeing Roger Styles and his wife together in town, almost as if they do it on purpose to upset me. It may only be three or four times a year but it's quite enough thank you, as a reminder of what might have been.

For years I have been haunted by a single thought, and with all the issues surrounding Edward it had reared its ugly head again. Had Roger Styles used me purely for practice? Was it true when he had said when he took my virginity one Saturday afternoon how it was his first time? It was pretty obvious as things turned out the lying hound was already in a relationship with pretty little Brenda. In times of real deep depression I constantly ask myself if I had been nothing more than somebody willing to offer Edward the practice he was after, so when he got it together with his bride-to-be there would be none of the fumbling about and missing the target I had endured.

Now I had to talk about another lost love. Probably something mummy in her emotional detached manner would have been quite happy to do, but not me and not with a young man. This could prove very embarrassing.

It took a little while for me to pluck up the courage once I had decided how I wanted to play this. I know people see me as a woman of self-confidence and strong opinions with a forthright manner I have inherited from daddy. Inside I feel a lot different much of the time.

12

First I had to establish with young Brandon sat opposite me how our conversation had to be in the strictest confidence.

Knew I really did have to talk to somebody, and when there was little choice this young man would just have to do.

'Please hear me out,' I started as I put down my knife and fork and lifted my glass. A sip first. 'I'm a silly old woman and…'

'Not so much of the old,' got him a look. 'Sorry,' he smiled.

'I don't mind admitting I do get lonely sometimes. Go to help out at the club as you know, but to be honest some of the time I'm the one in need. Anyway.' I stopped to sip again and knew this was in for a penny in for a pound time. 'I went on one of these…lonely hearts websites.' I had to stop and sipped more as my nerves go to me. 'I'm not going to explain what, why and wherefore at every little juncture or we'll be here all night, save to say I've been a damn fool. Just hear me out.' Another sip of my red wine and I was back to looking at the half-eaten meal on my plate I could have been sharing with a man who by now should have been my lover. 'Got talking to this guy, who turned out to be Edward, did it on line not talking as such at that stage, then he phoned, we met for coffee, then he came over one Sunday, then another.' I blew out a breath. 'Then he stayed for a weekend, then a couple of days, started to become a regular event almost,' I added quickly through nerves as if what I had just said was a deadly sin. I glanced up for the first time. Brandon was just getting on with his meal. 'Gave him the money for a horse.' I was embarrassed, dropped my head and sat there in silence just looking down at the table. The table Edward McCafferty and I had shared on quite a few occasions for breakfast, for mid-day snacks and our evening meals. Meals I had done my utmost to ensure he found appealing and enjoyed. 'You're quiet.'

'Thought you didn't want me to interrupt.'

'He went to France to buy me a horse at the yearling sales, the money's gone and so has he. Three card trick and I fell for it hook, line and stinker.'

'And you've got money trouble as a result I take it?'

'No,' I added with the hint of a chuckle. 'Bit of a blow if I'm honest but won't have me claiming benefits.'

I'd pretty much gone as far as I was willing to go. I was never going to explain how I'd have to sell a few shares to make up the shortfall or get rid of one of those terraced houses if needs must. With most of my wealth all tied into those trust funds daddy had set up to protect me from the unscrupulous, there is never huge piles of ready money I can lay my hands on. I'll just bide my time for now I'd already decided.

'And what have you done about this Edward character?'

'What can I do?' I asked in all honesty.

'How about the police for starters?'

'Don't be silly,' I put down my glass as I felt some of the tension weighing me down had been lifted slightly and then I returned to my meal.

'Why is it silly? It's what they're there for.'

'Serious?' I tossed at him with a smile, a fork full and a breathy snigger. 'Walk into the police station and say, excuse me constable I met this total stranger on the internet who persuaded me to buy a horse, now he and the horse and the money have gone, what you going to do about it?'

'And if he's done it before?'

'How d'you mean?'

I had to wait for Brandon to finish eating. 'They may have a file on someone they're looking for and you just might have the one clue they're after. Or can add to what they already know.'

'I very much doubt it,' and slipped a forkful into my mouth.

'Can I ask? How long has this been going on?'

'Three months or thereabouts, actually met him first time early August.' I looked at Brandon. 'I was so careful,' I insisted quite loudly. 'I didn't tell him anything, it was ages before I'd give him my number. First face to face was down in Newmarket for a coffee in broad daylight,' I added as I tried so hard to build a defence against being thought of as a complete imbecile.

'Problem?' Brandon queried softly with me sat there with my eyes closed.

'Think going to Australia didn't help,' I said and then opened my eyes. 'Been going with the same company for donkey's years to athletics all over the world, meet up with like-minded folk I've known for ages.' I stopped to sigh. 'I guess when I came back, another Commonwealth over with, all the excitement and camaraderie I enjoy on such trips was gone again and I was back to this hum drum life I lead.' I sniggered slightly. 'Great sport, thrills and excitement, lovely company, sightseeing, dining out, sunshine…'

'And this Edward was still there waiting?'

'Not exactly,' I sighed. 'First made contact on the web, then I went to Aus and when I came back…'

I saw Brandon close his eyes before he spoke. 'If this was all a con, I've got to say he'd been very patient.'

'And secretive.'

'I'll help you clear all this away,' he said getting to his feet. 'I'll get my laptop. Time me thinks to do a bit of digging into this guy.'

In the end I did all the clearing away and tidying up, did the washing up while Brandon walked home to collect his laptop and a few bits and pieces I didn't understand at all. Within half an hour he was all set up on my dining room table. Raspberries and cream I'd bought earlier once more in my naive hope of a sudden appearance were first on the agenda and our glasses had again been replenished.

I found it simply fascinating to watch Brandon on his laptop, the speed at which he slipped from one website to another, brought up all sorts of what looked like complicated formulae, but in the end all to no avail.

I'd learnt not to ask too many questions at times like these. Being told he was using an encrypted memory stick might as well have been double Dutch.

Interesting when I thought back to my school days and how boys I knew then would have laughed had anyone suggested they learn to type. Something of that sort in those days was considered very girly – like shorthand, one of the things daddy would never have done.

As I watched he sought information from a whole range of places from lonely hearts clubs and sites, through to horse breeding in

Britain, France and even Ireland. Couldn't look up the horse I was supposed to have bought as I had no idea of its name or lineage or whatever these horsey types call it. Brandon also phoned the number I had for this Edward to no avail.

'Looks like bad news,' he said after I'd watched him slide down pages of the website linked to yearling sales in France. 'He's not listed, nor are you as having even bought a rocking horse at the sales in Deauville.' He stopped, sipped his wine and as he looked at me I saw him pull his bottom lip through his teeth. 'As far as I can see there never was a yearling sale when you said there was.'

'He said it was a trade sale,' I meagerly offered and Brandon grimaced.

In the end, with his glass empty, Brandon sat back in his chair next to me and ran his fingers through his thick brown hair.

'Coffee?' I offered, but his hand on my arm stopped me moving for a moment.

He hesitated. 'How much?'

I blew out a little breath, was about to say *mind your own damn business*, but then I just blurted it out: 'Forty. Forty thousand…pounds.'

'Bloody hell!'

'Told you I was a silly old woman,' and I was on my feet wrapped in pure discomfort. 'Coffee?'

'Yes please, but before you go. Looks as though forty grand would have bought you a pretty decent horse by the look of the figures here and…'

'Brilliant,' I interrupted with amusement. 'Bit like saying your numbers came up on the Lottery pity you didn't buy a ticket.'

Of course I've no idea how I'll explain all this to my accountant.

Back in 2001 when the rat Roger married his pretty little Brenda I'd sat on my bed and cried my eyes out. I'm willing to admit I am still not too long in the tooth for the wet hankie routine. He wasn't to know and it most certainly all got to me, sat there with Brandon. Been tossed aside once more was what I already knew but somehow sat there it just all showered over me.

In truth I was much better off on my own in the kitchen, with my Tassimo as a comfort blanket.

13

Coffee served and with it more of those delightful oaty biscuits one of the ladies at the lonely folks club had recommended. Is it all my life amounts to, what I'll be remembered for? Somebody who enjoyed a decent biscuit?

'You know what you have to do?' brought me back to down to earth.

'No.' But I did. I guessed what was coming next from Brandon.

'You have to go to the Police. This has all the makings of a clever scam.'

'And what good will it do apart from bandy my foolishness around Spalding?'

'They'll not go telling all and sundry your business.'

'You can guarantee it can you?' I shot at Brandon for no reason with my self-consciousness in control.

'Just offering advice,' he shrugged self-excusingly. 'If the boot was on the other foot what would you be saying?' he asked.

I shrugged pink faced. 'Probably right.' I knew he was. 'Need to wrap it up a bit.'

'How d'you mean?' asked Brandon before he dipped an oaty biscuit into his coffee and took a bite.

'How stupid will I look going in there and telling them what a complete arse I've been?'

'Not as stupid as you could look if you don't go.'

'What d'you mean?'

'If the Police already know something is going on and during their investigations at some later date they come across your name and come knocking on your door. What d'you say then? Oh yes, I gave him forty grand but haven't bothered to mention it. They'll either think you must be loaded or you really are a complete fool.'

'See what you mean.' I knew there was no getting out of this.

'Tell you what,' he said and rested hand on my arm. 'Old friend of mine's in the force. How about I ask him to come and have an informal chat with you? Sort of off the record kind of thing, set your mind at rest. Might be able to offer a bit of advice and which way its best to play it from here.'

I sighed deeply. 'I suppose so. Have to face it one day, confess all and look a complete dipstick!' I took an initial sip of my coffee then a bite of crumbly biscuit without dunking it.

Eventually our conversation moved away from my situation and my obvious doziness and the world of technology crept logically into our discussions. I had wrongly assumed Brandon would be into all this 'gaming' you hear so much about, but had been surprised when he derided the subject. Suggested he had dabbled in his early teens but since then had preferred the real world.

The subject only came up because I'd recently read most people cannot for the life of them begin to understand why these gamers around the world get so excited about the launch of some role-playing game set a thousand years in the future.

This unlicensed skins gambling I'd also heard about is another very good reason to keep your children well away.

'Gaming is very transient,' Brandon advised. 'To be honest I went through a stage like many do, but then I matured and moved on. Same for almost everybody I know, to be honest.'

'Isn't it what the world has become obsessed by, reality with all these dreadful programmes?' I suggested.

'The problem for so many of these people is being incapable of distinguishing their world of fantasy from reality. In Japan apparently they have serious issues with teenagers becoming totally obsessed.'

'And we wonder why there are so many mixed up kids.'

'And adults,' Brandon added quickly to correct me. 'Apparently they lose their masculinity,' was not a concept I could begin to understand. 'They are rejecting the norm of men's relationship with sex and beer and apparently become disinterested in the world around them.' Brandon stopped momentarily and then went on. 'With very little social interaction it's an addiction like on-line porn can be and they both exclude female contact.'

'Not a good idea.'

'I've become interested in drone racing since I've been experimenting.'

Another thing I have yet to fathom about modern life, is the fervor generated about new smart phones. I think we need a new word, for such people – saddos is not nearly descriptive enough.

I just never imagined great swathes of seemingly intelligent young people would so easily succumb to the seduction of these little screens.

To be honest this online world is almost a foreign language to me. I grew up remember when communication was face to face the majority of the time or on a proper telephone.

Give their kids one of these all-singing all-dancing smart phones and it seems they immediately join the world of bullying or being bullied. The remedy is so very simple.

To be honest there are good many adults who could do with throwing their phones in the bin too. Complaining as they do about bovine trolls messing with their lives. Don't moan, dump it. Remember. No phone equals no trolls.

But in a world where some feckless parents are more interested in taking the little darlings to Disneyland than ensuring they have a good education are we surprised? I'm certainly not.

More than once during our conversation it did cross my mind how had I been twenty two rather than forty two, then Brandon could very well have been an object of my desires.

There were at one time people of my acquaintance with young children I would spoil with presents on their birthday and at Christmas. Not any more I don't. Seems to me basic good manners have become a forgotten way to behave these days. If these children cannot at least have the basic courtesy to say thank you, then in return I cannot give.

I can just imagine how both my parents would have reacted had I not sent thank you letters after my birthday and at Christmas.

What's the betting Brandon will? I am absolutely sure he will always say please and thank you and thank you for having me.

More than anything the evening with Brandon was a delightful opportunity to see the world from his perspective and from his viewpoint. Took me out of myself and away from what I had got myself into, except this was real life and it would not go away just by pressing *Delete*.

14

It had become almost a daily ritual between Inga Larsson and her tall shaven-headed Detective Constable Kenny Ford. She would look at him, and he would hold up a blank sheet of paper. No words were exchanged, just the tittering around the room following the convention.

So frustrated had Inga Larsson become, in the end she went back out to Washingborough to talk to Amber Coetzer about Gordon's employment record. Was there somewhere she had forgotten, somewhere he had worked maybe for a short period she had not remembered? Was she sure Lucas Penney had said he'd worked with him and was there any chance somewhere down the line he had said more than just "Grimsby"?

Then wham bam out of the blue like a bolt of lightning Amber just sat there in Myra Gaunt's scruffy lounge and casually remarked:

'Been trying to ask him,' she said. 'Tried phoning him but I just get a strange noise.' Amber Coetzer was starting to look more like the woman Inga had expected, having borrowed a framed photograph from her home to use in the Incident Room. There was no doubt this was a very attractive woman and had in her younger days been someone to catch any man's eye.

'He's not been in touch then?'

'No.'

'What do you know about him? Is he married?'

'Divorced.'

'Any details?' Inga posed and the answer was just a shake of the head. 'Does he know about what happened to Graeme?'

'No idea,' Amber said with a slight shake of her head. 'Not seen him.'

'How often did he get in touch previously?'

'Every couple of weeks or so.'

'And he's not been in touch since?'

'No.'

'Do that again,' she said and pointed to the phone. 'Phone him now.' Inga watched carefully as Amber selected him on her phone and then listened to the number unobtainable sound. Experience told her there was little point in taking the phone, she knew exactly what she would be told if she did, but to be on the safe side took it and the phone number with her to pass to the e-Team for a quick check and promised to return it to the woman post haste.

When Kenny Ford waved a blank sheet of paper at her when she walked in Inga was not at all amused. She knew as well as all the previous employers, Kenny had investigated everything he possibly could through all the police and government databases they had access to. To all intense and purposes he'd done both a Police and Open Source Search on the man. Inga's DC had been onto DVLA but the only Lucas Penney they came up with were far too old or way too young. He'd even been onto social media to see if anyone popped up who might be worth a closer look at.

None of Gordon Coetzer's employers over the years had any record of ever employing anybody by the name of or similar to Lucas Penney, except for one Michael Clayton-Penney they were quickly able to dismiss.

Amber Coetzer had described to Inga how this Lucas who visited her was around six feet tall with a full head of hair, she described him as being dark, clean shaven and oddly suggested he was muscly. She had no photo.

On Facebook Kenny had diligently discovered less than a dozen people with the name worldwide. One lived in Massachusetts, one in Newfoundland and one listed his whereabouts simply as Canada. One guy was trying his best to use the social media to sell a dune buggy, another could only talk about Liverpool football, one had no photo and one had a photograph of a young girl to worry Kenny. When DCI Luke Stevens' e-Team checked it out for him they discovered it was his daughter. They went for the one with no photo and Facebook quickly came back to the team upstairs with an American location so he was ruled out.

Kenny had even been to see the Amber Coetzer woman to check the spelling of Lucas Penney's name. She had absolutely no idea, had never seen it written down.

To be fair to him Kenny Ford was doing a good job, but he was still lagging behind DS Nicky Scoley, who'd been in his position before she went to Cambridge courtesy of the boss's pals down there. She had come on leaps and bounds since and the pair of them had continued to enjoy a fika from time to time – Swedish coffee, cake and chat when she had been in the area visiting her family.

Goodwin had suggested she hand the hunt for Penney over to Alex Kemp and his fraud team, but Inga was reluctant and didn't want those clever dicks thinking such a task was beyond her crew.

She'd steer clear of them as long as she could. The eTeam were hard enough to deal with. All their silly talk of perpetual portals, onion browsers and platforms drove her to distraction.

Later in the day it was Inga's turn to wave paper about as she strode from her office to bring almost instant silence.

'Here you people have a saying about bad luck coming in threes. Now we have them all. Lucas Penney has not been in touch and his phone is the pay-as-you-go burner he's probably thrown in the sea. Kenny cannot find anybody like him anywhere and now we have this.' She waved the print-out, then began to read.

'Our Gordon Coetzer was poisoned and...'

'I thought...' Inga's hand stopped whatever Jake was going to say.

'If you remember the pathologist said something was not right, the reason we were called in. It looked like a heart attack but now we have the forensics report.' She read carefully. 'It is something called Aconitum which is also known as Monkshood.' She looked up but there was no sign of recognition from any of her team. 'This causes vomiting, diarrhoea, paralysis of respiratory system, with convulsions and spasms. Aconitum mixed with strong tasting drink, victim would be dead before convulsions set in.' Inga looked up at Jake in particular. 'Gives the impression of heart attack most doctors would diagnose at point of death. It was all the vomit and diarrhoea which alarmed our pathologist friend.'

'Matey boy is conning Amber and the son works out what's going on...he turns up...'

'With a peace offering.'
'Bottle or two of Flying Horse and bingo!'
'Flying Dog you mean.'
'Whatever.'
'Penney turns up with a peace offering while the mother's away,' Kenny slipped in. Beside him on the desk was more than one morning's work. Evidence reports and witness statements alone were forming a neat tower of files.

'I told you Amber said her son was not too happy about him,' Inga reminded her troops.

'Has to be stopped eh?' Raza finished for Jake.

'Because he's a Man City fan you think? How sick is that?'

'Be serious!'

'Know's his mother's away for a couple of days, pops round for a drink,' Jake chuckled.

'Mother's away. Hmm convenient.'

'Don't you worry I've already thought about it,' Inga assured her new Crime Scene Manager Sandy MacLachlan.

Every now and again Sandy's vocabulary is joined by Scottish words and phrases if you listen carefully. This languid north of the border accent slips gently out like the intriguing scent of whisky passing by.

'Anybody else got a better idea?' the woman Sandy refers to as the high heid yen asked looking around the room. 'Good,' she said when nothing was forthcoming. 'There is good news. Forensics have plenty of DNA, fingerprints and fingertip sweat pores. All we have to do now is fit them to somebody.'

'Like Lucas Penney?' Sandy suggested, enjoying his opportunity.

'Whoever he might be.'

'Mr Blank Page, Mr Nobody or the man who never existed, take your pick, he's one or all of those. Certainly got me flummoxed.'

'Absolutely blinking nobody.'

'Raza, Ruth,' said Inga pointing at Raza in particular. 'Top priority for you, rip this competition business apart and the train ticket. Get onto Metro, Holiday Inn, LNER and anybody else you can think of. Anybody and everybody please feed Kenny with any ideas of how he might find somebody called Lucas Penney. Try asking these phone number people, tell them you want to talk to Lucas Penney, see what they come up with.'

'Just so you are up to scratch,' said a weary Kenny, 'this is where we are with him. The name Lucas is the 700th most popular in America for example, and only eight thousand people have the surname. On Facebook there's two in Massachusetts, one in Connecticut, one in California and just one in Kentucky.'

'What are you suggesting?' Inga posed.

'These days the eTeam are very much involved in people steeling identities as you can imagine. This has not been stolen, this is just a made up name. You've got hell on trying to find a Lucas Penney to steal. And before you ask, they tried Penney with and without an e.'

She always lived in hope but this time all Inga received in return from her team was bad news or to be more precise, no news.

'Bit of blue sky thinking?' she tossed back with a grin. 'Let's all try something off the wall, and if it all draws a blank then we take it this is the person who never existed.'

An hour later more bad news. Holiday Inn had never run a competition involving LNER and Metro and when her team then posed the same questions to the rail company and the shopping complex they ended up with a full house of rejects.

15

If Rebecca Faraday was perfectly honest with herself the break-up of her marriage after close on twenty two years had to a degree been down to her. Not been a bad girl, far from it. Never snogged the postman, committed adultery or been abusive or anything similar. It was what she had not done she now realized had been the basis of the undoing of the commitment she and Ronnie had made at St Mary's all those years ago.

She was sat in a deck chair in the unusually warm late autumn sunshine just inside the beach hut at Southwold this Keith had invited her to. Just in need of her thin cardigan today, but she could imagine what it must be like in the summer. This was glorious with the sound of the sea just lapping in way down the beach in the distance. He'd been into the Suffolk seaside town and bought fish and chips and they'd sat there together eating them out of the paper with a nice cup of tea she'd made on the primus stove while he was gone.

Rebecca wasn't dosing with a full satisfied tummy, just thinking back with her eyes closed and savouring the moment.

They'd actually met in the pub, her and her ex Ronnie Faraday. The Rose and Crown it was back in those days. Called something and Lettuce now so she understands. Ronnie played football back then for the pub team on a Sunday morning and played darts for them at least once a week. In fact 'Fingers' Leyton the goalkeeper had been Ronnie's best man at their wedding.

This was how life continued. Their life before and after marriage was based around the pub, the social hub of the community. Rose and Crown for three years after the big day but then when they'd managed to scrape enough together for the deposit and struggled to obtain a mortgage for the lovely little place on the new development, life for the pair of them had continued in the same vein – new location, new pub.

Then along came the kids of course. Victoria first and then David which of course pleased Ronnie. Married with two little ones under three, but her man still wanted to go to the pub. No, let's be honest. Ronnie insisted on going to the pub. He could see no further than going to the pub, it was his life, the hub around which he gravitated.

Forever coming out with hogwash about pubs always being the centre of the neighbourhood.

Rebecca sitting there in the sunshine wondered just how bad some of the cabaret acts had been once upon a time appearing at the Coot Inn on Friday and Saturday nights? One particular Country and Western duo she recalled were just awful thinking back now, but whatever the weather every weekend off they would trudge together to the pub.

Some of the stuff people endure these days on trashy reality shows are truly appalling but the old pair Ronnie and her sat through in their cowboy hats were really the pits. A series of babysitters left at home to listen out for the kids and watch tele and probably up to all sorts with their boyfriends.

The world gradually changed in time, everybody moved on, the pub never got into doing food and very soon deteriorated to become a den of iniquity full of loud-mouthed yobs with drugs and all sorts. No matter what, her Ronnie had to be there, reluctant to leave his womb.

People she could still recall were by then off on all sorts of great holidays. Take the couple who lived next door in those days, they had been off to Vietnam and even went on a safari in Kenya. Florida was a favourite for plenty of people with kids, except for her and Ronnie.

When her friends came back all tanned and bragged on continually about where they'd been, what they'd seen and how much cheap food they'd scoffed it really got her goat.

Those who weren't heading off to sunnier climes and places far far away were certainly going out for meals and spending weekends away, having extensions built or a conservatory added on. Yes, they went to a pub like Ronnie did, but places with a bit more about them; more family orientated. People they both knew socialized over a good meal, fine conversation and a glass or two of wine. Not for ten pints, dirty jokes, a packet of pork scratchings four or five nights a week, plus a god awful kebab at least twice from the dreadful place on the corner run by the Greek bloke.

Even though Mrs Crutchelow owner of the florists had been taken seriously ill and Rebecca had taken over Flowers by Felicity, they still could never afford it. What with the two kids, the amount they spent in the pub and then there was his gambling. Started with just the horses and now it's anything and everything. Ronnie even admitted to her brother at one time he'd spent fifty quid on the number of corners in the first half of a Cup Final a year or two back.

Enough eventually for Rebecca was indeed enough. Too many years of just putting up with a way of life for the sake of her marriage and to some extent for the sake of the children.

If only she had put her foot down when Vicky was born, maybe life would have turned out a lot different.

A little over seven years Rebecca had now been on her own and business even if she says so herself is doing really well these days, with both the kids at uni now. It had been a struggle for her and she'd certainly come through some hard times, but to be fair to Ronnie he had paid his dues on time.

'Penny for them,' she heard from Keith next to her, but she daren't relay what she had really been thinking about. Her previous life, her previous love.

'Just making the most of this. My idea of heaven, they can keep Torremolinos and all the rest of them, this is perfect.'

'That's the problem.'

'In what way?' she asked.

'My friend Russell who owns this has put it up for sale. Wants to get it off his hands before winter sets in, be more difficult to sell with snow on the ground and howling gale off the North Sea.'

'Which means..?'

'Probably my last visit.' He shrugged his broad shoulders. 'Sorry.'

'Ow,' she sighed.

'Bad timing to be honest that's all,' said Keith softly. 'Any other time and I'd see if I could raise the cash. But you know...'

'If it's not a rude question?'

'Cost an arm and a leg these places. So sought after I can tell you.' Without opening her eyes, Rebecca sensed Keith was on the move, getting up. 'Thought I'd have a bit of a wander, see if anybody can give me a heads up on value. Know what Russell's asking, just need to see what the going rate is. Won't be long.'

Rebecca hadn't mentioned it to the kids and of course daren't say a thing back at Flowers by Felicity. What would they think?

Been a good few years now since she's been with a man, and a year or two since she'd even had a date. She is well aware these days she tends to get too wrapped up in the business, making sure the kids are well looked after to worry about herself. Then by chance she came across this dating website.

Internet has a strange compulsion sometimes as she had discovered. It was through the web she'd met up with Keith Bradley. Chatted on the internet for a couple or three weeks it was. Then they met for coffee.

Rebecca was struck right away. Yes she knew from the website what he looked like, but in the flesh he was even better. Liked the unshaven look about him, great hair with those little whisps of grey above his ears.

Based down near Bristol working all hours with his hot tub business he was trying to expand he'd explained. When they met for coffee over in Kettering he told her how just eight years ago he had decided to take the plunge and branch out on his own. She knew from talking to him he had found it tough going at times and now he was involved in opening a new depot in the Lake District he seemed really excited about.

Keith's marriage like hers had gone for a ball of chalk. Except his was a bit different, his ex-wife had run off with a chap from work. Keith had admitted the first time they'd met how he'd found it difficult to build a relationship where he lives, as it seemed every woman he knew was friends with or had some contact with his ex-wife or her girly pals. Despite being the totally innocent party he was lumbered with hefty maintenance and all things considered, along with the recession a decade back he had done well to avoid the hot tub business being brought to its knees.

Keith had been different. One or two she'd dealt with through the dating thingy had been in too much of a hurry. One was a real throwback to Ronnie, wanting to meet in a bar he knew well and as a bonus suggested the place was always really buzzing. Thirty years ago maybe, but not now. Another suggested cocktails, but Rebecca wasn't sure she'd ever had a cocktail in her life, another even suggested clubbing. She immediately imagined trying to get to know someone by shouting over the din. All this of course after she had dismissed those quite obviously too young or too old and one who she guessed by his photo was far too short.

Keith had put the idea of meeting for a coffee to her in a far less hurried way. Left the date and time to her.

As she laid there in the deck chair savouring the peace and quiet her mind wandered to their first meeting. It brought a smile to her face when she wondered if Starbucks were aware they were matchmaking.

Then her thoughts went back to old Ronnie.

You'd never catch him in such a place, nor a coffee house either come to that. Too worried what his drinking buddies would think were he to be seen drinking a Latte. Rebecca knew for sure you'd not catch Ronnie sat in a deck chair in a beach hut opened onto the promenade, sandy beach and sea. There is no way he would have strolled around the town's high street window shopping as she and Keith had done and ventured onto the pier. First question when they arrived from Ronnie would have been what real ale do they sell and whatever it was he'd be down the pub or in the bookies, or maybe now he did it all on line. But there again she wasn't at all sure he'd be on line. Not his scene at all. He still thought the world was how it was when they wed. Wasn't entirely his fault, his parents had been drinkers. Thing they always thought of first before they went anywhere, can you get a decent pint, would there be a beer tent.

Ronnie Faraday was certainly nothing at all like this Keith. This man was everything Ronnie had never been. So sophisticated, so assured, good looking, smart and so very kind. A real gentleman, the sort of man she'd never seen herself with to be honest.

She'd never tried a hot tub and according to Keith there really is no better way to unwind at the end of a stressful day. According to him a Jacuzzi hot tub these days for many people is an absolute must have.

Since linking up with him on the web she'd mention hot tubs to people, but nobody she knew had even been in one let alone owned one. Might be good to be first for once and would certainly be something to tell the girls back at Felicity's.

This had been Keith's idea. A day trip over to Southwold, a place Rebecca had never been to before. A kind friend of his apparently had lent him this delightful beach hut for the day.

'You awake?' was whispered and she looked up to see Keith offering her a Magnum ice cream. 'Looks like a good deal from what I can gather,' said Keith as he sat back down in his deckchair. 'Apparently there are around two hundred and fifty huts all told and in great demand. Fetch upwards of a hundred and twenty grand and sometimes more, which kind of puts the kibosh on it.'

'Why?' Rebecca asked as she unwrapped her ice.

'All about cash flow. With the new depot opening in four weeks up in the Lakes I can't afford to leave myself short, as you never know what contingencies you'll need.'

'Would you have to pay a hundred and twenty thousand, right now?'

'No not at all,' said Keith after a few licks of his almond flavour. 'Russell says he'll let me have it for a hundred grand, wants twenty as deposit. Which is fair enough.' He shrugged. 'Any other time than this it'd be no problem, but the plan is, I think I told you, three depots to serve the country. One where I am in Bristol, one up in the Lakes to cover the north of the country and one over this side, maybe down in Essex next year or the year after will make life so much easier. Cut down on costs. Makes servicing a strong income generator with three depots, not to mention cutting down on overnight stays for the service teams.' Keith returned to his Magnum. 'Get the depot open in Kendal up and running and then you'll have to come over to me at Bristol. Bring your swimming costume and we'll enjoy a glass of wine or two in my hot tub.'

'How often do beach huts like this come on the market?' Rebecca felt she had to ask.

'Not very often. Just been talking to a chap down there. Handed down through his family he said, first came here when he was just a nipper. Reckons there's a waiting list of twenty or more all the time.'

'Popular then.'

'You can say that again and more expensive. Big advantage with this one according to the chap I've just spoken to, it's in the right place. Knowing Russell as I've done for many years I bet he's knocking twenty grand or even more off for me as a favour.'

'Have they always been here do you know?'

'Since the sixties according to Russell.'

'I could lend you the money to tide you over, how long we talking?'

'Don't be silly I wouldn't hear of it,' Keith insisted between licks. 'Just bad timing that's all.'

'Seriously,' Rebecca insisted. 'Be like a bridging loan, if it's just to tide you over.'

'Let's not spoil what we have. I don't know about you, but I feel we're good together and we don't want business and money getting in the way. What would you like to do when we've finished these?' he asked as he gestured with the remains of his Magnum.

'I'd like to come here again. In fact I'd like to be here a lot. So, what are we going to do about putting a deposit down?'

'Under normal circumstances there'd be no problem but just at this point in time what with the Lakes opening I can't put it all in jeopardy. I'll pop back and have a word with the fella, see if he knows how I get on the waiting list.'

'And wait a year or more and the price goes up another ten or fifteen, you know what they say about irons in the fire.' Rebecca turned her head and stroked Keith's arm with her spare hand. 'In a year's time we can be sat here like this lapping it up or sat down there on a towel on the sand wondering how long it'll be before one becomes available and for how much.' She looked at him until his fine head turned. 'Please.'

16

Some things are inevitable in this world and a visit from Detective Superintendent Craig Darke was just as expected as the sun rising in the morning.

Inga Larsson had organised her team's tasks after the morning briefing, and most of them were out and about attempting to move things on in their favour, sat peering at monitors or on the phones.

Having a first class relationship with her immediate boss was one of the things Inga was always pleased about. There's was a relationship filled with little idiosyncrasies they both were aware of, but never spoke about.

That morning was a case in point. He was never one to just barge into her office unannounced and she had worked out the reason why over time. He would phone and suggest a meet at her place say in half an hour to give her time.

To give her time to organise coffees. Coffee exactly as he liked it, and coffee in cups rather than in grab and go cardboard containers because he knew this was something the Swede could not abide. He also knew the chances were she'd buy biscuits as well or come up with two or three he knew she kept in her desk drawer.

So it was, with two Americanos on her desk in white mugs and a packet of bourbons she greeted him for his briefing.

'Before we start,' said Darke. 'According to the media, this is a football related murder and to be honest some of the rubbish I saw last season on Match of the Day was also absolute murder.' He pointed at her. 'Time on this one for you to be more strategic, you have no need to get your hands dirty with this one. Leave it to your team, leave it to the lads.'

Inga sucked in her breath as a note of caution. Apart from having sexist leanings she didn't know why it should be the case. After all she was better at it than all the others.

The DI was not a fan of strategy and politics. Not seeing another crook face to face was not a path she wanted to go down in a hurry. Knew if and when she allowed it to happen she'd be bored senseless.

'Jake is almost leading this anyway,' she said and wondered if he'd notice she used the word *almost*. Inga knew if she let go too much she might easily lose her affinity with all the strands of the investigation. 'As we both know he's not too keen on old cases. Says they lack the adrenalin boost of brand new evidence.'

'Just make sure you do,' came with the hint of a grin. He'd know how difficult this delegation business was and she did wonder if it was him ticking a box. Someone on high had told him to ensure she delegated and he'd told her. Box ticked, job done.

One big worry was him offering her a journey to a less demanding workload he may well wish to fill with all the admin nonsense he was probably sick and tired of.

Inga knew how a great deal of his work would never put the guilty behind bars. Spending his days on research and evaluation linked to progressive challenges he'd told her about recently. Not a road she ever wanted to go down.

Murder she knew from experience, if that was what it was, is quite often done for petty reasons which take some fathoming. Football has so many connotations of rivalry, of tribalism particularly in Britain, of hate even, of religious interface and if you then throw in the modern mix of social media and betting this one more than likely had moved on a great deal from just being petty. To some people it's more important than life or death; winning is not a bonus, it is everything.

It had simply never occurred to Inga how football fans get themselves in a peculiar aggressive state over match results not because their team has won, but because they will have won or lost at the bookies.

'Twenty eight year old IC1 male Graeme Coetzer dead in the kitchen of the house he shared with his mother in Washingborough. He was all packed ready to go off to watch Man United play Juventus in Turin in the Champions League. His mother who lost her husband four years ago, was conveniently away for a couple of days in Gateshead, having won the shopping trip to Metro in a competition. Spokes in the wheel are motive and someone to carry it out. His mother had a fancy man who called now and again, she claims is an old work colleague of her dead husband.'

'Have we looked at it being related?' Darke asked. 'Dead husband and dead son?'

'Industrial accident in 2014 and a poisoning? Hardly. Techy lads are going through everything right now.'

'Football?'

'His father, the one who died was a Man U supporter too. He introduced him to it all.' Craig Darke had always sensed a particular energy about Inga Larsson, and hoped the message he was trying to casually pass on to her would in no way dissipate such enthusiasm.

'What did he do this lad?' Darke realized they weren't dealing with a bit of a kid. Was this all really necessary when he'd had all her reports?

'Worked in a warehouse. Seems fairly popular but didn't really mix with workmates because he lived and…died I was going to say,' Inga was smiling. 'For his football team.'

'Man United season ticket would cost a fair bit. I assume he had one.'

She nodded. 'Plus petrol and a bit of grub.'

'Latest new shirt I bet he'd got.'

'All he did though. No woman apparently, just him and his mother at home plus football and real ale.'

'What sort of life is it?' Darke scoffed. 'And I guess he bet on them, bet the score on line. How many bookings.'

'We'll check it, but not sure bookies come round to get you if you win.'

'What about the mother?' Darke asked then lifted his coffee to sip.

'Attractive woman in her late forties who is as obsessed with taking part in competitions as her son is with Man United. We take her out of the equation because she was away and what have we got?' Inga sipped her coffee but her blue eyes were still on her boss. 'To be honest we're struggling for a motive.'

'Not to mention a suspect.'

'Except for this Lucas who has a blank page all to himself.'

'Good man is Jake, he'll do well with this I'm sure. And you, how's life suiting you these days?'

They then moved on to discuss Adam and his business and then they moved over to talk about Darke's wife Jillie the stunning red-headed former banker, now some sort of financial consultant and their young daughter Holly.

Eventually when his coffee was finished he was on his feet, and Inga somehow got the feeling he was going back to his office with some reluctance. Craig Darke no longer had his finger on the pulse and it was obvious he wasn't happy and she had no intention of eventually going down the same road if she could help it.

'It's all right for you,' he said stood there with his hands on the back of the chair he had just got up from. 'Coventry beckons. Not for football unfortunately but the delights of another conference.'

'Enjoy,' said Inga with a broad smile.

'No chance.'

Should she one day take the bull by the horns and just come out and ask the aching questions? All done in the name of austerity or so Darke had assured her.

Inga found this delegation business difficult, particularly with a case going nowhere very fast. She did of course have the assurance of Jake Goodwin as her right hand man and even if she had poked her nose in more than Darke probably required her to, he was doing well under the circumstances.

Inga appreciated the high principles by which Jake lived and worked. Not somebody to suffer fools gladly was plainly obvious and so much of modern life attitudes annoyed and infuriated him. Obviously he was not someone you'd want to meet had you been driving whilst drunk or drugged up or dared to be behind the wheel of a car and texting at the same time. He was also dead set against litter louts, against people expecting to be served in shops whilst blathering on their phones. He had no time for the able bodied parking in disabled bays and a whole host of other anti-social acts.

Inga knew from experience if Jake Goodwin asks you a question and your bog standard reply like so many bozos offer is "What's it to you?" then make no mistake, you are in serious trouble.

She knew if she actually let him take the daily briefings with her out of the way, then questions would be asked by the team and she had no intention of lumbering him with the whole shemozzle without warning and putting the team under more pressure.

'What have the search teams come up with?' Jake asked.

'Billy Upjohn has a date with me in about an hour,' said Inga and looked at her watch.

'Something new you think?'

'Seems like it. All tied in with social media by the sound of it. Be all Man U stuff no doubt. My team's better than your team is just unintelligent nonsense.'

'Darke mentioned betting. Get someone to give it a whirl. Keep him quiet if nothing else.'

'The eTeam have his laptop, they'll highlight if he's been busy being daft.'

'Phone and laptop, did he have anything else?' Jake shook his head as Inga looked all around. 'Think what we need Jake are Graeme Coetzer's employment records over and above this warehouse job and anything we can find out about his friends. Must go to football with someone surely. Wait for me to see Billy, see what he has to say then take it from there.' Inga was careful not to suggest who should look into it. *See Craig I am delegating.* 'Then the mother, what else does she do apart from entering competitions and we need to dig a bit deeper with those. What has she actually won, or is this just a gag, a cover maybe? Last but not least our Lucas Penney, who is this guy?'

Time she realized if she was not running the show to stop talking or the team would lose interest, get bored and switch off.

'Answers about this time tomorrow suit Jake?' He looked a trifle bewildered but nodded, and nobody mumbled.

Inga sat sipping her coffee with the door to her office open as she tended to and was pleased to see how well Jake operated. She had decided this delegating business is not as bad as she thought it would be, as she pulled another biscuit from her top drawer and dipped it in her coffee.

17

Hello there. This is Jacs back with you again. Now where was I? Oh yes I remember now.

I'd had my evening with young Brandon and Thursday came round again which meant it was time once more to feed the hungry, homeless and destitute.

I knew my parents if they were still alive would not be at all happy with what I had become involved in, and daddy Arthur in particular.

In his world, idle and desolate ran hand in hand. As far as he was concerned you never had one without the other. Couple of years National Service would according to him sort out these good-for-nothing layabouts with daft haircuts.

Two or three times a week I was cooking for and serving to what daddy would unfortunately describe as life's scroungers, the dregs of society, those he would consider to be a complete waste of space who were not deserving of anybody's help and most certainly not my financial contribution.

Thoughts of Edward were always on my mind but working with the homeless at least occupied me to a certain extent. Without which I'm quite sure I'd have gone barking mad. The homeless of course is a constant catnip issue with politicians of all persuasions. Few of them can resist the temptation to grab it and shake it up. But of course nothing gets done.

I am always really surprised my charitable endeavours have remained a total secret for the few years since I had been introduced to the plight of so many good people, down on their luck mostly. Once I had become aware of the desperate need to provide food and shelter on an almost permanent basis, I had become angry with the food waste from the big supermarkets which so easily could be put to far better use than it already was. Penny pinching was a sad reflection on society and I think I've already mentioned daddy's views on all that business.

This St Joseph's Sanctuary I had been working for in my spare time were absolutely desperate for money constantly, unable to provide decent cooked meals due solely to lack of funds on top of all the expense of providing shelter. The whole thing had really come home to me when I was being served with Christmas Dinner at one of the area's finest hotels with all these people fussing around me getting on for four years ago it was now.

What you and I would normally regard as basics such as cranberry sauce and Brussels were in the hostel regarded as luxuries. This would be a token gesture if you like.

Funds simply would not run to those kinds of added extras. Basic Christmas fayre no doubt being served to murderers, terrorists and sex offenders in every prison in the land, but not available to a few good folk down on their luck. They were not bank robbers, rapists or child abusers these were good decent human beings treated a lot worse than the scum behind bars.

Best these good folk could expect was probably a slice or two of tough turkey, a couple of small spuds, a spoonful of white cabbage followed by rice pudding if they were really lucky. All put together in haste and served up quickly by folk understandably wanting to get home to their loved ones and a decent proper festive nosh.

Get home to a scrumptious offering and a cracker to pull before the flaming Christmas Pudding came in. Be no red and white wine in the shelter and certainly not the Bucks Fizz I had thoroughly enjoyed on Christmas Day back then.

Within a month or two the refuge had been contacted by a long established local butcher, followed within a few days by a greengrocer and soon after a popular local general goods wholesaler to say they had been tasked to provide products on a regular basis by a benefactor who wished to remain anonymous.

Now twice a week at the very least or more I am in their kitchen cooking up good wholesome meals with food I have in fact paid for on the quiet.

Can I please ask you to keep all this to yourself? I'm not looking for praise or an MBE like some self-importants are doing it for. Just doing what I can to help the less fortunate, trying in my own small way to put back into society what my greedy ancestors have taken out over the years. Please don't go embarrassing me by spouting about this, and don't make good people feel obliged. Keep it as our little secret if you will. Thank you.

Enough food as it turns out to feed those seriously in need of sustenance every other day of the week. Now at Christmas you will find me and my willing team of volunteers, cooking up and serving up the best dinner I can muster. So good in fact the local hotels have lost a Christmas Day customer and I sit at the table and enjoy the fare with those I have cooked and served the food up for.

We're talking properly cooked decent wholesome food here. This is not the 'ping' cuisine nonsense we hear controls most households these days. That and Deliveroo.

We have turkey with all the trimmings followed by Christmas pudding and then mince pies and tea or coffee. We even have crackers. What we don't have is alcohol, for I am obviously aware the demon drink is the very reason some poor souls are now on their last legs. To start opening bottles of Pino Grigio would not be fair at all. Very nice of course, but not a wise move. I can always open one of my Californian Zinfandel's when I get home.

In my estimation you meet a better class of people at the refuge for Christmas lunch than some of the opinionated and self-obsessed buffoons who dine out.

I do worry when I read how most people these days don't even have a kitchen table let alone a dining table and I wonder how they handle Christmas lunch. Is it the same as all the other days of the year, sat in front of television dross with a take-away perched on their knees?

These 'millennials' find such basic behavior so peculiar, many of them deliberately describe eating decently at a table as knees-under eating. The mind boggles at some of their puerile nonsense.

Of course at the refuge there is always a degree of education involved at meal time. We get some folk using just a fork to eat with, even some who prefer to use their fingers and to a lesser degree nowadays want oodles of nasty synthetic gravy splashing about.

Can you imagine the finest French chefs serving up big jugs of onion gravy? I thought not. Lathering the whole meal is such an uncivilized way to savour any roast meat to my mind and nowadays is regarded as little more than a relic of post war austerity.

Here's another thought about feeding at Christmas. I wonder how many would opt for a take-away on Christmas Day given the option?

There's a thought. Can you order a pizza on Christmas Day? What about McDonald's, if they close how do some people survive the day without their staple diet?

Something I've never done. Eaten food from a plate on my knees and I find it difficult to understand the reasoning behind it. What do you gain by such behavior? I hear tell scouping from bowls rather than using proper plates is the stylish way some conduct themselves.

It'll not happen all the time I'm in charge of meals at St Joseph's I can tell you. Remember these people are in the main looking to improve themselves, to up their station in life. Learning to converse with people including strangers, eating and drinking to acceptable standards will all hold them in good stead in society as they aim for a better future.

Being slovenly and eating out of bowls whilst gawping at a screen has no acceptable outturn I can see and will only hinder their life progress. A bowl of rice and fancy named bits and pieces of next no nothing may be all well and good in a paddy field in China. In Spalding it most certainly is not. Quinoa, most people didn't know how to pronounce and Capuaçu were all the rage at one time as part of a fad.

Eating food should be an experience and an important element of life and to do so you need to see what you are eating not just stab at something and shove it down your throat with a fork or their fingers while your mind is on another rowdy shouting match on *EastEnders*.

Tell me. How on earth would you eat a proper roast dinner from a bowl with a plastic fork? Just imagine classics such as Beef Wellington and Eggs Benedict in a naff bowl. When you see high-end restaurants dishing up their signature dishes in a bowl you let me know. Until then I rest my case.

The introduction of smartphones and tablet computers hasn't helped along with the dire attitude of so many parents. The thought of doing anything at the dining table other than eating and drinking is beyond my comprehension.

I simply cannot imagine I would ever have allowed a child of mine to tinker with a gadget at the table during meal time. How thoroughly rude it would be, and if you bring daddy Arthur into the scenario he would have been apoplectic.

I'd have done it but once and from then on I would have had a good hiding to remind me never to be so downright rude ever again.

When these people go out for a meal, do they not think it strange why restaurants serve food to people sat on chairs at tables with cutlery and not to scruffy herberts dossed down in a dirty filthy onesie in a threadbare armchair?

Perhaps when I consider all these modish ideas it is probably best I have lived the life I have, as all this tardy uncouth behavior is not something I think I could stomach.

I am not a Royalist by any stretch of the imagination, as genuflecting and everything which goes with it to just one family in perpetuity is something I have never been able to accept is the right way to behave. I am sure however our dear Queen would never sit around stuffing cheap scooter delivered vindaloo down her throat with one hand and thumbing her iPhone with the other.

Good manners don't cost money.

In the early days once I had become the secret benefactor I had to be very careful those in charge did not work out my role behind the scenes. There were those of course dictated by their religious beliefs who tried to insist these starving people were served fish on Fridays or Halal meat and I could sense other suggestions creeping in over time.

St Joseph's like so many of these things is linked to a church, but I want nothing to do with that side of things at all and to their credit they have never insisted I do. Sorry, but I have no time for anything ultimately responsible for virtually all the troubles in the world in one shape or form.

18

'Said to my old man, I said. They'll be back,' was the reaction Sandy MacLachlan received after introducing himself at the first door. This tall willowy woman in a garish pink jogging suit she had probably never jogged in and an array of cheap bangles on one wrist stepped back and held her front door open wide for the pair of them to walk in. 'What you after this time?' she asked when she pushed past them and walked into her lounge.

'You asked our officer if we knew....'

'Officer?' she scoffed with a grin. 'Plastic copper I thinks you mean, love?'

'You asked our PCSO if we knew about a fancy man,' Ruth Buchan repeated. 'Could you please explain what you mean?'

'Had his nose put out and no mistake,' was no reply.

'What do you mean?' she pressed.

'Lover boy at forty nine.'

'Mrs Wright,' said DC Buchan slowly. 'Would please just explain what it is you are talking about?'

'Josef Dudek...old Jo,' she said as if they knew exactly who she was talking about. 'Got his feet under the table good and proper and no mistake.' For some ridiculous reason this blonde straggly haired woman looked all about in her own lounge as if somebody might be hiding behind the sofa or peering round the green curtains. 'When Man U was playing o'course.'

'Have I got this right?' a puzzled Buchan probed. 'Are you suggesting this...Josef Dudek might have been visiting Amber Coetzer when her son was away? Is that what you're trying to say?'

'No might about it, me duck.'

'And why would we be interested in what two consenting adults do in their own time?' MacLachlan asked.

'I thought it was obvious. While the cat's away.'

'Are suggesting Mrs Coetzer was having an affair? With this Josef Dudek?' She nodded with a look of excitement about her face. 'We are looking into the death of Graeme Coetzer, so why would his mother's love life be of interest?'

The sigh was huge. 'Graeme couldn't stand the bloke.'

'Because he supported another team?' Sandy tried even though it was such a tedious issue they'd come across before in this case.

'No,' was loud. 'Yeh he's fancied her a long time like, but now she's got the money her Graeme's dreams have come true. He's heading off to Europe with them and he don't want Josef poking his oar in and have her spending it on him. It's his footie trip money. Been telling everybody like.'

'So before all this, what happened?' The bluff copper got a look which said explain. 'Up to now what matches has he been to?'

'Only here don't you see? Goes to Old Trafford course and some away matches he can get to like, but never had the bunce to go abroad like since his old man died. Now she's got all the money the world's his oyster. Juventus was to be his second trip this season like. Went to …'

'Berne?' said Sandy having become an expert on Man United fixtures.

'And you think this Dudek will be after her money?' Ruth Buchan guessed

'Ah no, be fair. Didn't say that,' she said taking a step or two back and wagging a finger as if they were naughty thoughts. 'But I'm sure Graeme could see them going out for meals, weekends away and all. Amber was talking about going on holiday, Greek Islands think she was talking about, so I hear. Got a brochure down the travel they say. No good to Graeme now is it? Be his footie money Jo Dudek is spending.'

'Is he still going round there?' Buchan wanted to know.

'Not as much so I hear, like she's frozen him out lately.'

'Any idea why?' Ruth Buchan asked. 'Apart from the business of her son's death.'

'Bet your life it's Graeme putting his foot down once the season started. All she's got now see…sorry, he was all she had. Doted on him big time what with his dad being dead.'

'Now of course the scenario has changed,' said MacLachlan more as a thought than a question.

'Seems like a lot of money but it won't last, you know what people are like. Be a new car next, then what? Soon be gone and what good will it all have done her?' There was more than a hint of envy within.

'Have you ever heard of someone called Lucas Penney?' Buchan asked. Stella Wright just pushed out her bottom lip and shook her head.

'Not from round here I'll wager.'

'Been known to visit Amber,' said Sandy. 'Naebody else?'

More pouting. 'Not what I know of, not much gets past us.' *I bet.*

Once they were back in the car Sandy MacLachlan decided to phone it in and Jake told him to carry on with their list and he'd get back to them.

Two more houses they called on but there was very little to go on and when they mentioned men visiting the house: this Josef Dudek and the famous Lucas Penney they just got more grimaces. Two relatives from Lincoln the team had encountered during those first few hours after the body was discovered on the Sunday evening and the next door neighbour had mentioned this mystery man. The two relatives had even admitted they'd never seen him, and Ruth remembered from the report wherein the next door neighbour said something along the lines of *'I'm pretty sure she had somebody visit.'*

Proof positive was needed and they were a long way off. Being pretty sure would never stand up in court with a barrister in full flow. Trace, Interview, Eliminate was the procedure but the system just hits a brick wall when you can't even come up with a Trace.

'Don't mess about,' said DS Goodwin on the phone when he called back. 'Boss says go and rattle his cage, see what he says. Think out of the box for once. What's the chances he's our Lucas Penney?'

'The Wright women knows this Dudek but has no idea who Penney might be.'

'But the relatives who say they think someone has been calling, do they know this Dudek? Could be one and the same.'

The door had been painted black badly and the front garden was very neat and tidy had it actually been a garden with a mowed lawn and borders full of pretty flowers. Somebody had paved it over as a parking place for their little Renault.

'Mr Dudek? Mr Josef Dudek?' big DC Sandy MacLachlan asked as he looked down slightly at the man who had answered the door.

'Who wants t'know?'

Warrant Card held up. 'Detective Constable MacLachlan, Lincoln County Police.'

'Hello pleased t'meet yer,' was part of a smirk.

'May we have a word?'

'If yer like,' said this Dudek leant against the doorpost in a black Black Sabbath *'Burn'* t-shirt and old worn blue jeans, who had still to confirm who he was. Sandy looked at him in expectation of an invitation inside.

'And?'

'And what?' he shot back.

'You happy for t'neighbours to listen in just now?'

'Can if they wants.'

'Tell me about your relationship with Amber Coetzer.'

'What's to tell?' This balding dark haired lump of a man just stood there sucking his teeth as if he had a bit of grissle stuck between them.

'And?' Sandy waited but his patience was rapidly wearing thin.

'And what?'

'Amber Coetzer.'

'And?'

'I can play this game all day Mr Dudek, but if I do for most of it you'll be sitting in an interview room with a tape running and you'll stay there until we get some answers. Only person to suffer will be thissen.'

'Listen son, I choose who I speak wiv. It's free country and if I dunna wanna talk then I won't.'

'I ask again,' said chunky MacLachlan slowly and deliberately. 'Amber Coetzer. We understand you've been having a relationship with her. Tell me 'bout it.'

'Like I said, don't like the look of yer son. Am I under arrest? No I'm not, so I'm not gonna answer any o'yer daft stupid questions. Why should I?'

'Because I'm asking.'

'You from t'over river?'

'What?' Big Scot Sandy threw at him with a grimace.

'You a yorkie pig?'

'You're not too hot on accents are you?' For a moment Sandy thought he was going to spit his dislike.

'Yorkie shit,' he chuckled.

Ruth had seen cops pull a few strokes on Friday nights but never seen anything quite so fast. From nowhere MacLachlan produced handcuffs he thrust onto the wrist of Dudek hanging limply against the doorpost, and with one yank he was outside and face down on his path.

Time living down in England had tamed Sandy's Dumfries accent somewhat, with now the odd world or unusual phrase standing out as strange to colleagues.

To suggest he was from Yorkshire was a real insult to the big Scot.

Nicky Scoley was convinced in interviews he put his burr back on to confuse the less intelligent individuals they dealt with.

Well before the van Ruth Buchan ordered had turned up, a small crowd of thin hooded youths had gathered to form an audience of grey jogging bottoms this Dudek delighted in. Buchan took her chance to go into the house to carry out a quick sweep through for other occupants, right in the face of idiot Dudek shouting demands of how she needed a search warrant and following his instructions found his house keys, so they were able to leave the building safe and secure.

19

Fifteen questions Jake Goodwin asked this Dudek in the stark interview room in Lincoln, and fifteen times this scruffy dope smirked, chuckled and said 'No comment.'

Inga who had been sat beside Jake quietly turned off the tape and video and stood up to look down on both men.

'Tell you what I'm going to do Jake,' she said to her sergeant, stood with her hands planted firmly on the grey table beside this Dudek. 'I'm going to get one of the team to rustle up a cuppa and a few biscuits for just us two. While I'm at it I'll sort out an early morning rota. In pairs I thought would be best, so everyone gets fair dibs. Five o'clock every morning they'll knock on Josef Dudek's front door, drag him out in his knickers and march him down here. Every afternoon we'll let him go home for a kip. What d'you think?'

If Jake was perfectly honest he'd never experienced anything quite like it. Thought his boss had lost her marbles. She was tough and uncompromising, but she played by the rules. Normally.

'Tell you what might be an idea,' said Jake up to her having decided to play along. 'Get Kenny to do tomorrow for starters and he can bring the big red key with him and knock the bloody door in.'

'Give Dudek something to do in the afternoon,' she suggested and chuckled. 'Bit of DIY.'

'Get a new door from B&Q and….'

'We need a new wood saw, p'raps he could get one for us at the same time if I give him the money. Bring it in with him when we send the lads round to collect him.'

'Then next day when we knock it in again he can…'

'All right!' Dudek shouted and covered his ears.

'Tea?' Inga asked Dudek so calmly it must have really annoyed him. 'One lump or two?'

'No sugar,' was mumbled.

'Thank you, sir,' she said and left the room.

Jake Goodwin just sat there with his arms folded trying to fathom what was going on. There had been a change in atmosphere recently and he had wondered if all was well at home for Inga. He'd mentioned it to his wife Sally only the previous evening about how Inga seemed to be backing off from the case. They'd even discussed the possibility of her being moved and this was her preparing the ground. Yes, life working under a woman was different to what he had been used to over the years with some of the rough and ready clowns he had been lumbered with and working with a good looking big blonde Swede with her little idiosyncrasies had taken some getting used to. He knew from what he'd said the Detective Super Craig was a great fan of the woman, plus he knew there were many in the force who fancied her like mad.

There was certainly something going on and if she was being moved he would be thoroughly disappointed were such a good team be broken up by the powers that be, who so often did not understand group dynamics and the need for good relationships between team members.

Darke had moved Nicola Scoley down to Cambridge for a good while to gain alternative experiences and now had chosen her to attend this specialist course in Scotland. Now Jake had to give thought to the idea the DI would be next. Was she off to pastures new, destined for higher things, courtesy of the dark boss?

She was true to her word. Detective Inspector Larsson walked back into the interview room with a tray and three white mugs of tea. A job usually reserved for a DC or just a plod of a uniform constable.

Jake just sat there watching her. This was a good looking very astute Detective Inspector with a great record in major crime clearance rates serving tea to a two-bit donk like this Dudek.

Having handed them round like a very accomplished waitress, she propped the tray against the wall and turned the tape and video back on.

What was going on?

'Josef Dudek, let's start again shall we?' she said as she sat back down. 'I'm Inga Larsson, I'm the Detective Inspector in charge of this case.' She rested her hand in the crook of Jake's arm for a moment. 'This is Detective Sergeant Jacques Goodwin my right hand man, my number two.' She stopped to take a sip of tea. 'Perhaps in your own words you'll tell me about your relationship with Mrs Amber Coetzer. But before you start, might I suggest repeating what you've seen in some cheap jack television programme with criminals saying no comment time and again won't work here. Do that and there'll be only one loser.'

Jake was staggered when Dudek after a few tentative sips of tea, went straight into his story. It was as if Inga had slipped a magic potion into his cuppa, or perhaps it was just a case of giving him enough time to think about it and to consider his situation and review his options. Not to mention the thought of being dragged from his bed on a daily basis.

'Knew her just after we left school, went about as a bit of a gang sorta thing. Went out with her fer a bit, then when it started getting sort of serious her old woman stepped in.' He sipped. 'Where you from?' he asked Inga. 'What country?'

'Sweden, why?'

'I was born and bred in Lancashire, then we moved down this way with me dad's job. Was me grandfather what was born in Poland, but weren't good enough for old Mrs Hewson like. I was foreign as far as she were concerned, not good enough for her Amber.'

'So it ended, you and her?' Inga queried with Jake sat there sipping strong tea still wondering what was going on with the boss.

'Pretty much overnight, duck.' He gathered his thoughts and continued head down looking into his mug. 'Gillie and I moved here around twelve year ago now,' and Inga noticed how he was becoming slower in his delivery.

'Gillie?' she asked as the story appeared to have jumped.

'One what I married. Seven years it'll be come March since she upped and left and took the kids with her. See 'em of course, been no nastiness or anything, but means I've been over here on me own like.' He looked up at Inga, as if sending her a message.

'And Amber was already here.'

'Pretty much,' was a strange phrase Jake thought but he was utterly surprised at the complete turnaround by this man. 'Mid-life crisis, whatever you want ter call it and things are not too good in the Coetzer household it would appear.' He sipped his tea again and licked his lips. 'Football's ter blame. Once Gordon had his lad reach an age where he could take him with him, think he was like a pig in clover. Got his football, got his lad and a few jars what more could a fella want?'

'And Amber?'

'Played second fiddle to Man United.'

'While the cat's away…'

'Pretty much.'

'And what was your problem earlier?' she hoped would not return him to his initial state.

'Sorry. Just a bit…well you know. Been there for her all this time and she gets what's due to her and it's like I'm out the back door. Blame it on the lad, God rest his soul.' This Josef sat up straight and crossed himself twice. 'He can see the world beckoning, anywhere he wants t'go now. Any damn place Red Devils wants to play he'd've been there.'

'You're upset because your face doesn't fit any more?'

'Bit hacked off. All folk round here wanna talk about, just getting to me a bit. Played me part now I've been tossed aside.' Then he mumbled.

'Pardon. Please speak up for the tape.'

'Second time it's happened like,' was sarcastically loud. 'Lightning strikes twice eh?'

'And Amber is funding it all, and you've missed out.'

'I've not missed out,' and his hands went up in an act of surrender. 'I'm not in it fer the money,' Josef said and allowed his hands to return to the table and his mug. 'Heck I went with her when she didna have two ha'pennies to rub together with the amount they used ter spend on the football rubbish, but it's not so much the money, seems suddenly her love has dried up. Like cheque arrived one day and I was yesterday's chip paper the next.'

'What is it you do?' Jake asked.

'Drive lorries. Done it for years but got the team leader job few weeks ago now so couple of days a week I'm back at base. If we're short-handed and in holiday times I'm driving all the time.'

'So when Gordon was alive you were driving lorries?' Inga asked him.

'Yes,' he said suspiciously.

'This mean you were away a lot?'

'Sometimes yes, but free more often than not at weekends when they was off to the match.'

'Have to ask this,' said Inga looking at the few notes she had made on her pad. 'When you and your wife Gillie were together were you seeing Amber?'

'No way,' was adamant.

'Talk to me about Lucas Penney,' was the switch of subject she'd learnt from Craig Darke.

'Who?'

'Somebody of that name has been calling on Amber.'

'When was this?'

'Six months or so apparently, pops in now and again. Appears nobody's seen him, but we'd like a chat.'

'How d'they know who he is then?'

'Did you get on with Graeme?' Jake slipped in under the radar to unsettle him.

'Not a lot t'do with him to be fair.'

'Why?'

Josef chuckled. 'Allus went round t'see Amber when they were away at matches of course. Amber felt it best if I didn't intrude when her Gordon had his accident. Didn't want any talk of a secret lover getting in the papers, so I had a low profile for quite a while.'

'And you think it was Graeme who stopped some o'money coming your way. D'you have plans for it?'

'Not plans as such. She was talking about having a decent holiday somewhere rather than Gordon and the lad going off following the damn football on some foreign tournament like they'd done a time or two with England.' He sipped his luke warm tea. 'Thought she might take me. The lad'd not want to go o'course unless United was playing on Majorca or somewhere.'

'And she'd not go on her own,' said Inga and Dudek shook his head.

'To be honest, thought we'd be a couple. Seems it were wishful thinking on my part. Gets t'me a bit, marriage fell apart and now all this business has gone bottoms up as well like.'

'Did Amber go on these foreign trips to follow England?'

'Don't be silly.'

'Anything you want to tell us?' Inga enquired calmly.

'Night they say Graeme lad met his maker my daughter was over fer the night if I need an alibi.'

'What did you do?'

'Got a take-away, watched a film, not my scene but there you go. Nothing special just what me kid wanted.'

His belligerent manner had all gone

'Sorry,' said Inga to Jake the moment they were alone in her office. 'Sorry, but I just got so pissed off with the no comment garbage, he just got to me.'

'Everything all right?'

'I'm fine, just too many prats I suppose, and the sheer frustration of all this. Quite sure the Darke boss thinks this is one we should have cracked by now. Trouble is of course being a super sleuth he probably would have. Now this Josef's another one we can cross off the list and forget. When we started off with him being a berk and after what Sandy had said I thought we'd got a live one.'

'Why d'you think Amber has eased him out?'

'Absolutely doted on Graeme apparently. D'you see the door-to-door report about some woman saying what a shame it was Amber Coetzer had those miscarriages, now she has no family to fall back on. If it were the case, could be she's over protective with Graeme, or was. Gives him everything he wants and probably decided there could only be one man in her life and poor old Josef got the heave-ho.'

'Just when the money arrived.'

'And just when our Lucas is on the scene siphoning off her money most likely.' She looked at Jake. 'Everything all right with you?' He nodded. Now was not the time to say anything. 'Here's another thought. What if this Amber starts handing over money to our mystery man and realizes if she carries on with her relationship with Josef the two things might clash. He's going to ask questions maybe?'

'Probably right if the relationship develops more than just…sex or whatever it was.'

'Now he's thrown England into the pot, first time it's been mentioned.'

'Must be those Euros he's talking about.'

'Where we talking do we know?'

'Have them all over the place, year or two back it was France. Perhaps father and son went wherever it was.'

'Have we actually come across anybody apart from the two relatives and the next door neighbour who have mentioned this Penney?'

'No. And none of them have ever seen him, neighbour talks about him as if he's some sort of shadowy figure in the moonlight.'

'If he does exist, there have to be nosey neighbours in the area who would have made a mental note. Stella Wright woman who Ruth spoke to and how many more knew about Josef playing away every time Man United were playing at home? Yet nobody saw this Penney.'

20

'Jacqueline, this is Chris the friend I was telling you about,' said young Brandon Wishaw at my oak front door after a day fresh from producing beef stew and dumplings with cabbage, swede and locally grown potatoes. With rhubarb crumble and custard plus tea and fresh fruit to follow.

To be honest I thought I'd heard the last of it all, but it just shows how wrong you can be doesn't it?

This tall light haired man stepped forward and shook my hand firmly.

'How d'you do? I'm Detective Constable Mackinder.'

'Come in, come in I'm Jacs,' I said and stood aside to let the two young men pass and followed behind as Brandon led his pal down the hallway and into my drawing room. 'Coffee?'

'Yes please,' they replied almost in unison.

'You Natalie Mackinder's son by any chance?' I wanted to know.

'Most certainly.'

'Good,' I said with a smile. 'You from the Spalding Police Office?' I checked.

'Sorry no. Lincoln,' he said to relax me a little, for I had concerns about who locally just might get to learn he'd called in for a chat. Well you know what some of these gossips are like. 'From Spalding originally obviously, but stationed in Lincoln now.'

Coffee served to the two young men sat side by side on my big squidgy old leather sofa and my nerves were just a bit on edge I can tell you.

I'm not like you. I expect you've got friends you can talk to, chew over the cud with. Not something I've ever had for two reasons really. Nobody I went to school with lives within a hundred miles and having never had a job, there have never been work colleagues I've socialized with at all – yes there are other helpers at St Joseph's but it's not quite the same. Just me on my lonesome trying to fathom things out for myself all the time, and as you can see so far I've not made a very good job if it.

This is where I guess a girlfriend or two would come in useful to answer daft questions which come to mind like what on earth is a beauty blogger? Just saying it gives me a fit of the giggles.

I'll just have to remain ignorant.

'Before we start,' said this Chris. 'This is only an informal chat as a favour to Brandon, but rules still apply. I can't just ignore anything I hear but also information I do become party to will be treated in strictest confidence.'

'Thanks,' I said and to some extent it helped calm a trickle of concerns but was nowhere near abolishing them completely. His brusk demeanor didn't help.

'Would you like to kick off?' this Chris asked and sat back. 'Can I take a few notes?' he asked as he raked around by his feet to open the bag he'd had over his shoulder when he arrived.

'Of course.' Another tendency I could never imagine daddy ever accepting, like so much these days. A man with what amounted to a handbag. 'Lonely old woman,' I started and immediately knew I'd said the wrong thing and a frown from Brandon confirmed it. 'And when I get down and depressed sometimes probably like many others I've done silly things. But nothing as stupid as this.' I smiled and looked at Brandon. 'All your fault this,' I chided him. 'You told me to get all techy and come up to date.'

'Thanks.'

'Anyway I went on this lonely hearts website for want of a better word and over a week or two got talking on line as it happened to this man.'

'We know who do we?' Chris asked.

Before I could respond Brandon was on his feet. 'Don't think I should be here,' he said down to the pair of us. 'I know this is just an informal chat, but I shouldn't know all your business. Sorry, that's not fair.'

'You don't have to leave on my account,' I assured him.

'I know I don't.'

'Television in the lounge,' I offered. 'I'm sure we won't be long,' and polite Brandon left us to it. Just another example of how well the young man had been brought up.

This is a case in point to be honest. This lonely hearts thing. If I had a couple of pals I could have chatted to them about it over a glass or two. They'd have probably told me not to be so ridiculous and I'd not be in this mess at all.

'Edward it was, Edward McCafferty,' I told Chris once Brandon had closed the door. 'Anyway, one thing led to another, I was away for a bit and after a few weeks I met him in Newmarket for a coffee. He was there on business.'

'And he was from where?' he asked immediately.

'Worcester's as near as I ever got.'

'Carry on,' Chris told me. All seemed a bit more officious than I had expected. Too formal, not relaxed enough for my liking.

'Then I invited him here for a day, lunch and tea. A Saturday I think it was. Really nice bloke, told me all about himself, what he did for a living and all the rest of it. Then…in for a penny, he stayed over. Just happened a couple of times and then he was going off to France to buy horses and I transferred funds to him to buy me a horse.'

'Two questions, one…'

'No.'

'Sorry?'

'You were going to ask about sex,' caught this lad by surprise. 'No,' I shook my head. 'Never happened.'

'You're into this?'

'What? No sex?' relaxed the whole situation.

'No,' he chided me with a grin. 'Buying horses.' Chris had to wait for an answer as I was in need of a something to wet my mouth.

'No,' I said and took another drink of coffee as I watched Chris' look of confusion.

'How long ago we talking?'

'More than a fortnight now.'

'And all your money's gone,' Chris went to speak on but I beat him to it.

'Only the money I gave him. Forty thousand.' I saw the surprise in his eyes because I thought I knew what he was about to say.

'Hasn't taken anything from any other accounts?' was not it.
'No.'
'You sure?'
I was emphatic. 'Yes. In fact this past week I arranged with my bank to move my current account to another new account number, just in case.'

'I'll need the details, your bank, his bank, how much.' I scampered upstairs to the smallest attic room where I keep my laptop and made a note of all the information I had on the transaction Edward has organized, then downstairs to borrow Chris's notebook

'Anything else?' he asked after he'd looked at the scant information I had provided.

'How d'you mean?' I asked.

'Has anything else gone missing?'

'No.'

'Can I ask you this?' said Chris and leant forward, mug held in both hands. 'How would he know you had enough money to invest such a large amount in a horse?'

'I've no idea.'

'Did you talk about money in the early days? Just thinking if he made contact with say a dozen women, asked the right questions and then concentrated on those who gave the answers he was looking for.'

'You think he's done this before?'

'Quite possible. Some of these people are very clever. They have a set routine of questions they ask and from which they can deduce what it is they want to know.' He must have realized I was finding it all a tad confusing. 'Some people are obsessed with what religion people are and ask particular questions which appear to have nothing to do with the matter but give them the answer they're looking for.'

'People really do that?' I asked.

'Could have happened to you, not in this case maybe, but in life. You may well have come across somebody who then doesn't want to know you. You might think it a bit odd at the time and wonder what you've said. Truth is they've discovered or rather think they've discovered what religion you are and if it's not to their taste, ignore you and move on. What bigots do.'

'Have people really got nothing better to do with their lives than this kind of mumbo jumbo?'

'In a word.'

'How sad, but I can't imagine I did. Not the sort of thing I do, talk about money to somebody who was still virtually a stranger. What annoys me is I was very careful, particularly to start with, one of the reasons I met him in public in daylight in a café in Newmarket. I suggested where and when.'

'Then what?'

'I came home.'

'How?'

'How?' I repeated. 'I drove.'

'From a car park near the café.'

'Quite near.'

'Did you and he go to the car park together?'

It was months ago, so I had to think about it. 'I don't think so. No, I don't think we did. I'm pretty sure I walked to the car on my own, Middle of the afternoon, then drove back here. Not easy to remember, this was ages ago. Came back from the Commonwealth Games and life back home compared with all the excitement and sunshine was flat and tedious. Stupidly thought I'd spice it up a bit.' I just looked at him. 'Probably got fed up after coming back and rushed the relationship,' I admitted.

'You went to Australia you mean?'

'Yes,' I responded to an odd question. 'To the Gold Coast.'

'You go to things like…?'

'Yes.'

'What about Olympics?'

'In Rio?' I asked. 'No,' and he looked at me in a peculiar manner. 'Just didn't fancy Brazil, did London of course, and Beijing and the others. Too many issues for my liking, incomplete facilities, strikes and then the Zika business. Stayed up half the night watching television.'

'I've never met anyone who's been…well to the Olympics.'

'Strange as it may seem, people do.' He nodded with a hint of embarrassment. 'When I heard friends were planning to leave personal items at home and were concentrating more and more on security I had serious doubts. I also realized my normal access to tourist sites may well be compromised I knew it was one to dip out of.' I sighed. 'Lost a deposit, but hey ho,' I shrugged.

'And your car?'

'One friend who like me decided against Rio then spent the money on a campavan.'

'Your car?' he insisted.

'A Mercedes, much to my father's chagrin.'

'Sorry?'

'German.'

'What reg?' came with a chuckled smirk. I can't imagine what daddy would have made of Angela Merkel. A German *and* a woman.

'How old is the car?'

'18 reg back in March.'

Chris sat back in his seat and smiled and left me wondering what I had said, as he then sat forward and began on his coffee. Was the German remark one of these dotty things you're not allowed to say these days?

'And you met him when?'

'August first time for coffee.'

'Driving your new car?'

'Yes.'

'My guess is,' Chris said as soon as he'd had a good drink. 'He follows women to their cars. New Mercedes tells him you're not on benefits, not on your uppers and you're worth a punt. And when he came here,' said Chris looking all about. 'You were ripe for picking. Just had to gauge how much.' Chris took another drink from the mug still in his hands. 'Thought so. If its right, you've been stitched up by a cool operator,' didn't exactly make me feel full of the joys of spring but I felt slightly less foolish. Chris looked all about him. 'Excuse the phrase, but you don't get a place like this on housing benefit.'

Brandon rejoined us and we drank coffee, and in the end spent perhaps another hour and a half together.

I am not at all sure I had ever been alone in my home with two young men smartly dressed in polo shirts with logos even I recognized and snazzy trainers, yet no matter how delightful it had been, I felt I was in need of a break.

Just to quell the tide of interrogation as much as anything else, I went off into the kitchen and returned with more coffees and a plate full of apple and walnut scones I had buttered earlier. I had got it absolutely right, young men seem unable to ignore good food.

'What are we going to do about your problem?' Chris asked me and he had us back on track.

'What can you do?' I asked. From my point of view I had learnt my lesson the hard way and it was time to pull up the drawbridge and keep myself to myself. When winter arrived I knew life would not be good at all, and it just might have to be back to the Bridge Club. I'd not left under any sort of a cloud, just put other non-existent commitments up as an excuse.

'I can ask about,' said Chris. 'See if anyone else in the force has come across anything similar. County wide,' I probably grimaced at. 'No names, no pack drill, just pose the questions, announce what I know just see what pops up. May be nothing of course, you may well be a one-off, but it does seem very elaborate to just be you. This is either a tried and tested scam or this Edward is starting out and will be looking for more...'

'Suckers?'

'Be fair Jacs,' said Brandon quickly. 'You took precautions, you didn't just take him at face value, invite him in first day, hand over cash your pin number and your passport.'

I knew what I had to do, and if somewhere down the line folk got to hear what a silly bitch I'd been, so what? Some good might come of it, maybe somebody somewhere was being set up right there and then. If that was the case it was time for me to stick my oar in.

'Maybe I was just gullible, but he sounded so knowledgeable. He talked as if he knew all about horses. Said something about the dam of the horse he'd bought for me had already produced Group 1 winners and talked about putting it into a stakes race first time out.'

'Thought you didn't understand it all?' Brandon posed.

'I don't,' I responded. 'I'm quoting, just the sort of thing he said or something along those lines.'

'Maybe he is in the industry, or was,' said Chris now all ready with small pad and biro. 'Could be he was just a stable lad, picked up all the jargon and this is what he does now.'

Inside twenty minutes they were back to talking about anything but my utter ineptitude. We all had those second cups of coffee, and at the end of the time the two lads had spent with me there was only one scone left.

Among the matters we discussed had been my idea for introducing the world of technology to those at the lonely club. Brandon suggested it would be best if such an event were held right where we were and he had a couple of pals who would willingly attend and bring their tablets with them for people to try.

All good things come to an end, and although it had been a form of inquisition I had certainly enjoyed the company of two decent young men.

Perhaps you'll think I'm now being a bit snooty, but it is certainly not the intention. Those two young men, Brandon in particular are not the average young men you're likely to see dragging themselves around town in back-to-front baseball caps.

21

'This Jacqueline Epton woman or whatever her name is. Any suggestion of violence?' Chris Mackinder was asked by his Inspector, slumped in his chair annoyingly tapping his biro on the desk.

'Violence?' he repeated.

'At inter-sector briefing, MIT's woman was talking about the Man U murder they've got. Said they'd nothing except for some geezer known to the mother who nobody had ever seen. Mr No Show the silly bitch is calling him. The man who doesn't exist nonsense.' He chuckled. 'Be bloody Invisible Man next!'

Chris knew his boss Detective Inspector Robert Bowring had no time for the female DI running MIT. She was Swedish and too good by half it seemed to him. All Bowring ever went on about was the fact she's *only* a woman, has great legs, a fabulous arse and had *'just been a lucky bitch'*.

'No suggestion of anything like it.'

'You reckon whoever it was followed her to her car just so he could suss what this old woman's worth?'

'Just my guess. How else would he know?'

'What you basing it on?' Bowring chuckled and Mackinder worried he was about to be belittled. 'What d'you think it would tell him? Might be a hire car, might be a rental,' he pointed his pen at Chris. 'I could afford to rent a Lexus and who's to know? D'you know if all the blokes in your road own their own cars? Chap I knew once ponced about in a new Astra, turned out his mother-in-law bought it for them. Sorry son, it's no bloody guide to anything.'

'He wanted her to buy a horse. How else would he know she had enough money for something as expensive as they're likely to be when he'd only met her for coffee? Sorry sir, she's not the sort who'd rent and as she doesn't work it's not a company car. Maybe she told him she didn't work, so when he saw the car it had to be a clue surely.'

'Told him's my guess, you know what women are like. Bet the silly bitch bragged about what she's worth on bloody Facebook. It's what them garish big bags are all about, just showing off like they do, sometimes think they're on bloody social media all the time. Bet a pound to a penny it'd cost a small fortune too.'

'Don't think so, sir, not the type I shouldn't imagine.'

'Don't talk wet. She's woman isn't she? Been bragging online to all her girly pals, you know what they're like for crissakes.'

'Sorry guv, but I don't see her on social media. This Epton-Howe had no idea how he knew what she could afford. Said all he'd done was give her a guide to how much yearlings are at these sales. She says thinking back she now realizes he must have had some idea almost from the outset and when he turned up at her house he probably added a few noughts to what he thought when he saw the size of it. Big place in its own grounds, granny annexe as well nearby where my pal lives. Wasn't as if she was in a Corsa or Focus, she's driving a brand new Mercedes which would be just months old when they first met and I reckon he followed her to where she'd parked it. Says until they talked about buying a horse, money was never mentioned.'

Chris knew Bowring wasn't interested. Chasing after con men who'd fiddled old ladies out of their life savings was not his idea of proper policing, and if he was told it was a waste of time he had no idea where he'd go next. Chris certainly didn't fancy going back to Brandon and the Jacs woman with his tail between his legs.

'Sounds to me like she's got more money than bloody sense. Big house you say?'

'Yes it is big, got a cellar and five or six bedrooms my friend who knows her said, and rooms all which way and tother. Drawing room and a scullery and bags o'fancy stuff. Plenty of land too, and a long drive up to it.'

'Look son,' and he pointed his pen at Chris. 'Things like this are a pain in the backside. Couple of years back we had some scam to do with wood plantation in Brazil or some crap. Just like this is, nothing but greed. One fella heard about this money making idea in a car park, and a woman if I remember right answered a knock at her front door and was taken in by all the nonsense a bloke she had never met in her life was coming out with. If it's too good to be true, you know what they say. Can't be like you and me and stick their spare cash in a building society what pays out bugger all in interest, got to go for the big money. Like I said son, it's just greed.'

'Do I tell her we're not interested or what?' Chris shrugged.

'Not exactly my cup of tea by the sound of her, more money than sense. Tell you what, we're a bit full right now. Take it down to the blonde bitch in MIT stick it under her pretty little nose, sort of nonsense she'll be interested in. Leave us real coppers to get on with important stuff.'

The envy was there for all to see. Was it because Inga Larsson was a woman, because she was good looking and wouldn't look twice at the likes of Bowring or was it all down to her clear-up rate? People often use the word jealousy when they mean envy. The resentful feeling they have when someone else has what they want.

This Inspector Bowring was one of those who derides others possessions and achievements and try to discredit them.

DC Chris Mackinder didn't just go bowling in amongst the Major Incident Team as Bowring probably would. Instead he looked around for anyone who would tell him about the lie of the land with this foreign woman in charge. If they were up to their ears in this murder, chances are they'd not welcome a DC like him just popping his head round the door with a half-baked idea. In the end the advice was to chat to DS Raza Latif, give him the heads-up on what it was all about and see what he thought.

'Have a seat, tell me what you've got.' As it turned out it really was painless. When he'd spoken with DS Latif he had not suggested they were desperate for a new lead or were clutching at straws just how in their world anything and everything is considered. He'd seen this DI Larsson about but never as close as this sat looking at her across her desk with elbows planted and her fingers just touching at lip height. What people said was right, she appeared both very attractive and formidable all at the same time.

Her informality made it all a great deal easier than he had assumed it might be and he felt able to refer to his notes. She sat there unmoved but was obviously listening intently.

'Jacqueline Epton-Howe,' she said slowly when Chris hesitated. 'Mercedes, big house please forgive me if I'm inclined to sterotype this woman.'

'What it sounds like I admit, but to a certain extent she's not like that at all. Think there's money there and no mistake and I understand she went to a private girls school, but she's an only child and the guy who told me about all this says he reckons the truth is she's actually quite lonely.'

'Little lonely rich old lady, falls for the three card trick possibly.'

'Great deal more to her than that,' Chris said. 'Money in the family but Brandon the guy who put me onto this still lives at home in a cottage in the grounds of the house. How he knows about her. To be fair, she was wary, didn't meet this chap for some time, then in public in daylight, then for odd days. Didn't rush in hook line and sinker like some love torn bit of a kid. Probably not as worldy wise as she likes to make out, probably due to her upbringing. From what I have been able to gather her old man could be a nasty piece of work and was a real one for the ladies and it seems this Jacqueline, who prefers to be called plain Jacs by the way, was stuck with acting as sort of chaperone and carer for her mother. Now she's in her forties they're both dead and is wanting to see a bit more of life away from the WI ladies she's sort of stuck with.'

'Briefly, this is what we've got,' said Inga, as she dropped her hands onto the desk. 'We have this Mrs Coetzer and her dead son, and it appears there was this gentleman friend called Penney who used to call,' she waved her hand towards the Incident Room. 'Lads'll bring you up to speed on it all, but even with all our efforts and all the man hours wasted what we have is this.' Inga picked up a book on her desk and held it up. 'Packed full of information, interviewed everybody from a pig to a dog, ' she said and flicked the pages. 'At the end of the day what have we got?' She didn't wait for a reply and flipped over to the end and held it up. 'The blank page. And what have you got, lots of stuff from this Epton-Howe woman and what else?' She closed the book waved it again and then opened it up. 'Another blank page. We have no name in the frame no scores on the doors, no suspects we can even consider naming or even some creep we're suspicious about.' Inga signalled with her fingers to those watching and Jake Goodwin was on his feet and entered her room.

'Jake, this is Chris I was telling you about. I'll let him fill you in on this woman who had forty grand filched on some horseracing scam, another Mr Blinking Nobody seems to me.'

'Bit of a dark horse is he?' was not an unduly wise remark at that juncture, but for once he was lucky as Inga just ploughed on.

'Take Chris here under your wing please and let him explain everything he knows, and you give him the bullet points from our Coetzer case.' She stabbed her finger down onto the book. 'Two blank pages is not a coincidence, you with me?'

'I agree with you there,' said Jake and Chris Mackinder was on his feet.

'May well be nothing in it, but it's worth a look,' said Inga very seriously. 'We're chasing moonbeams it seems to me. All a bit like trying to catch up with your own shadow, something all kids try to do. Going after something which doesn't actually exist.'

'Thank you ma'am,' Chris said down to Inga and followed Jake out into the Incident Room wondering as he did so if this astute woman knew what Bowring thought of her.

Alone with her thoughts Inga was always aware how to find out *why* someone died you have to ask the living. To find out *how* someone died you have to ask the living. The latter was the easier of the two with the pathologist, crime scene people and forensics on your side.

The former was always the more difficult. Not asking *why* someone had died, but finding the one person who *might* know or better still the one person who *would* know.

With needles in haystacks you can look, you can search as much as you like, and even make use of metal detectors and magnets or you can rummage about and feel a prick. Searching out the one person in a million or more is never as easy.

You're looking for the prick and there's plenty of them about.

22

How are you finding my story? If you remember I did warn you early on there'll be plenty of moaning, because of the way I am. There's still a good way to go yet, so I'd better get on.

Right then, where were we? Oh yes of course, modern technology.

Before I got to know Brandon I was sadly of the opinion surfing the web took you into a world of grimy sex, filth and more sex. He put me right, by explaining how more people watch cats on the web than anything else.

I'm quite sure Mummy would have simply pretended none of this business even existed, so set was she in her ways.

She was very much the mother and I was just a child. Good manners were everything. I'd never ever dare leave the dining table until given direct permission and there had to be good reason. Not something you can expect from a child when you can't be bothered to buy a table. I was the one who could be seen but not heard, would only speak when spoken to and always on my very best behaviour, total obedience with impeccable manners.

I'm not so sure a lot of the lessons in correct behaviour did me any harm, and almost daily I see children who could do with a good dose of it. Perhaps not into adulthood though as I had to suffer.

If I remember correctly a greeting from mummy would be little more than a nod of recognition and a soft handshake to anybody whether it be me or someone she knew from the church.

Was it all an essential part of my problems, in that I have never been able to properly develop relationships? Had I been too formal in my attitude with Roger to some extent; had I lacked emotion and had it once more reared its head in my alliance with Edward?

All things to ponder as I sit alone with a cappuccino watching the comings and goings around me. As I observe the interaction between people I knew for sure my parents had never ever behaved in such a manner with anyone. Watching two men greet one another with a hug, I knew Daddy would most certainly not have deemed such behaviour as anywhere near acceptable in polite society or impolite society come to that!

But I have to admit I'd never seen him in casual attire. Even sat watching cricket locally on a summer's afternoon when he deigned us with his presence, daddy would wear a collar and tie, a good blazer and sharply creased slacks. He would doff his hat and shake hands. Shirtsleeve order was for those actually playing the game and in his world nobody else.

Daddy Arthur would most certainly not be the group-hug type I know some go in for. I laugh to myself when I see these people making themselves look utterly ridiculous with their foolish oblique posture and can imagine what would happen to one of his employees were one to be stupid enough to hint at some bonding nonsense. Do that and I know for sure they'd be for the high jump and sharpish.

No way, absolutely never ever would Arthur Epton-Howe give anybody a hug and please just don't get me started on all the horrid kissie-kissie luvvie business even I'm appalled by.

I'm never going to be part of this insidious kissing cheeks hypocrisy. All started they tell me by dozy women desperate to attain status with purveyors of the celebrity cult.

First time somebody tried it on with me I wondered what on earth she was up to. I froze and guess the message has got round as hardly anyone has ever tried since. If I spot any fool thinking about it, I now just turn away. They soon get the message. Public affection or emotion I find quite unnecessary and to a degree because of my upbringing, embarrassing.

There you have it then. A problem with relationships has probably been with me all my life and the way others behave is not intrinsic.

There is no doubt how I had become more aware during the last decade of his life how much grumpier daddy Arthur had become as a result of the way the world was turning out.

Right now my guess is you're thinking I'm taking after him!

All the standards by which he lived had been gradually eroded and unfortunately replaced by attitudes which even annoy and confuse me at times.

Had Arthur Epton-Howe lived to experience the life I now have to endure I am sure his blood pressure would have gone through the roof and his rants would have been a delight to observe, providing you were not on the receiving end!

He like me would have never been able to understand why people are quite happy for total strangers to overhear their totally uninteresting phone conversations.

I would never want my drivel to be inflicted on others, and if my father were able to do anything about such crass behaviour I cannot imagine what he'd think of people eating in the street, stuffing vast amounts of fast so-called food down their gullets The putrid smell of cheap curry and the stench of fish and chips pervading a train carriage is about as much as I can stand, and know it would have had Arthur in a rage. Anybody behaving in such a manner in his presence would have got their head in their hands to play with and no mistake. He was just the sort of sharp intelligent giant of a man nobody would argue with let me tell you.

Another thing people learnt to their cost; don't get him started on the EU. Any conversation on the subject was just littered with unpleasant old school words for the French, Germans and Italians and his politically incorrect descriptions could be a great deal worse if he was truly angry. He hated Ted Heath nearly as much as Thatcher which was really saying something, just because the poor fellow was a bachelor and had taken us into the Common Market. What was wrong with Thatcher in his eyes I hear you ask? Her being female, father running a shop and having attended a Grammar School for starters was more than enough for my old man.

Think it's probably a good job daddy has moved on what with all these women now in charge. With Theresa May of course and up in Scotland with the very astute Nicola Sturgeon, and not forgetting Germany's Angela Merkel.

Not at all sure he would have coped with all those. Would most certainly have given him something to chunter about.

He'd have been in his element with the EU Referendum business batting alongside Boris for the Leave Campaign.

I guess there are some who are already planning a Back In campaign right now.

As the days passed it has begun to dawn on me how my life was being altered through no fault of my own.

Edward had given me such hope on a personal level only to destroy all the pent up innermost hopes and desires with one wholly unwarranted and cruel act.

Now perhaps it was time to reconsider other aspects of my life.

Providing meals at the shelter was one facet of my being I had absolutely no intention of changing. If anything I might well double my efforts in some way. The club for the isolated using a rejected lonely woman as a put-upon unpaid helper was I am increasingly convinced doing me no favours.

Just last week was a case in point. At the end of the session I had set off round the building doing all my usual security checks; trying all doors to ensure they had been properly locked and the same went for windows and of course pulling out all plugs. When I returned to the main hall it was empty. When I'd set off there were four other women chatting near the entrance, now there were none.

Club for the lonely and they'd just upped and left me on my own, and not for the first time.

I know what I should have done. I should have gone about my business as if nothing had happened. That morning I had decided once the club activities were over I'd stroll round into town, buy apples and bananas and stop off for a coffee somewhere. Had actually told myself to take the bull by the horns and quietly ask the girl in the coffee shop what drink it is people have with piles of cream squirted on the top. Then buy one.

This is when I'm at my weakest. Rather than do what I had planned, I simply got in my car and drove home. Do you understand why?

There was always the possibility of bumping into those who had beaten a hasty retreat in the street or I would discover them all sat together in whichever café I chose, talking about me. Sorry but I'd not want to meet such a scenario head on so I retreated back to my big empty house alone. How ironic eh?

So much of what I enjoy in life is being eroded by the selfishness of an increasing number of people.

For all their faults my parents were not all bad, and certainly better than some I read and hear about.

It worries me how some parents with no consideration of what their actions may lead to, purchase phones for their offspring, in the same way mummy bought me shoes. A must have. I cannot imagine why parents do this? We're told it's a safeguard which of course is utter garbage.

Paedophiles are not and never have been hiding behind a lampost on the way to school, the vast majority are online or in the family.

One of the really good things daddy Arthur did for me which I have always truly appreciated has been demonstrating to me the power of major sport at the very highest level: Wimbledon, Ashes Tests, The Open, World Championships in a whole range of major sports, Commonwealth Games and Olympics had been a necessary part of the ethos of who I have been for most of my life.

I was so enamoured by Edward I had foolishly considered talking to him about us going to the World Athletics together due in Doha next year. The paperwork is due any day now I would expect, so it looks as though it will be back to me on my lonesome heading for Qatar in September. In itself it's not really a problem as the people I go with are such a friendly and sociable bunch being a singlie has no downside.

What was really strange however was for someone who would be offering experience of sport at a top level, daddy had chosen the school he did for me. Their main sport was Lacrosse. Oh how I envy young women these days who can play football and cricket at such a high level.

Can you imagine there ever being "Lacrosse of the Day" on BBC? Wouldn't it be something, with main presenter Tiggy Dewdrop-Bidcot and her match analysts the right defensive wing Dee Dee Sanctimonious and Lubiloo Greene the well-known left attack wing, talking about cradles and dangerous propelling? The nation would be fascinated. Not.

There's no need for you to look it all up, it's all just Lacrosse talk and I hope for your sake it's nothing you're ever likely to come across.

Talking of sport and the numerous trips I've made abroad over the years has reminded me of something else which annoys me these days. Picture postcards, and the fact people no longer send them.

It used to be so nice to have a card pop through the letterbox out of the blue, rather than all the take-away pizza bumph we get these days.

Pictures of places at home and abroad friends had been to. Now I understand it's all about taking selfies with your phone, to put them on Facebook, Instagram, Twitter and whatever the other things are. I read somewhere or perhaps it was one of the volunteers at St Josephs who was saying recently how they understood one in three people send a text or an email to their pets.

I really do find it difficult at times to get my head round some of this cobblers young people in this selfie-obsessed society go in for.

When they're not on their phones all you seem to get these days from some people is the ridiculous 'Wow!' they come out with about everything. The word which doesn't actually exist means nothing at all. How ludicrous.

Heard about sick people taking selfies at funerals, making sure they get the coffin in the background. How on earth did people get to be like that?

Went to a wedding earlier in the year where the couple insisted on no smart phones. Such a request was necessary to stop the phone-wielding numpties destroying the once in a lifetime wedding pictures with their vulgar me me obsession. I hope more people will take to the unplugged fashion.

Yes, I know I'm out of step, don't have a degree in street cred and I'm sure some will tell me there's no harm in it. I don't own a phone capable of taking such nonsense but I did send a load of postcards from Gold Coast when I was in Australia earlier in the year.

Guess there are some amongst you who will think I shouldn't have done it. I bet you think it's showing off. You can think whatever you like, but I'll still send loads of postcards. What is posting look at me, look where I am on the internet all about then?

Truth is it was probably silly old me once again thinking psychologically how it might just spur friends onto reciprocate. Can't see it working of course. This past summer I had just one measly postcard from a woman I hardly know at the drop-in sessions who had spent a week near the New Forest and sent a card with ponies on it.

At least there was no sign of a coffin or some poor soul's ashes.

Be the smartphone obsession brought us to this state of affairs of course. They're all gone now of course when some toerag tore the phone from your grasp as you were texting as you crossed the road, or when you dropped it down the loo or left it on a bus. All your yesterdays' gone in the twinkling of an eye.

Don't come crying to me. You did it.

Of course on the positive side, real proper cameras nowadays are thankfully making a serious comeback, and those who see the light'll now not lose their memories for ever.

Be like vinyl records and record players being the hot property being sought by a whole new generation.

I've got a friend who still has all his original albums on vinyl, all the great classics such as *Sgt Pepper*, *Dark Side of the Moon*, *Pet Sounds*, *Machine Head*, *A Night at the Opera* and *Abbey Road*, all of which he can still enjoy to his heart's content.

Maybe if people see sense about phones and vinyl then given time they just might start sending postcards again. Rather than telling millions on social media with a selfie taken in Magaluf you're away on holiday, leaving your home empty, unattended and vulnerable to burglary.

From what I can gather all this Twitter stuff is just a case of one person's response to a subject all based on their particular prejudices and personal agendas. Will never be what millions think and it looks less than pointless nonsense to me.

Read somewhere a year or two back how the Simon Cowell fellow had not used his mobile for months. The one I have will only receive and send calls and texts, but I use it so infrequently anyway, so I'm never likely to rudely bump into folk in the street because I'm gawping at it. To be perfectly honest I don't ever use it away from home, nor do I scoff food as I walk along.

One thing I don't understand are these adverts telling you to save data, which I assume is something to do with mobiles. I don't have a clue what they're talking about but as it's never likely to be anything for me to get over concerned about it matters not. Just a bit annoying having people spouting nonsense at you about a ten gig SIM which might as well be in Arabic for the sense it makes to me.

23

If I wished to be young and hip, wearing flip-flops in the rain with a tattoo sleeve I suppose I'd come out with the tawdry "Hi Guys!" to welcome you back.

What exactly does 'Hi' mean? Worse when stupidly aimed at the fair sex of course, but I always cringe at the sound of the supreme gut wrenching presumptuousness of the awful 'Hi there!' If you think about it 'Hi' linked to 'there' is at best complete banal nonsense

I'd had good days and bad days, but we all get those don't we? Sundays can often be the worst. Just wish politicians would open up Sundays like any other day. Why do we have to cow tow to what a decreasing minority of religious folk want? These shop opening hours are plain daft if you ask me. One opens at ten but'll not serve you for thirty minutes, another half past, some at eleven and so on. Why don't they all open at the same time for goodness sake?

Edward and how I'd been treated by him, were still subjects constantly returning to mind to annoy me, but gradually I was pre-occupied by such thoughts less frequently.

I had decided to get my hair done for starters. All the ladies amongst you will know what a good fillip such a simple act can often be. Not the usual trim or blow wave, this was time for a change. I've had my hair the way it is for two decades and I'm not suggesting I go for something outlandish or inappropriate but I feel a change will give me a boost and herald in my new life.

I even considered as part of a new me to maybe sup at a different café. When I ignored my usual coffee house and headed for another I noticed a sign in the window offering PANINIS. Sorry, quite enough for me. You simply cannot make a plural word doubly plural and I couldn't imagine what the coffee might be like in such case, so I turned tail and went back to one of my usual haunts.

The quirk I spotted was a thin woman sat at a table with a bearded man, with her cup perched on the palm of her hand as if using it as a saucer.

Bet next time you're joining in the coffee culture you'll be oddball spotting like I do. It's great fun because as you'll discover, there's nowt as queer as folk.

I had always enjoyed working with the homeless more than any other group of people I had become involved in over the years since mummy's passing. There were of course the good, the bad and those who were neither one thing nor the other, much as in any walk of life.

To be honest if when I turned up at St Joseph's Sanctuary there were less helpers than the ideal number, unless we were desperately short I'd try to see if we could manage with what we'd got. All the helpers are unpaid volunteers, doing what they can out of the kindness of their hearts and I have always felt we are better off just with willing volunteers.

If somebody hasn't managed to make it, then there has to be good reason. Phoning folk and badgering them is not how I tend to operate.

Tuesday was one of those days. We were actually two short of our ideal quota, which in truth amounted to a bit more than two as one of the women can only work up to the start of lunch.

Elaine Goode was there, but two others were not and when we settled down for a morning cuppa before I got on with prepping the main meal of the day we were discussing the situation. I could see Elaine felt embarrassed. In two hours she would be off and the situation would then be worse for those of us left behind.

'What d'you want doing Jacs?' I heard behind me as Holly Methven dished out mugs of tea to two of the homeless who had appeared at the hatch. When I spun round I realized it was a man I had seen a couple of times but had never been introduced to. Sort of new kid on the block.

'Can you peel fifty tates pronto and how good are you at making custard without lumps in it?' I just tossed at him jokingly to cut him short as Elaine sniggered behind her hand.

'Where's the peeler?' I looked at him. 'Do I need a pinny, miss?'

'Thanks for the offer…' and realized I didn't know his name.

'I'm serious,' he shot back to me. 'C'mon, let the dog get at the bone.'

'You're serious.'

'Of course I am, my dear woman,' was how I met Martin Pearson.

I was going to say he did the work of two men, but to be honest he was useful in so many ways. So hard working, so enthusiastic and he made a good job of the potatoes and came up with a great pot of custard to be fair.

To my mind there is just too much twaddle spouted about food these days. One priggish presenter reading from her auto-cue I heard recently said how people are always embarrassed to serve rice pudding!

Who fills these people's brains with such tripe? No pun intended.

Poor tripe. Something which has had to suffer from being handed a bad name and perception as a result. If you call it Tablier de sapeur or to you French crumbled tripe it has a whole new image. Serve it with fresh from the garden new potatoes and dressed with a good butter and a touch of seasoning it is delicious.

Families I grew up with had no need of these food banks we have nowadays, because they could cook. Been taught by their mothers from an early age. Stew was always a good hearty meal, cheap too and full of all the nutrients we all need, in particular the young. Things like toad-in-the hole I still make these days and of course rice and tapioca pudding

Nowadays they run short of cash halfway through the week and have to turn to the charity freebies because they'll not be able to come up with a decent nosh for their bairns. Stuffing a ready-made pizza in the oven or more often than not going on their mobile to ask some jerk in a clapped-out Renault to deliver a cheap and nasty excuse for a meal is not cooking, and despite what the advertising would have you believe, it's nothing more than extremely expensive tasteless garbage.

Problem always is, if you make use of the very people we are there to help there is always the risk they can take advantage, will feel they should be given special treatment and perks. This day I took a chance on this Martin, because quite frankly without some help I'd be struggling with just me, Holly and Elaine for a while. Just wished at the time I knew a bit more about him, his background and history in order to evaluate the risk.

I am always well aware I need to treat all these people with dignity. When suddenly having a real bed to sleep on to some of those I deal with is often the biggest thrill they've had in years.

I've talked to men who have never spoken to their own child. Two or three have told me in confidence they have absolutely no idea where their offspring live.

Please take a moment to just think about it. What if it happened to you, how would you feel?

Desolate is one word which springs to mind and so is utter cruelty, but who actually cares? "I'm going to make sure you never ever see your daughter again!" is nothing more than utter spite and child abuse of course.

Same sort of thing goes on here and now every day in our modern sophisticated educated world amongst seemingly decent human beings. I bet animals never behave in such a manner.

As it turned out I had no need to worry about this Martin. He asked for no special favours, never hinted at special treatment or extras, and in the end it all went well. A hard day certainly with it being understaffed but it was still good.

Elaine is too fussy to my mind and we were better off without her as she frequently insists capriciously about things to get what she wants as if we are there to serve her not those in dire need. She really is too much to deal with at times in such an environment.

What I liked about this Martin was a distinct lack of clamour for sympathy. I appreciate these people have been through hard times. Life in so many cases has not been at all kind, but sometimes you just need a bit of peace from it all. I don't need chapter and verse about their misfortune, about how people, the authorities and government have treated them apparently.

With this Martin at the end of the day I knew no more about him, his background and his tragic life story than I had the moment he had called out to me through the hatch.

I had not seen Brandon to speak to for a day or say and guessed all this police business had probably gone the way of many little unimportant cases in this day and age and been swallowed up in bureaucracy. With all the things you see on the news, hear on the radio and read about was it any wonder with all this terrorism, corruption, paedophiles and goodness knows what going on, dealing with the dopiness of an old batty woman would never be given top priority?

That is of course if any of it can wheedle its way amongst all the sheer boredom of Brexit.

I am adamant children need to play outdoors, to climb trees, build dens and race soapbox carts and we as adults need to close their digital bedrooms. Since when did fresh air do anyone any harm? Children living in the wilds of places like Africa tend not to suffer from the allergies our young mites are said to have these days which we never did. Perhaps there is a message there somewhere.

I'm sure I read how kids are frequently diagnosed with asthma who actually have nothing of the sort and even, believe it or not, how inhalers are in some cases seen as some sort of dotty status symbol!

We somehow need society to return to the old standards to protect our young. Back to when there was a world for adults and one for children, with none of the tedious cross-over we suffer nowadays.

We have absolutely no need for the utter bunkum some spew out about the young needing opportunities to navigate the space and the need for these little kiddy winkies to have a good digital footprint.

Have you heard the like I ask you? Please excuse me while I laugh.

I know I'm wasting my breath as nobody will listen to a daft old fool like me of course. Just pretend to be concerned, wring their hands and then harange the world on social media with utter bilge about their kid being better than your kid and organise an upgrade for little Titania-Louise.

How on earth I seriously want to know have we arrived at a position in society where outdoor play is regarded as irresponsible? Who are these idiots obsessed with child safety and is it just pure coincidence we have this to deal with at the same time as a supposed increase in child abuse?

I Jacqueline Rosemary Miriam Epton-Howe do not believe in such coincidences and would scream my warnings from the rooftops. It's never going to happen, the self-important bores of this world are alas not the sort of people I wish to mix with.

How on earth I would want to know from a council with more and more ridiculous child protection rules in and out of school, do we finish up being more at risk than ever before? Guess there is a message there somewhere they constantly ignore.

Just one of dozens of serious reasons why I never entered politics - those useless parents would never vote for me because I talk too much common sense. Don't let the little darlings climb trees, just hide them away in their bedrooms so they can talk to paedophiles. Is it me or is that absolutely crackers?

Perhaps I'm starting to sound a bit too much like my own father.

Pupils turn up for school starving hungry or so we are told. Because of family financial pressures these days they can't afford food.

Please don't suggest I open up a Breakfast Club too! What's the betting some of those who reckon they can't afford a bowl of porridge for their kids have got the latest iPhone and a television the size of a shed?

24

Amber Coetzer's attitude when he arrived at Myra Gaunt's home along with auburn Julie Rhoades surprised DC Chris Mackinder even though he had been well briefed. He knocked at the door, and when surly Gaunt opened it he had only started to introduce himself when she promptly turned around without a word and walked off down her hall.

Chris stepped inside, with Julie closing the door behind them and the pair walked in the direction they'd seen Gaunt take.

In the drab lounge Amber Coetzer was sat in an armchair waiting, legs crossed, arms folded, looking none too happy. Chris having dealt with the introductions then got himself organized with notebook and pen and sat down on the sofa with young Julie. He started off with a bit of chatty schpeil about the weather and being sorry to disturb her and how it wouldn't take up too much of her time.

'Can you tell me what it was you and Lucas Penney did together?'

'Talked pretty much me duck,' was no use at all.

'What about going out? Where did you meet for the first time, where did he take you for instance, can you remember?'

'Nowhere,' was plain and simple.

Julie was looking at the Gaunt wifie sat there in her chair taking it all in, and repeating it no doubt in the local supermarket or at the doctors. Dressed in a pale yellow twin set, it was a long time since she'd seen one of those. Her mum had a photo of Auntie Maud in a twin set, but it'd been taken years ago.

'How about the first time?'

'Came here.'

This was not at all like talking to Jacqueline Epton-Howe and there was no decent coffee on offer or any of those delicious scones of hers he'd munched his through down near Spalding.

The surroundings were absolutely worlds apart. The Epton-Howe house was probably the largest Chris Mackinder had ever visited with rooms running of in all directions. He was sure it was the first time he'd ever been in a Drawing Room and the kitchen was big enough for a dance and the requisite centre island estate agents go on about. Brandon Wishaw had said there were at least five bedrooms, with a couple more in the attic apparently each with en-suite and two family bathrooms.

The Gaunt's place was a nice enough three bedroomed house, but it was fairly basic and could well have been a council house at one time. A drab wallpapered lounge-diner and a kitchen was pretty much all there was to the place, apart from an entrance hall loaded with pictures with the stairs running off. There was no cellar or scullery he was aware of and no acres of land with orchard and the place where the Wishaw's lived in the grounds.

'He turned up here the first time, is that correct?' Chris enquired, and all he received was a nod. 'Then what?' she just looked at him. 'Where did you go after that?'

'Nowhere.'

'You didn't go out for a coffee or a meal; what about the pub, did you visit your local?'

She smirked. 'No, I'm sorry. Apart from the odd occasion when we went to a pub somewhere for an evening meal once by a canal on holiday I seem to remember, Gordon and I didn't frequent pubs.'

'I meant with this Lucas Penney.'

'I was hardly likely to do such a thing with him when Gordon and I never had, now was I?' They had to wait for her to gather her thoughts. 'Sorry, but Gordon was never one of these who has to prop the bar up all night, he had a lot more about him let me tell you. Anyway his father was an alcoholic.'

'Was Gordon teetotal as a result?' Chris queried.

'Could never see the point of it,' was not actually an answer. 'Drink caused so much trouble in his family when he was young which I'm sure you can understand. Going to a pub to down pints just for the sake of it was never an option for Gordon. Hardly welcoming sort of places and as far as I'm concerned – think they just lack atmosphere. Probably all seems a lot different when you've had a skinful. Not our scene at all sorry, just don't see the point in it.' Amber lifted her hands momentarily. 'But I hope you can understand why.'

'Yes I do. Makes sense it really does. You never went anywhere? Not even out for a coffee maybe?' Chris had never expected his remark to receive the reaction it did.

'What's that all about?' Amber sat back with a self-satisfied grin all over her face. 'Have these people never heard of a jar of Nescafe or if they really do think they're something special, there are plenty of those expensive machines on the market these days they tell me to brew yourself a cup of coffee. You seen how much they charge?' She tried to whistle but there was no sound. 'Well over two pounds in some places I can tell you. How ridiculous is that? Yet the poor fools pay it, got more money than sense seems to me. But then I'm not at all surprised, when you see the sort who buy handfuls of those scratch card things.'

'I probably drink too many Americanos as it happens,' Chris admitted. The no alcohol to some extent made sense with it probably having destroyed her husband's family, but now it was no coffee which was harder to fathom.

'Not to our taste I'm sorry, and I'm never going to pay through the nose for idiotically named coffee, I'm sorry.' She sat there blowing out her breath and shaking her head as if it was a major problem. 'You seen those coffee places, what they call them? To go is it? Now there's a disaster waiting to happen and no mistake. Driving up to buy a cardboard cup of expensive hot coffee. I'm sure somebody's having a laugh telling folk to drive with one hand.'

'What about if you're out shopping say?' he asked for something to say. 'Don't you never stop off for a rest and a nice cup of coffee?'

'When there's one at quarter the price waiting at home you mean?' she chuckled. 'Sorry son, but I just don't see the sense. I dinna float down the Witham on a biscuit.'

'I've no idea what they are,' this Myra Gaunt joined in. 'Where do they get all those silly names from, a coffee's a coffee as far as I'm concerned.'

'Same people probably who take out these pay day loans and no mistake.'

'You need a loan by the look o'some of their prices,' Gaunt considered amusing.

Chris Mackinder had fallen amongst the anti-pub anti-coffee brigade and if he wasn't careful they'd rope him into joining in a protest march on the parish council. He was in desperate need of common ground and his endeavours with this woman were getting him precisely nowhere.

'What sort of time of day would he turn up?' He asked Coetzer to change subject quickly, because if they asked him what a Mocha Cortado was he didn't have a clue. 'This Lucas Penney.'

'All sorts,' gave him the impression she was being deliberately awkward. Yes it was difficult, yes she had lost her husband and her only son, but was that it? Was this woman just willing to let it go and then complain later about the force's lack of effort as some do?

'You and this Lucas,' said Julie suddenly. 'What did you do exactly when he visited? Have a chat was it, watch a bit of tele?'

'Mostly,' wasn't an answer one way or tother.

'Did he turn up on a particular day? Saturdays was it when Greaeme was away at a match?'

'Midweek usually.'

'But when Graeme was away?' She nodded. 'And you've heard nothing more from him since the tragedy?'

'No.'

'Are you upset about it?' Julie continued. 'I know I would be.'

'Not really,' Coetzer replied. 'Not easy for him with what happened, not as if we were related, probably doesn't want to intrude. Never easy you know.'

'Did this Lucas Penney know about you winning the competition?' Chris remembered.

'Of course me duck.'

'What do you mean by of course?'

'Well I told him. Why wouldn't I?' was not what he wanted to hear. 'Why d'you keep going on about him, he's got nothing to do with all this. Shouldn't you be out looking for whoever killed my Graeme?'

'We need to cover every eventuality,' said Chris. 'And we need to talk to Lucas Penney.'

'Why?'

'He might have seen something, might know something, know somebody. Perhaps Graeme told him he was having trouble with somebody. Whatever it is, we need to talk to Lucas Penney, and to do it we need your co-operation.'

'I wasn't here and Lucas wasn't here. Why would he be?'

'How d'you know?' Chris threw at her.

'Because I told him I'd be away.'

'We still need to talk to him. We've talked to your neighbours and relations, we've done house to house, but as yet the one person we haven't had a chance to talk to is this Lucas Penney.'

The conversation just ambled along to nowhere in a manner which clearly said the woman had either had enough of questioning or just couldn't be bothered with it all and in the end the pair quietly slipped away.

'Did you notice something?' Julie posed as Chris drove away. 'No cards, no flowers,' she answered her own question.

'Not her house.'

'You saying cards and flowers are at her empty bungalow?'

'Possible,' Chris glanced at his young assistant. 'She's grieving remember.'

'Can we go and have a look?'

'At what?'

'Her place.'

'What d'you hope to see?'

'Flowers and cards. Her son's been murdered, I know most people will be lazy and send messages on social media, but plenty'll have sent flowers and cards with it being in the papers and on the web.' Chris slowed to take a right turn.

'What will it tell us?'

'Has she actually received them, has she read the cards, in fact has she even opened them? Gave my mum a lot of comfort when my gran died, reading all the nice things people wrote. She seems very cold and it's as if she's just not interested. I felt we had intruded and my guess is she didn't want us there.'

'Probably fed up with us by now.'

'Doesn't she want to help?'

'Her son's dead, nothing will bring him back could be how she sees it.'

The Coetzer bungalow was easy to pick out. It was the one with flowers, remnants of flowers and a whole load of Manchester United memorabilia with scarves the most prominent feature hanging from the porch, propped up against the front door and strewn all across the open plan lawn.

If he was honest Chris had seen enough, but Julie insisted on stopping and peering in through the front window.

'Not a card in sight,' she said when she slipped back into the car.

'And?'

'Bit odd, don't you think?'

'Maybe she's got them round at the Gaunt woman's house.'

'Where are they then?'

Chris started the car. 'Would you put all your cards out in someone else's house?'

'Not right.'

Chris drove away and neither of them spoke for a while.

'What if it was all made up? What if the Coetzer woman made up about winning the competition so she had an alibi for when they did for her son? How about if she and our Lucas Penney are in this together?'

'Chances are he's stolen her money remember,' Chris popped in as he chuckled at the suggestion being formulated. 'So what's the point?'

'To get rid of Graeme.'

'Because neither of them can stand Man United? You're kidding me,' he sniggered.

'She wants to get it together with Penney and the son is having none of it, doesn't want a new dad, so the pair of them came up with this scheme to do him in. She has an alibi for those few days and he's the man who doesn't exist. We still don't have a clue who he might be.'

'And my Jacqueline Epton-Howe, where does she come into all this?'

'Your case has nothing to do with this one at all.'

'You telling the boss this?'

'Might do.'
'Only might?'

What Chris Mackinder was finding difficult to get used to, was a Detective Inspector who would listen. Inga Larsson may not agree with you, she might well dismiss it out of hand, but at least she would listen, or if she was busy get one of her Sergeants to hear what he had to say.

From where he was sat in the Incident Room, the view was far from perfect but from what he could see he got the gist of the reaction DC Julie Rhoades received from DI Larsson, and it didn't look at all pleasant. This was a boss willing to listen but then he saw a reaction he had not as yet come across before. He could hear nothing but the body language and gestures told its own story.

'If I tell you I'm not at all pleased with you coming in here with all this nonsense, do you have any idea why?'

'You're busy,' Julie offered.

'You really have no idea do you?' Inga threw at the young brunette. 'What does Chris say or haven't you discussed it with him?' was sharp.

'Doesn't agree with me.'

'At least one of you has a bit of sense.' Inga commented as she leant forward onto her desk. 'Do you read the overnight reports?' Julie nodded but it was not very positive. 'How come then you don't know we've already got CCTV of her catching the train to Newcastle? One of the first thing's we obtained was LNER confirmation of when the ticket was bought. We have more CCTV, getting on the train and getting off and more of her turning up at the Holiday Inn. We have a report saying Metro can search for her on their system if we want.' Inga hesitated for a moment. 'What do you think the team are doing all day?' there was no response. 'People like Ruth and Raza are not gleaning such information for fun,' she said loudly, but not so loud she could be accused of shouting. 'In an enquiry like this they are the basics, why don't you know that?'

'Sorry,' was mumbled.

'Are you suggesting this Amber woman pretended she won a competition and then went through with it all as if she had? What about her sister she met when she got there? Was she in on it as well? She part of this subterfuge, played her part in creating this alibi, and if she did, why do you think it was? Has Amber got some hold over her sister do you think?' Julie could only shrug. 'You need to think these things through young lady. Did you think you had to come up with some out of the box nonsense, is that what this is all about?'

'No.'

'When all this came to mind, didn't you think, maybe I'd better read the reports see what they've found out about the Coetzer woman?' Julie just shook her head. 'Do the men intimidate you?'

'No.'

'We're one team and I'm not into creating little girly groups.' Inga sat back. 'I'll put you with Ruth. She'll report back to me, so watch your step young lady. Make use of her, pick her brains. If she comes up with some off the wall idea ask her why, ask her where it came from and see where she researched it all.' Inga licked her lips. 'This is the first team and right now in football parlance you are on loan from PHU, but at this rate you'll go back at the end of your loan period.' Inga sighed obviously. 'Enough. Off you go, think about it, decide what it is you really want to achieve, if anything and I'll speak to Ruth.'

'Sorry', she muttered as she turned.

'Julie,' stopped her with the door half open. 'You could be a much better copper than you are right now.'

This was not all one way traffic. Inga knew Ruth was ambitious and to add this mentoring element could only be good for her. To some extent it was not entirely Julie's fault as she had been stuck in PHU (Prisoner Handling Unit) for some time and all their multi-various acquisitive crimes. The dour world of shoplifting, domestics and burglary.

Once released from the wrath of the DI it was a very somber auburn Julie who slumped down in her chair, and Chris decided to keep well clear. He could only guess it was her theory about Amber Coetzer and it had all blown up in her face.

25

'What have you got?' Chris Mackinder's mentor Jake asked to disturb him watching freckled Julie out of the corner of his eye.

The DC sucked in hard before he dare speak as fair warning the news was not good. 'Nothing, which if you look at it one way is a good thing.'

'How do you make that out?'

'My Jacqueline Epton-Howe admits she never stepped outside her front door with this Edward fella. Earlier when we spoke to Amber Coetzer she told us how she and this,' he had to glance at his notebook. 'Lucas Penney, never went anywhere either.'

'Crafty sod. If by sheer chance this long shot turns out to be the same person he's a cool customer and no mistake.'

'And very careful.'

'Sit down,' said Jake, 'you're making the place untidy,' and Mackinder pulled up a typist chair. 'Tell me why they didn't go out. Or is this something else we don't know?'

'According to Jacs this horse trader is racing about all over the country all week, when he got to her she said he just wanted a decent meal and to sit back and relax with a glass or two of wine. Lovely house let me tell you with big grounds. Wouldn't need to ask me twice to just kick my shoes off and relax in there.'

'And this Penney, what about him?'

'Didn't give a reason, except remember he never stayed over, probably wasn't there so long. Three four hours at the most I should image. But she had a lot to say about not going to the pub?'

'Why?'

'Her father-in-law was an alcoholic. As a result think Amber's husband was virtually teetotal; his childhood could have been an absolute nightmare and it seems it turned him off the booze. Gordon and his wife never went to the pub just for a few jars, she doesn't like them, simply can't see the point in supping lager all night.'

'Could be she wouldn't go even if this Penney suggested it.' Jake just allowed his head to wobble.

'More than likely.'

'Not something we do to be honest, go to the pub unless we go to a country one for a meal. We're never going to just sit there with a pint each. Better off at home to be honest.' Jake sighed. 'What else have we got to link the pair?' He guessed there was more to come so Chris bided his time. 'Perhaps it's me but a booze boozer always has an atmosphere, something I can never put my finger on, just one way or another it feels as if I'm intruding, never feels quite right.'

Not something Mackinder had ever encountered. 'This Lucas knew she'd won the competition.'

'Really? Well...'

'Not so fast,' said Mackinder to stop him going on. 'He knew because Amber Coetzer said she told him.' Jake simply exhaled in frustration. 'Cars are different.' The look of anticipation on the Detective's face made him go on. 'Our Edward McCafferty drove a top of the range Skoda according to Epton-Howe, but Coetzer doesn't know one car from another.' He put a hand up to stop any comment. 'Young lad two doors down fortunately reckoned it was a metallic grey Mazda 3, you know what some lads are like probably tell you the brake horse power and fuel consumption rate as well.'

'Bugger,' said Jake and began to shake his head. 'Haven't got two things the same have we?' Mackinder left him to his thoughts for a few moments. 'We've got Raza looking at the football connection for Coetzer and right now it looks like our best line of enquiry. Don't suppose there's been a hint about football from your Spalding woman by any chance?'

'Certainly likes her sport. According to my mate she attends all the big matches. Rugby, Cricket, Open Golf and all the rest. Been to several Olympics and even the Superbowl once. One of the prawn sandwich brigade is my guess,' he sniggered. 'She'd not rush out to grab a pie at halftime,' he chuckled.

'Football?' Jake smirked. 'Please tell me she's a season ticket holder at Old Trafford.'

Chris Mackinder didn't like to admit it but he had to be honest. 'Do you know, I haven't a clue. Could be couldn't it, she's also a Man U supporter? Then it would be more than just a coincidence.'

'Is this how Man City cut down the Reds support by having their avids murdered and ripped off?' made them both chuckle. 'Check it out,' said Jake as he saw Inga approaching. 'Is your Jacs woman a secret Red Devils fan?'

'Where are we then boys?' was the DI behind Chris. 'Found a link?'

'Still up a gum tree,' said Jake in response to his boss as Mackinder spotted Julie out of the corner of his eye, head down at her desk. 'Different cars, but the only spurious lead we have really is Jacqueline Epton-Howe's guy. This Edward whoever, never went out of the house when he visited and same goes for this Lucas Penney character with Coetzer.'

Jake Goodwin had become concerned at how disinterested his boss appeared to be with the case. Had she just given up on it already? If true it was unlike her, in fact it would most likely be unique.

'And why wouldn't you step outside?' Inga asked in a manner which suggested she already had the answer to her own question. 'According to friends and relatives Ruth has been interviewing he was never there, in as much as one woman said she thought there was someone in the house once when she called and Amber Coetzer was very furtive and couldn't wait to get rid of her. As if everybody knew this Penney called but nobody ever made contact with him.' She looked at each of them in turn. 'He didn't want to be recognized.'

'But,' said Mackinder. 'Where would they go? She apparently doesn't go in pubs, places like Starbucks are closed at that time and anyway she's not into cappuccinos and lattes, and he's only there for two or three hours.'

'And if your lover called round for a couple of hours...' Inga smiled knowing she had no need to finish.

There was just a few moments of silence as she gathered her thoughts and peered at her tablet. Just enough time to hear raised voices in the corridor outside. Normally it would have passed off without comment or even knowledge.

'Somebody's not too happy,' said Raza Latif and Inga showed no irritation at how his concentration had moved away and went on as if there had been no break.

'Evidence we've got so far is all a bit flaky to say the least.'

'The other one never stepped out either,' Inga suggested as she looked at young Mackinder. 'Am I right?' He nodded.

'The Coetzer woman says this Penney character called midweek.' He saw the DI point at Jake. 'I reckon it's obvious it would be when Man U had a midweek game and Graeme wasn't there.'

'And why our Mr Dudek has never seen him,' the DS reacted. 'He visited Coetzer at weekends when Graeme and his dad were away at Old Trafford, and even though he's had his nose put out of joint he lives three streets away so he'd not just see this Penney knocking on her door.' She turned to others in the room. 'He's a lorry driver during the week and probably only had weekends free to visit, which was convenient with her old man off to Manchester once a fortnight.'

'Have we checked for CCTV?' Jake queried.

'Done it all early on if you remember,' had a tinge of annoyance about it. 'On a housing estate. No chance. There's a camera outside the Co-op shop but analysts upstairs tell us it's aimed down at the front door if you remember, to pick up any shoplifters and low life hanging about at night. Doesn't show the road at all, so he could have driven up and down there dozens of times.' Inga looked down at the DC. 'What about your woman? I suppose there's no chance.'

'Couple of miles outside the town, not a camera for miles I shouldn't imagine.'

'Don't complain about a lack of wind,' said Inga. 'We always say, learn to sail.'

'That's all very well,' said Jake not fully comprehending the Swedish line of thinking. 'Where do we go now?' he asked, and Chris Mackinder could see he was about to be shunted off back to the nasty world of Inspector Bowring and his attitude. Guessed he'd have to get in touch with Brandon and ask him to tell Jacs Epton-Howe there really was nothing to go on. Be another unsolved case Bowring would put his name on and tell him it was the waste of time he'd said it was in the first place and make fun of the fact the foreign blonde bitch had got nowhere just as he'd said she would.

'We go back to the woman,' she told Mackinder. 'Might not be football linked but they both appear to be sports enthusiasts.' She smiled and put a hand up to stop Jake. 'Don't say it, what has football got to do with sport?'

'Would I?' he grinned.

'I know you Baggies supporters,' she slipped in and was back to Mackinder. 'Do a DVLA search for the two vehicles. Need somebody called Lucas Penney who owns one and this Edward McCafferty and his…?'

'Skoda,' said Jake shaking his head. Inga waited. 'We've done DVLA if you remember. There's no Lucas Penney with a valid driving licence.' Inga's facial expression asked the question clearly. 'You think maybe…'

'How many skurks do interceptors pick up every day for not having a valid licence?' she asked.

Jake blew out his breath. 'Risky.' He turned to Mackinder. 'Skurk by the way is Swedish for crook.'

'But still worth a check.' Inga turned away from giving Jake a look, to Mackinder. 'Do we know anything more?'

'I can try Jacs, see what she remembers.'

'Jacs? Sounds all terribly girls private school nonsense and no mistake,' Inga chuckled. 'While you're at it, talk to her about football, about maybe going abroad to support Man United. I've said to you before, we have two cases and between them the case files have little more than a few blank pages. My budget doesn't run to the cost of chasing moonbeams. Two cases surely cannot be without a link somewhere down the line.' Inga turned. 'Keep at it. Thanks.'

Forty minutes later and DI Larsson appeared once again and this time called for hush.

'I know we're not getting very far in either of these cases and we still have nothing to tell us they're linked,' she looked at Chris Mackinder. 'Looks like we've got a live one with yours. Tell them Ruth.'

'According to the Economic Crime Team, the bank account your Jacqueline Epton-Howe had transferred her funds into had the account holder living at an address in Glasgow,' dark haired DC Ruth Buchan advised those present. 'Got onto Police Scotland who passed me over to their Greater Glasgow Division who kindly sent a couple of their lads round to ask a few questions. No Edward McCafferty of course sitting there in a kilt, Irn Bru in hand with his feet up waiting for us,' she commented and went on reading from her screen. 'Turned out to be in the area of Bridgeton a village which sprung up in the 1800s and then became part of Glasgow's East End where foundries and factories rose to create some of Britain's iconic constructions. All in the past now and the area now no longer resounds to the clanking of chains and hammer on steel which at one time was all a critical part of the hard life in those parts for more than a century…'

'This a history lesson?' Tigger piped up.

'No,' said Ruth grumpily. 'This is just the report I've got back from the DC up there. Listen up, you might learn something,' showed her annoyance. 'This proud working class community was then regenerated to host much of the Commonwealth Games back in 2014 including the athletes village which is now home to social and private housing. One resident is an old boy named Finlay Currie.' Ruth put her hand up. 'I know, I know sounds unreal, but most certainly it really is his name. Been told he's a lovely old fella apparently, but a bit of an old cuss living alone now where the old house used to be. Turns out he's in need of new glasses. A kindly neighbour explained to the lads up there how old Finlay could very well have received material from the bank but the likelihood was it had somehow gone stray or this old fella had just thrown it all in the bin.'

'Thanks Ruth,' said Inga then glanced at Julie hoping she'd taken notice. 'And how much has the account got in it now?'

'A quid.'

'This is close to the sort of scam some of us have come across before,' said Jake. 'I've heard of postmen having to deliver mail to addresses which in effect don't exist.'

'Come across it more than once,' Inga reminded him.

DS Goodwin was not for stopping. 'Rather than carry them round all day and take them back, they simply post them through letterboxes as close as possible to the address. A road ending at number 47 often has mail addressed to non-existent 49. Regular scam I hear, often used to create an address for benefit fraud.'

'By my reckoning, your Jacqueline has been done over good and proper,' Inga told Chris Mackinder.

'D'yer ken we tie it to this Coetzer?' Sandy asked.

'Good question.' Inga looked down at a glum Chris Mackinder again. 'Need more info from your woman. Need everything she has on the Lonely Hearts thing she got involved in and borrow her phone. We'll let the e-boys have a search through it, you never know what might pop up. Did you say he'd phoned her or she'd phoned him?'

'I'm pretty sure he phoned her.'

'And what's the betting if you ask Coetzer she'll tell you Penney phoned her all the time.'

'We ever done this before?' she asked everybody. 'Built cases against people who might not exist? Get to it.' Inga looked all around. 'Rest of you need to find something, any damn thing to link Coetzer to this horse scam.' As Inga walked past Julie Rhoades she bent down. 'Which includes you young lady.'

Inga did exactly the same to Jake at his desk next but with an altogether different tone and message. 'We going with this being one and the same? This Edward McCafferty and Lucas Penney?'

'What else do we have?' Jake whispered back. He had noticed his Scandinavian boss did not understand what his use of gum tree was all about but let it ride. 'Give it a whirl, see what happens.'

'Still a worry this Penney doesn't actually exist. At least we know McCafferty or whatever is real according to the woman.'

'Don't suppose Craig Darke has dropped any hints about how he'd tackle something like this?'

'Don't be silly.'

'Just a thought,' he grinned.

'Leave it with you then.'

To be summoned to the boss's office less than an hour after she had last briefed him on progress normally meant just one thing to Inga. Trouble.

Often a complaint from the public or a solicitor had reached his desk or there was some new staffing edict or new system to be introduced instantly.

As a result she found under such circumstances it was mighty difficult to walk into his office with anything like enthusiasm on show.

So it was she entered with a degree of trepidation, but when he immediately offered her a seat, she knew from experience it was not completely bad news.

'Talk to me about Sandy MacLachlan,' he said while she was still on her way down to the sitting position.

Inga sucked in a breath noisily. Was she about to lose another?

'Doing fine so far, but it is early days.'

'Good,' Darke sat back in his big chair but Inga was not for moving yet.

'Replacement?' she dared to ask, and this was where the downer would come. She'd have to suffer a load of guff about austerity and budgets and word from on high. More civilians she knew about most on zero hours, scrapping old clapped out cars which were always useful as decoys and scrutinizing every penny of expenses. Two more years of this Darke had already threatened.

'Irons in the fire, can you leave it with me,' he sat back up and leant on his desk. 'You won't go short in the long term, but I feel we need something less than a bit of brute force, so I'm looking for the right type for you,' made it sound as if he was doing her a favour which was highly unlikely. 'Anything more to report?'

'Nothing much,' Inga said as she pushed herself to her feet.

Inga knew every time she went up to see the eTeam it was like a different world. "The future" Darke had said more than once. With all their techy equipment and more superior flat screen computers than you can shake a stick at. A peculiarly British phrase she'd borrowed from Adam.

'Biggest bollocking I've ever had,' a miserable looking Julie Knowles admitted more than an hour later when Chris followed her to the canteen and offered her an ear. 'I feel so stupid, bet she's telling them all now. Why didn't you stop me?'

'Stop what?' he asked but guessed he knew.

'About the Coetzer woman.'

'What'd she say?'

'All about checking reports.'

'And did you?'

Knowles grimaced. 'You know what it's like.' Chris was shaking his head. 'God she was angry.'

'What you doing now? I've got to go back to my Epton-Howe woman.'

'I've been put with Ruth.'

'Use her,' Chris offered. 'She's fairly new apparently and once was Family Liaison. Learn from her.' He saw a look of disinterest. 'Tell you what, I'd swop working with Inga rather than the dope of a DI I'm lumbered with normally. Make the most of it or you'll regret it soon enough.'

'S'pose so,' said Julie and sipped her tea.

'Know anything about Ruth off duty?'

'Bits,' Mackinder responded. 'But remember I'm only here for the Spalding element. Somebody said she's divorced.'

'Kids?'

'No idea.'

This Julie Rhoades was too thin, too pasty faced to Chris's mind to be attractive or to be what he considered appealing. The PCSO he'd spoken to last week was more up his street. Time maybe to hunt her down and try his luck, because although he'd thought about her a great deal he was convinced Ruth'd would never give him the time of day, and divorce was always an amber warning light to his mind.

'Never gonna be me meeting the boss for coffee some place is it?'

'Why not?'

'Like Scoley does?' she queried. 'I should coco.'

'No reason why not.'

'Never teacher's pet, not even at school.'

'You think she's teacher's pet?' Mackinder asked and Julie nodded.

'Way I hear it is they had to visit a café out somewhere once to get information. Since then they say Scoley has provided a shoulder for the boss to release some of her stress. Do it in Sweden so DS Goodwin was telling me, meet up for cake, coffee and a chin-wag.'

'So why'd she sent her off to Scotland now?' Julie probed.

'Nobody seems to know.'

'And you seriously think she'd let me tag on? Be serious!'

'From what the DS was saying he understands in her homeland it's as likely to be men meeting up.'

'For coffee and a chat?' Julie smirked. 'You're joking!'

'Different world apparently.'

'I can just imagine what my Steve would say if I suggested he meets his pals for coffee and a fairy cake.'

Although she was totally unaware of such comments Inga Larsson decided to send out Ruth Buchan and Julie Rhoades as a pair which pleased Chris no end.

Their job was to ascertain from the people he worked with any aspects of Graeme's life they were unaware of. Scant information was the result as they confirmed the ManU man had a two track mind, footie and ale. Except for a very occasional celebration at work staged for somebody leaving or getting married, he never attended any run-of-the-mill social events involving staff. All just a repeat of what they'd discovered in the early days of the investigation.

26

I think I've told you before, but I was fully aware how change was needed in my life. Exactly how to go about it was my overriding question. Up to which point it had been somewhat characteristic of a merry-go-round.

I most certainly went to the wrong school for starters, which has been obvious to me for years. Probably the right school if I want to be a top civil servant or be in the Cabinet, but my only real schooling issue was mental arithmetic for some reason.

Even so I could still probably get a Ministerial post or become a judge. Not a lot of mental calculations I shouldn't imagine and from what I've seen not a lot of mental anything.

Strange how some events from your schooldays remain in your memory bank. I was jealous at one time of girls who got chosen to be taken into the tuck shop next door by the geography teacher when they needed a new exercise book. Then later as I became more mature and understanding of the ways of the world I appreciated why it was always the pretty ones and what the exchange rate was for a free tube of Love Hearts or Spangles. Do you remember them? Rounded square boiled sweets in a paper tube individually wrapped. Strawberry flavour I can remember, orange and lemon come to mind and probably blackcurrant. Whatever happened to Spangles?

One distinct advantage of being sent away to school was I was never subjected to all the nonsense some parents get involved in at the school gates. This feverish one upmanship between mothers and the silly notions they try to foster about parenting and the price of houses they'll never own because they'll never save and want it all now.

I'm quite sure had I been schooled locally, maybe for the first week or so mother would have walked me to school. I'd certainly never have been part of the absurd school run or come out to find her gossiping about others at the school gates all dressed to the nines. Mother Miriam would most certainly have never become one of those obnoxious uber-mummy types we hear about.

Anyway I digress, again. Even though in my form at school I was the first to develop breasts I never received an invite into the tuck shop, but all the girls in my year wanted to have a look and two wanted to have a little poke about at them.

The school merry-go-round ground to a halt as it inevitably does for all, and off I stepped along with all my friends, they now call peers and for why I cannot imagine, because they are not.

Alas it was where those relationships ended. No university for me, no Oxford to study Economics and Management which I would have thought would have been useful to daddy. Edinburgh for Medicine had interested me at one time but looking at the NHS now I'm not so sure. My path was clear and had been since my early teens; my role in life was as a domestic.

The phrase in itself is so typical of what little I gained from a private education? I still at my age refer to the social climbers I was at school with as 'chums'. Not school mates, pals or friends, but chums. All chums together don't you know, except nowadays I have no contact whatsoever with any of them. Nor would I welcome it if I'm perfectly honest. I may be lonely at times but I'm not that desperate.

Somebody told me recently how on the internet some of these hyper-sensitive young women have been dubbed the snowflake generation. This is because for ridiculous and immature reasons they believe they should be forever protected from anything slightly unseemly.

What I find offensive is quite the opposite. The bleeding hearts brigade like poking their noses into my life. Such as the patronizing voice popping up uninvited on my television having the temerity to advise me how the programme I have chosen to watch contains material of a distressing nature.

Do people really become genuinely upset by antics on their tele? If some of the content is too real life for them, then switch off. Surely we all know what to expect from the programme you plan to sit down and gawp at.

Wasn't there a TV serial about Guy Fawkes at one time? When a few irritatingly soppy folk complained about distressing scenes. Nobody wants a cozy version of history. If being hung, drawn and quartered is what happened, then show it or don't bother to make the programme at all.

If this is all done by do-gooders to protect children, they've got it completely wrong. What they're doing is highlighting real life episodes in dramas. The moment the silly warning comes on what's the betting surly kids become avids for a minute or two. Kids of today would not take their eyes off loathsome nonsense on YouTube for some of the prissy silliness on BBC2.

Nobody comes on to warn how you could die of middle-class prudery watching some of the soppy old maid dross they serve up.

There was no health warning when Theresa May suddenly called a wholly unnecessary General Election a few years back which the TV bores used to stupefy the nation for weeks on end.

While we're on the subject, mummy always used to make me walk in front of her when I was very young sometimes in order to check my gait and correct it if necessary. With such seriously bad deportment somebody should have done so for our PM, but I guess it's too late now.

You'd have to watch a lot of episodes of *Escape To The Country* to come across blood, guts, nudity and what some weary willies consider to be bad language. Anti-social behaviour is there in front of us every day of our lives so why is it such a big deal? It'd have to be jolly rotten to upset me let me tell you.

There's nobody in the high street with a loud hailer warning you some scruffy goon is gobbing outside the Post Office.

What would really infuriate me would be if I was to come across one of these offensive trollops who go to the shops in their pyjamas. Next time I see one it's more than likely she'll get a mouthful from me and no mistake.

Daddy Arthur could see no point in my attending a seat of learning. As he would frequently point out, those who have created great wealth – his watchword for everything – have not spent years reading from books and learning from tutors. They in turn have never ever made more in life than their measly salary of a few shekels…his wording not mine. Theirs was not a doctrine he wanted any child of his to follow.

So it was I stepped onto the slow roundabout of being my mother's companion. Almost akin to a lady in waiting to be summoned at her beck and call.

He did however pay for me to attend a residential Cordon Bleu crash course during the summer holidays in my last two years at school.

Do you really have to ask what it was all about?

That in itself is quite ironic, my father paying out a small fortune to have someone teach me how to eventually cook for the destitute he loathed!

As mummy's health slowly deteriorated over the years I had felt less and less able to break free, seek pastures new. I had never been employed, had never had to work for a living, not once had I received a pay packet or salary cheque in my life, just an allowance.

The 'family' allowance my father paid into mummy's bank account each month was more than enough for the pair of us to live and maintain the big house and grounds, while he lived it up in London, Rome and New York where he had business interests and numerous women's beds he would make use of apparently.

Then I had the Jeremy Dale episode. How on earth had I fallen for it? We've all heard about the best man at weddings making a bee line for the pretty bridesmaid, well in truth it was along those lines. He wasn't the best man and I have never been a bridesmaid or pretty. I ask you, is anybody likely to be quite so desperate?

Anyway it was Georgie Davenport's wedding when she wed her father's dopey accountant and most probably because it was one of the very few opportunities I had to get away from the clutches of mummy for a night, I went a bit mad. Made too much of the bubbly and then a good white wine flowing freely.

Without going into boring detail like they do apparently in those *Grey* saucy books I'm still thinking about by the way; there was this good looking lanky Jeremy Dale there. With more than a little help from the alcohol one thing led to another and he bedded me. Just once in the hotel bedroom he was staying in. Even cheekily took me down to breakfast the following morning and it was the last I ever saw of the rat.

Found out much later it'd been a dare with a bottle of the finest malt whisky to anyone who could bed me and produce my knickers as proof.

Please don't ask how anybody would know for certain they were my undies. All I know is, I arrived home without any, and as I did the washing I never had to face awkward questions from Mummy about what had happened to my pink drawers.

27

The late night call from daddy Arthur's solicitor was another episode in my life I will always remember. It was more about ensuring I toed the party line about exactly where he had been and with whom, than any concern about us not seeing the head of our family ever again.

The funeral was organised like some obscene military operation and because mummy would never discuss such matters I have never known her feelings. I felt like an invited guest intruding into somebody else's grief. I was treated as though I was just a casual inconsequential independent observer rather than his daughter, his only child – that I'm aware of.

Mummy was never the same from then on. All down to the shame which I guess must have been wallowing up inside her she would never admit to.

Much later I was told by a family friend it was all to do with share prices, an impending take-over and daddy's involvement in intense negotiations; the stress of which probably did for him in the end. He had to be seen as whiter than white, and dying in some tart's bed in Islington of all places would certainly have muddied the waters apparently not to mention hitting the share price. Perhaps he really did have Apple in his sights!

The roundabout of my life had stopped once more and it was a little over twenty four months of increasing ill health controlling mummy and her desire not to go anywhere, not to do anything. From only child, baby daughter, out of sight, out of mind schoolgirl to companion and now carer with no life and no achievements behind me.

Then just a few days after the London Olympics had got underway she quietly slipped away in the nursing home which for me meant the wheels had come off again.

All the sport I have watched first hand over the years as far away as the Louisiana Superdome for the Superbowl or Melbourne for Ashes cricket and mummy had to go and die during a home Olympics. Not any Olympics, just the never to be repeated in my lifetime one in London. As it turned out I managed to miss some amazing spectacles but also fortunately I was not subjected to some of the utter garbage the media spewed out.

I fortunately was there in the stadium to see Mo Farah, Ennis-Hill and Greg Rutherford win three golds in a row.

Mummy was dead, the end of an era and suddenly I was in my thirties, a rich woman but all alone in a big rapidly changing and to some extent deteriorating world.

Looking back it was then I really should have set my stall out to change my life, when all I really did in fact was to carry on as before but in different directions.

Mummy had been into her church and it was for them she put in all her efforts over the years. Organising this that and the other, forcing people to perform duties they had no interest in or talent for. A flower rota, coffee rota for the after Sunday service cuppa. A Spring Fayre, a summer garden party, bring and buy, Dickens Dinner with readings from a Christmas Carol close to the festive season.

It must have been my reaction to her intensity, for the world of religion is not for me. Not a case of not believing in God, more a case of not being taken in by stories which appear to be little more than centuries old tales from wandering minstrels. All knocked up into one big book. A bit like those box sets some people seem to enjoy for reasons I have yet to fathom.

I did at one time read a great deal about ancient astronaut theories and past alien contact. As a result I have become very sceptical about a one man creation and tales of loaves and fishes. To me there are too many unanswered questions particularly in a world where a 'god' allows such terror particularly of the young and innocent in this day and age.

Quite frankly I don't care to know what religion people are and I have no idea what they all believe. Couldn't tell one from another to be honest. If you wish to worship a bunch of stinging nettles please go ahead, but do not involve me and please don't try to ram tales of Nasty Sting the King Nettle down my throat.

After mother died I carried on helping people but in a different direction. I've not been to church again since her funeral save to attend those of a few people I have got to know. Now I put all my efforts into helping those less fortunate than myself, rather than throwing money into a church wallowing in stockpiles of land, gold and precious gems.

To he that hath shall be given really does annoy me.

I know for sure I'm out of the loop, not snazzy or fashionable yet at the same time I'm not daft, but I do find life a strange place in which to live at times. I have just two handbags and can see no reason whatsoever to have another as most days I don't carry one at all. I won't ever ask why the young have damn great big ones as I really cannot imagine what they contain hanging stupidly in the crook of their arm. Please don't get me started on shoes or we'll be here all day.

I'm quite sure the average woman is like me and probably just goes to a shoe shop and buys the first pair they see. That's how interested I am in shoes. Think what you will about me if you are a slave to all the hype, but it's what I do.

Why on earth do people think nonsense such as ridiculously big handbags, angry eyebrows, mobile in paw ready to be snatched, high heels to ruin your physiology, ridiculously big TV screens and walking about with a cone of coffee are all important?

Think it was Einstein who once said he feared the day when technology surpasses our human interaction. When it happens he reckoned the world will then have a generation of idiots. I reckon that day has arrived when you look about you, what say you?

Just look at our future generations spending hours simply wasting the one life they are given on line or sat in a silent transfixed state on an expensive phone. All part of what somebody once called the cotton wool culture.

Maybe this is where I'm going wrong. Should I go in for staring at a phone and bumping into people in the street in total ignorance? Time perhaps to start watching *I'm A Celebrity* (but who gives a toss), and anything involving more people I've never heard of?

These are such tawdry times, with every man jack chasing tacky celebrity nobodies for no sensible reason.

Should I get a fake tan, have my hair dyed red and be inked with tattoos to cover my left arm? Have my nails painted different colours, get a ring put through my nose and five studs in one ear? The new me.

How about if I join the smartphone louts? Perhaps I should stop being irritated by the ubiquitous whistling alerts I am exasperated by or behave in a seriously dangerous manner and pay a small fortune for earphones, the sort some parts of America have sensibly banned.

Then I can quite easily step in front of fast moving traffic and not hear or feel a thing until the huge four by four on an elephant hunt through Spalding splatters me all over the A151.

What about if I go off on holiday to the place which advertises high octane thrills; whatever such drivel might mean! Join queues of people in garish un-ironed polo shirts with the short sleeves rolled up. I could wear naff shorts in the rain along with flip flops.

Next time I'm in a big store and some skinny scary painted doll offers to puff perfume at me I need to welcome it all for once in my life rather than steering well clear of the stench.

Tweeting is something else I have always kept well away from. Perhaps I should become one of these trolls you hear about and send scurrilous messages to all and sundry and the cruder the better. Those I've seen quoted in the press have never been very far removed from the realms of adolescent garbage.

Anyway I'm not at all sure if having your smart phone welded to your hand can be done on the NHS.

Yes I know, I'm being facetious. But it is how it feels to me right now. Most of what I see appears to be completely pointless nonsense and I want no part of it.

One of the things I love about modern technology is the utter folly which surrounds it quite often.

When I receive a text advising me if I top-up this month I'll receive five hundred free texts the absurdity always makes me chuckle.

I top-up maybe once every three or four months sometimes even longer, therefore five hundred texts would probably last me for years.

Never been sucked in by it all, but it still makes me chuckle to think what an absolute waste of time it all is and I wonder how many other people feel exactly the same.

I fully appreciate the efforts young Brandon has made and wonder if he feels the work he put in was in the end all in vain? His pal Chris the policeman seems to have disappeared off the face of the earth and no doubt in the cop shop they're having a good laugh at my utter stupidity. I'm probably the silly old bat with more money than sense they talk about in the canteen. Bet I've been the butt of many a good joke, what say you?

Everybody does foolish things when they are young and I am probably more guilty than most. These days however it seems to me the youth, and females in particular are making ineptitude a lifestyle.

28

Madeline Dorsett felt her best friend was being somewhat over protective, paranoid even. They'd been friends now for going on thirty years, way back to when Nadine had been at playschool, so she knew Angela had her best interests at heart. When she'd admitted after one glass of Shiraz too many how she was in touch with a lovely man on a lonely hearts website, the response was full of noisy sucks of breath along with *please be careful, watch your step, are you that desperate* and *do you really need to*?

It was all right for Angela, she appeared fairly happily married in a very stable relationship with a lovely caring husband and had never been subjected to the torment she had suffered regularly over the years.

She is however the sort of woman who when not getting her own way in her relationship, then tries to foist her attitudes on others.

At one time she was as thick as thieves with one of her nieces as she attempted to be the young blonde's mate rather than her aunt.

The poor girl, must have wearied of all the bizarre nonsense and like all teens preferred to be at odds with anything adult.

This lonely hearts business was not something Madeline had done with little thought. In the same way she dealt with all aspects of her life and her business in particular she had considered all the options including risk. Almost carried out her own risk assessment on the matter.

This David she'd come across had suggested they meet for coffee in Hemel Hempstead, not too far from her and he readily admitted his choice was purely for selfish reasons. He was in the area involved in the early stages of a new contract for his CCTV installation company and had a need to be available for any issues which might arise.

He had suggested a small chic café rather than one of the big multiples and it was with a degree of trepidation she entered the coffee house.

Thankfully it was immediately obvious who David was when a man rose to his feet as she walked in. He walked up to her and they shook hands.

'Good journey?' he asked

'Fairly good. At least the rain held off.'

'Coffee?' he asked as they both sat down. 'What will it be?'

This is where Angela had poked her nose in. *"Keep the coffee uncomplicated, don't let him think you're into all the usual machiattos and frappe business, and don't go for something with cream and a flake! Just play it very cool."*

Did it really matter what coffee she chose?

'Just a filter coffee will be fine,' Madeline said up to the woman who had made her way quickly from behind the small counter. This was not one of those where you queue up, give your order, wait for it to be dispensed into a cardboard mug with your name scribbled on it, then have to hunt down all the bits a pieces you need, including in some cases, milk from a communal pot all sorts have had their grubby mits on which then refuses to work properly; but to be fair you do get a wooden stick to stir with.

'Anything with it?' this David asked.

'No thank you. Coffee will be fine.'

Madeline had decided to try to concentrate conversation on him this time not on the advice of her tutor, and was how she started the conversation as the woman wandered off back to her station to create the coffee.

The jacket she was wearing was on the instructions of Angela, and in fact was one she had meant to take to the charity shop some time back but had never got round to it. She doubted whether he'd realize how outdated the style was.

'Family well?' David asked after he had advised how well the initial stages of the contract were going so far.

There were no instructions for this. Telling him her elder brother Richard was manager of a mobile phone shop and he and his children were all well, helped her to relax. Probably something she'd already revealed over the internet but it mattered not.

This was certainly a good looking chunky man and he spoke well, as he sat there in a very nice grey jacket and black trousers, and looked every part the businessman he was.

When the coffee arrived Madeline was not surprised by the addition of a tiny almond biscuit on the saucer. A couple of the small independent coffee houses she represented did so and had explained for just a couple of pence the biscuit hid the fact the price of the coffee was more than you'd have to pay if you visited a chain. At least it is what her clients thought, but Madeline had never been totally convinced. If it were the case the big boys would have done it in a flash.

As she looked all about Madeline wondered who handled their marketing. With just two other customers mid-morning on a Saturday sat at one table, they were either not good at their job, the location was all wrong with poor foot-fall or the owner had simply not bothered to thrust the business out into the marketplace.

'Problem?' he asked.

Madeline dropped her voice to a whisper. 'Just wondering who does their marketing.'

'Not working, obviously.'

'You can say that again.'

'Think it has to be something we get round to talking about at some point,' said David. 'Not at all sure my marketing is all it should be, but we can leave it for another time.'

"Watch out for the questions about you and money, your house, where you go on holiday. If he's a gold digger he'll want to know. Just be careful. And another thing, don't use your car. You turn up in your Lexus you'll have him slavering all over you"

The suggestion from Angela made no sense for as far as she was aware she had no intention of going for a drive with him. Just a coffee had been her decision from the outset, dipping her toe in the water so to speak and nothing had changed. In the end under pressure she had agreed to borrow Angela's little run about she used for popping to the shops and little errands.

Sometimes with Angela she felt she was so cautious she shouldn't really travel upstairs on a bus without a parachute, but it was just her way, loved her dearly and wouldn't change her for the world.

'I don't have CCTV on my client list,' she admitted.

'For another time,' he said as she bit into the tiny almond excuse for a biscuit.

'But I do have two independent coffee houses,' made him smile.

Conversation then moved away from talk about either of them onto the world in general without it becoming at all political, a sort of general synopsis about the state of the nation. It was slowly but surely turning into a very nice casual conversation, with little probing and she had to admit it, this man was most charming and laid back.

To be fair the coffee was fairly good, and yes she would have much preferred a good cappuccino and a biscuit or a piece of flapjack, but she was being a good girl and hoped Angela would be proud of her.

Towards the end of their conversation David had asked a few questions about her business, but it was nothing too probing and to her it appeared quite natural and she felt perhaps she should have been more enquiring about his world.

In the end he was a real gentleman, he paid the woman and insisted on escorting Madeline down the side street to where she had parked Angela's little Honda.

There was no silliness at the car, he just leant forward gave her a peck on her cheek and promised to keep in touch and suggested perhaps they could meet up again once he had got this new contract all bedded down and they wouldn't have to meet up somewhere unfamiliar to both of them. Suggested perhaps next time they could meet for lunch, which seemed to Madeline to be a very good idea indeed.

She agreed, got into the car and she watched as he simply turned and walked off across the car park and disappeared up a side street.

29

I must admit I do now benefit from working closely with the other volunteers at St Joseph's and I guess they have recognized a change in me, and probably for the first time in my life I can consider them as work colleagues.

My time with them has certainly broadened my perspective on life and the things we discuss nowadays would in the past have simply passed me by. Our conversations these days are less catty, less invasive of the characters who were not there at the time. That particular day had been a case in point.

One of the women had mentioned how her married daughter had applied for a job somewhere away at a big school with a new fancy name. Probably one of those academies I expect to cover up the fact they are pretty ropey.

In this case not the issue with her children now at a senior school, it was the job and her role. None of us were at all sure Helen had got her facts right when she told us they were seeking an Attendance Assistant to work as part of an attendance team at the school and the job description included implementing strategies to improve children's attendances.

I am still finding it hard to quantify the need for not just somebody to count children, but for them to have a team of them, all one assumes computer literate. The undemanding monitoring and recording of the day to day absences of children is such an utterly ludicrous concept it has left me speechless, and that's saying something! Has the world gone mad? What on earth is wrong with teachers calling a register? How long does it take? One minute?

So you can see these days in the kitchen at St Joseph's we seem to have moved on from pernicious gossip and idle chit chat to things which tend to be more often than not, ridiculous examples of the strange world we now live in.

It was still early afternoon when I returned home and by chance I spied Pru Wishaw in her garden when I looked out from my kitchen window. Saw her bending down in the distance and then pull herself up straight and hold her back. She did this a time or two.

The kettle had yet to boil and I was out of the back door and tramping across to her. It was pretty obvious Pru was suffering from a bad back but was still trying to do what she could in her vegetable patch. I could see from her face when I walked up to her she was grateful for an excuse to stop.

'I think that'll be enough don't you?' she smiled through her obvious discomfort. 'Cup of tea's in order for you, my friend.' She looked reluctant, almost ill at ease and went to move away. 'We'll get you a cuppa and have this all sorted. Your place or mine?' was a question but my neighbour was unaware there was only one answer. 'Hang on to me Pru,' I said and slipped my arm in hers.

To be honest I was probably a tad too blunt initially but it's my nature and you can see why I'd be too much for the Council. Not proud of my attitude sometimes, but you can take it or leave it, I'll not change now. Call a spade a shovel me.

Kettle of course had boiled by the time we got back to Oakdenne and I honestly believe it was the first time either Pru or her husband had been in my home. How awful an admission it is when you think about it? I actually feel utterly ashamed now every time it comes to mind.

Tea was soon made, a good mug of strong what they call builder's tea, none of this fruity or minty business. Sat there sipping, Pru admitted she'd been suffering for a week or more and before she could turn round I'd taken over.

You be the judge and say I was just making up for lost time, but within a few minutes I'd made an appointment for her with my physiotherapist.

'No arguments,' I said when Pru protested. 'It'll all go on my account. Now this garden of yours,' I went onto quickly before she could argue. 'I'll get my Derek to take it on, give him a few more bob as I'm sure he could always use a bit more beer money and he'll get it all sorted for you.'

'Please er...'

'Jacs.' You can see just how silly the situation was. They'd been in the cottage a good three years and she didn't even know what to call me.

'Sorry. Jacs. Please I'm fine.'

'You will be, but not now you're not. What about work?'

'Sitting down it's not a problem and they're very good.'

'Pleased to hear it. You still at the seed place?' She nodded.

'Please I can't let you…'

'Here's the deal,' I said and took a good drink now the tea had cooled a little. 'When you're back to full fitness you can do me a favour or two in return.'

I then went on to explain exactly my role with St Joseph's without admitting I paid the food bills, and how it was all volunteers and we can always do with an extra pair of hands.

'It's a deal,' she said and I was pleased to recognize enthusiasm. Yes I could add her to my list of volunteers. Pru's admin job with the big seed producers and distributors was only four days a week and she admitted she could do with an interest. Like me she said she wasn't interested in going to yoga or signing on for a gym, find she didn't like it but be stuck with paying out for a couple of years at least.

While she was there I received one of those nuisance phone calls. All so silly really when you consider how cautious I am normally. I never buy anything over the phone and these people usually get short shrift from me. How daft therefore when you consider I had been groomed in effect by Edward over the internet.

Do people actually respond to these calls? Why would you wait around for a phone call if you were in need of their nonsense? Wouldn't you source whatever it is for yourself?

'Between you me and the gatepost, I'm very lucky I have services available to me,' I told Pru. 'You go to my physiotherapist he'll charge you top wack. Put it on my tab it'll cost me nothing like. Way of the world I'm afraid, and Derek doing a bit of extra with your vegetables will be doing him a favour as much as you.'

We then got on to talk about her gardening successes and we'd both read somewhere about tomatoes. According to a magazine we'd both read the average tomato you can buy is now considered by some twerps to be dull and dreary. We both chuckled about people heralding black Russian or Cuban toms, all simply because they are seen by these pretentious fools as being on-trend. I was pleased to hear Pru remark about the nauseating nonsense people spout.

Pru had also read somewhere how some tedious restaurants charge a ridiculous price of these black tomatoes which she understands taste far less interesting than those who grows.

I guess this is what friends do. Am I right? Guess this is what women are up to when I see them chatting over coffee, a bit of you pat my back, I'll pat yours. I'm a bit new to this and maybe I'm sort of thrusting all this at Pru all of a sudden, but it'll settle down.

We had a nice couple of mugs of tea, had good old chin wag firstly about the business of a school employing people to count children and pay them a decent salary and she told me about her sister getting a degree with the Open University.

Pru was quite right, the school most probably was desperate for funds for worthwhile projects but chose to waste goodness knows how much on such futile nonsense.

During our chat we mentioned all the on-going tedious Brexit farrago with that Rees-Mogg gink doing his utmost along with a few chums to unseat Teresa May but failing miserably. Even Pru was of the opinion somebody with such quirky mannerism as a leader of anything, was an appalling thought.

We shared and thoroughly enjoyed a slice or two of malt loaf and I gave her a tube of Voltarol I had in my bathroom. Between me and Gavin my physio we'll have her fixed up in no time.

Just like me you've probably been thinking the police had most probably filed my case away in the cabinet marked 'Waste of Space' so it was a surprise to hear Chris Mackinder's voice on my answerphone when I got home the next afternoon.

Remember him? He's the copper friend of Brandon's. He wanted to pop round, suggested Thursday but as it happened was when ironically Brandon Wishaw and two of his friends were due round to talk technology to my bunch of lonely cronies. So far nine had said they were interested, and I had a bit of baking to do in preparation.

I phoned him back and we arranged for him to call on Friday morning first thing before I went off to the hostel.

My Silver Surfers evening was quite successful. Mary Latimer didn't make it in the end, so we finished up with eight; some very enthusiastic, others starting to build their confidence.

It was interesting to listen to the three of them talk enthusiastically about technology and how it is developing, but they also had tales of the absurd. Micky knew of someone who used Skype on a regular basis to communicate with a work colleague in the same building rather than meet face to face.

Whilst in itself they agreed it was a bizarre concept not to be encouraged, it did emphasise to those I had managed to gather together how it was not simply a form of communication they could use when dealing with those living abroad.

When I just happened to mention how they did not appear to me to fit the image of the average young person of today. Instead of coming to their defence they were quite scathing.

Brandon explained the norm is a world of self-containment and young people's issues surface the moment they leave the cloistered school or university environment to discover they are often than not by then the square pegs employers now disregard.

Micky explained to me how sadly some can never face the challenges which always lie ahead in life and therefore as a result they have to retain the self-regime through their beloved technology comfort blanket which had actually trapped them in the first place.

'You don't need a degree,' he said with a snigger. 'To kill creatures from outer space. In fact such skill is below GCSE level.'

To the lads' credit they kept everything as easy as pie and I kept them fed, which turned out to be a satisfactory arrangement pleasing both parties. By the close of play all eight wanted more and the three lads willingly agreed to retain their status as tutors for the following week. Same time, same place, more baking.

True to his word Chris Mackinder was on my doorstep well before nine on the Friday, and once I had poured us both a coffee we settled down in the Morning Room for his inquisition.

'Can we start with Edward McCafferty's car? A Skoda you say, but do we have any more information?'

'Silver grey,' I said and knew it would be of little help, how many of those were there? Hadn't I read how choosing such a colour signified dullness in the driver's character or was it the black? The ones always in need of a good clean.

'Would you recognize the model?' Chris asked.

'Might well do, it was a sixty-seven reg I know.' I then waited while Chris set-up his tablet and found Skoda websites, and we then skimmed through a number of different models. In the end I plumped for a Skoda Rapid on a pre-owned website as being as close as I could remember.

To be honest I'd never ridden in Edward's car. Simply seen him turn up in it and then when he headed off throw his overnight bag onto the back seat and drive away each time. In fact the final time when he headed off for France I had remained in the kitchen I remember, as parting was an increasingly difficult time for me.

'Talk to me about your interest in sport, and football in particular.'

'Football?' I threw back at him. 'You mean what have I been to, like the Cup Final, Champions League?'

'Any team in particular?'

'Saw Fiorentina play one time, when I was in Italy. There for an European Cup athletics as it happens. Did Rome and Pisa think it was on that trip.'

'With Edward?'

'Don't be silly, this was years ago.'

'What about Manchester City?'

'What about them?'

'Are you a supporter?'

'Sorry, don't go in for all their blinkered tribal nonsense. If it was them against Barcelona who I saw one time I'd cheer them on, but I don't have a team I follow through thick and thin like many do.'

'Pity.'

'Why?' I struggled to fathom the reasoning. 'What has any of this got to do with Edward McCafferty?'

'We think maybe he was a Man City supporter.'

'Don't be silly!' I shook my head. 'Not at all sure he was interested in football, certainly never mentioned it. Horse racing was the only thing we discussed to be honest. Came from somewhere near Worcester, not even sure what his local team would be.'

'What about Manchester United?'

'What about them?
'Were they mentioned?'
'No.'
'Tell me again why you never went out when he stayed over?'

I blew out a breath. 'He was always tired from a week working and then travelling all the way over here. Just wanted to relax if I'm honest with good food and a glass of Merlot. Sat out on the patio a time or two in the autumn sunshine, talking, drinking coffee and reading the papers. Daft really, because I'd been thinking it was about time I introduced him to some of the sights and sounds of the area.'

'Next thing,' said Chris and I assumed he had a list in his notebook the way he kept referring to it. 'I need to know everything there is to know about the lonely hearts club you joined and I need to borrow your mobile.'

For a second I almost told him there was a phone in the hall he could use, then realized it was not at all what he meant.

'Hardly ever use it,' I admitted as I got up to find it.

'Did you ever phone Edward?'

'Tried. On my proper phone.'

'But he phoned you?'

'Yes, he always phoned me, regular as clockwork, always about six wherever he was.' I went off to get my mobile phone and returned to him. 'No rush,' I said as I handed it over. 'People know my real number and there's always the answerphone.'

I saw Chris bite his bottom lip. 'Have you got any numbers on here?'

'No, sorry. Not the sort of thing I'm used to doing, ask people for their number and then fiddle about putting it on mine.' I shrugged. 'Didn't do very well did I?'

'Might be an idea in future.'

As far as I'm concerned it was purely a suggestion. Could see no advantage to doing all that business. At most there are a dozen phone numbers in my life and I have an index card system by the phone in the hall which has served me well all this time. If I receive a text from somebody as my phone is always turned off when I'm out, I obviously do not deal with it until I return home, so see little point in having people's numbers on my person.

'Anything else you need?' I asked. I top up so infrequently I often forget the process. Not something I was about to admit to.

'Really anything you can think of, and while you're having a think I have to tell you the bank account he paid the cheque into is in the name of an old Scotsman who's as blind as a bat and he's listed at a ficticious address and has just one pound in it.'

'Done up like a kipper and no mistake,' I said sadly as I allowed my head to shake slowly.

'Seems like it.'

'Where was this?' I asked casually and Chris sucked in noisily.

'Glasgow.'

'Where?'

'Athletes village for the Commonwealth Games up there, he's living in now.'

'Be serious!' I exclaimed. 'He's really taking the michael. I went to the Commonwealths up there.'

'And my boss will tell you it's another coincidence and let me tell you she doesn't believe in coincidence.'

'She?'

'Well…' he waved his hand about. 'Sort of temporary boss, kind of thing. One I'm working for on this.'

'Bet she's a tough cookie.'

He sniggered. 'She certainly is.'

30

'What would you say if I suggested our Edward McCafferty, Lucas Penney and Blinking Nobody are the same person and he is scamming people nationwide?'

'I'd ask how you come to such a conclusion, ma'am.'

'Glasgow,' was all Inga Larsson said and hesitated. 'Think about it, if he is the same person we know he's been to both Spalding and Washingborough in Lincolnshire and suggested to one woman he lives in Worcester and uses a false address in Glasgow and Amber Coetzer told me he was from Hull and worked with her husband in Grimsby but we don't know how true it is. Let's stick with the three we know for certain. He operates in two places in Lincolnshire so we have to ask ourselves why he chose an address in Glasgow.'

'Would it be where he actually comes from?' Jake Goodwin suggested sat opposite his boss in her office.

'Too risky probably. Remember the old adage, don't do it in your own back yard.'

'How about he's also scamming somebody up in Lanark say and while he's in the area hunts down the address for the bank account. While he's down this way he's searching out non-existent addresses he can use in the Glasgow scam and so on.'

'Say that again,' said Inga. 'When he's down here working a scam he's on the lookout for an address for false mail and buying a cheap phone for when he does say Bournemouth. When he's in Glasgow he's fixed up the old Scots boy for his Lincolnshire scams.'

'Kills two birds with one stone each time would certainly save on time and petrol. But we have no proof it is one and the same person, and Worcester and Hull are just places he just happened to mention, picked them out of the air most likely, we have no proof.'

'Thanks,' Inga said and as a result she had more food for thought. 'We both on the same songsheet with Penney making all the arrangements for this Amber to win a non-existent competition?'

'Very much so. He speculates to accumulate and he's certainly no fool this one.' Jake grimaced at his boss. 'This is becoming more and more complicated with these different scams, these phones and websites, the names and addresses dotted here there and everywhere.'

'According to the analysts in the eTeam they came up with the IP address for McCafferty, but it wasn't straight forward,' said her DS reading from his monitor. 'From what they can gather it would appear matey boy wants to avoid leaving a digital footprint. Went through what they called a virtual private network whatever it means, so he is hiding. He'd have paid for it I'm told but to him it must be worth it.'

'Why can't they talk sense? Virtual this, virtual that.'

'Ephemeral Messaging is my guess. Remember?' Inga's blonde head was already shaking. 'Mobile-to-mobile transmissions of multi-media messages which automatically disappear from the recipient's screen.'

She sighed noisily. 'This is under the name McCafferty?'

'Yes. Edward McCafferty.'

'Confirms he's up to no good. He's hiding his IP address which itself is linked to a false house address.'

'Belt and braces if you like.'

'What does that mean?' the Swede sighed.

'Means being careful, not taking any chances.'

Inga still considered it a strange saying. 'Somehow somewhere down the line he's made a mistake or we give him more rope and he'll make a mistake, and then we'll have him. Remember a bee has both a sting and honey,' made Jake smile.

'Could be he's already made his mistake with Graeme Coetzer.'

'Things got out of hand somehow you think?' she posed as an idea.

'Sandy was just saying earlier, if you were him and you start on this scam and discover the woman you're trying to rip off has an adult son who's Man United bonkers would you go in there shouting the odds about Man City, or anybody else? Wouldn't you keep your mouth shut, even if you supported Liverpool or Arsenal? Pretend you're not really into football, keep the lad on your side.'

'Can't help themselves some of them.'

'They do say if you walk into a room where men are watching football, you can ask the score but not who's playing. Men they say always know who the teams are.'

'All this tribalism you don't get with other sports. Could be his approach has let him down, his attitude's put Graeme's back up and he's sussed him or said something to worry him.'

'Why not just quit, he's already ripped her off for twelve grand.'

'If we've got this right, and I'm not at all sure we have. I don't like the idea we're dealing with someone who doesn't exist.' Inga sighed and looked as though the efforts of her and her team had been fore nothing. 'I'll have a word with Stevens see if I can chivvy up the e-boys with the phone.'

'This a deposition?' Inga asked as Jake and Ruth walked into her office.

'Just more bad news,' said her DS and Inga ushered them both to sit down. 'You first,' she motioned to Ruth.

'Edward McCafferty's phone. The e-boys pulled off calls to the Epton-Howe woman and traced them back. Not only is it a pay-as-you go probably bought off a market stall or in a pub but it's registered to a middle-aged woman from just outside Derby who doesn't have a mobile because she's very deaf, and as you know deaf people can't hear on mobiles.'

'Hang on a minute,' said the DI and sat back in her big chair. 'This guy goes all the way to Glasgow to find the address of an old man who should have gone to Specsavers, so he can register a bank account there. Now he finds a deaf woman who won't have a mobile. What's that all about?'

'He's chosen somebody who will never have a mobile.'

Hardly surprising, thought Inga. She knew all too well how some of these phone companies train their staff to ignore the customer's preconceived ideas about what they want. Selling whatever is the latest money maker was always a priority, not the customer and not customer service.

'Her husband has a phone,' Ruth continued. 'But his number is completely different. How many more people have phones registered in their name who are never contacted by the manufacturer or the service provider by post or email or even pigeon? Have you ever been?' Larsson just sat there shaking her head. 'All their contact is by phone.'

'To make your phone your normal mode of communication.'

'Go on,' was aimed at Jake with a long sigh.

'The website and corresponding email address Epton-Howe had used initially to make contact with this lonely hearts club was based at an address in Sheffield. Stevens sent somebody over there, reason it's taken a while. There the next door neighbour confirmed the house on the end of the road had been demolished as unsafe some two years previous after a gas explosion. The neighbour a Steven Cottam was as helpful as he could be but had no idea who Edward McCafferty was. All part of an elaborate process and no mistake, and we've finished up with blinking nobody.'

'This is certainly not one of those cases where these con merchants pretend to be some love torn soul on a dating website. Looks like this is the website, because if it was the normal con the hearts and kisses website would still be there. This guy or whoever have created their own, so god knows how many others he's conned.'

'Is this all worth it?' Ruth dared to plop in. 'We thought it was fairly straight forward, now we have Derby and Sheffield added to the mix.''

'Same sort of scam as I mentioned when we looked at Glasgow. Let's assume this is one and the same,' said Inga. 'Taken twelve grand from Amber Coetzer and how much from this Epton-Howe?'

'Forty thousand,' said Ruth and three sucked in noisily.

'But there's all this effort, all these arrangements. Sandy!' Inga shouted and they all waited for him to appear.

'How about another spanner in the works?' Ruth tossed in. 'Why Man City? How do they fit into anything? It's as if there's no pattern at all, as if it's all been deliberately muddled up.'

'Think it's just all jiggery-pokery. Bet he's not a City supporter at all, does it just to add to the confusion I bet.'

'Thought I was doing well too. Manchester is a bit like the mention of Sheffield, Derby and Hull. You may be right, odd ball places tossed in for no rhyme or reason to ensure we can't work out a pattern.'

'Take a bit of remembering by him too. Was Manchester chosen deliberately to start a row?'

'Would it?' Inga mused. 'Time for a bit of brainstorming', and she shuffled about in her seat as if getting herself comfortable. 'For this woman in Spalding we have him living in Worcester, then we have the bank, phones and websites registered in Glasgow, Derby and Sheffield. What we don't have is anything for Penney except mention of Hull and Grimsby maybe. No bank, no phone, no website for him, just a vague mention of Hull.'

'City of Culture,' Inga ignored from Jake.

'What if Penney uses the same places, same addresses?' Ruth probed.

'Like your thinking.'

'Does the Coetzer woman really not know anything more than her husband worked with him in Grimsby?' was her next question.

'You've met her. Not exactly gushing is she?' Inga reminded her. 'But its Grimsby where they worked together, north of Hull is where she said he told her he lives.'

'You're getting me at it now, see I'm confused. Like I said, could be the idea,' Ruth offered. 'Throws us off the trail.'

Inga looked at them both hoping for more, and then Chris Mackinder walked in to join them.

'How many times did this McCafferty visit your woman?'

'Got a note somewhere…' and he began to turn.

'Roughly.'

'Coffee first time,' he hesitated. 'Then a couple of day visits I think and two or three stopovers max.'

'Day visits? What days?'

'Sundays I think.'

'On Monday evening he's in Washingborough, then job done he pops down to Spalding…' Jake coughed and boss Inga looked at him.

'Problem. It was a Skoda the woman in Spalding says and Mazda we think in Washingborough.' Inga came very close to swearing. 'He switch cars?'

'You could run both these scams for just a few hundred in expenses and in the end it leaves a tidy sum he's made so far tax free for the two.'

'Is somebody this clever and organised going to commit murder for fifty odd grand?' Jake tossed in.

'People have done it for a lot less.'

'I know, but surely he's scuppered now. He knows this is not just a race horse scam a few novice DCs are poking their noses into, this is a murder enquiry.'

'What's to stop him using the Glasgow, Derby and Sheffield addresses all the time? Woman has no idea there's a phone in her name and the address in Sheffield doesn't exist. Use them all the time. Same with the old boy in Glasgow. Job done, dump the phone, go off to another market and buy another one, use the same name, same address.'

'All you need,' Chris Mackinder joined in. 'Is a bit of tape on each phone to say what the name is so you don't make a mistake. One phone has Amber on it, the other Jacs or whatever she called herself.'

'Try this one then,' said Inga after listening intently. 'Why is one in need of new glasses and one deaf? May I ask how does he know what they're like?' She closed her eyes when she saw Jake tapping his ear. 'Ask a stupid question.'

'Covers all eventualities, sees a woman with hearing aids in a corner shop somewhere and follows her home. Makes a note of the address. Could be really cheeky and ask someone what the post code is so when he registers this tu'penny ha'penny phone he's got everything.'

'And the old boy?'

'I'm working on it!'

'If we've got this right, he's certainly done his homework.' Inga motioned for someone to enter the office. 'Now then what good news do you bring?'

'Everybody by the name of Edward McCafferty who travelled on Euro Tunnel and Eurostar over the period have all been checked out, but hardly surprising when I tell you the next bit of news.'

'Go on.'

'You'll never be chuffed wi' this. We've discovered an Edward Roland McCafferty buying horses at yearling sales in Dauville, but it was years ago and when we investigated him out through the French authorities and the local cops back in the UK…' he hesitated to heighten the tension. 'We found he died in 2013. Natural causes.'

'Am I allowed to swear in mixed company?' Inga asked loudly with a chuckle.

'Of course.'

'Bother! Damn and bother!' brought chuckles from all of them. 'There has to be something, just something somewhere to somehow link us to this McCafferty and Penney or McCafferty or Penney. How often have we been desperate for a bit of DNA, a fingerprint, a bit of snot just something and this time we've got what the techies and Forensics have come up with which is more than enough. We just don't have anybody to pin it on. Back to the blank page again.'

'Is there a route we've not thought of?' Jake asked. 'Horseracing.'

'Something like, the truth was McCafferty had always wanted to be a jockey, but he just grew too tall, too big and there was nothing he could do about it. Working in a yard was no substitute because he also wanted to be top dog, the one people would be envious of. For him next best is to own his own racehorse, own a real winner, be there in the winner's enclosure and for that he needs money.'

'With us finding this other horse trader with his name we have to ask is this name assumed?'

'Quite possibly.'

'McCafferty's dead, so he's taken his name. That what we're saying now?'

'Takes people's addresses.'

'Need me anymore just now, gaffer?' Sandy asked.

'Thank you Sandy.' Before he had closed the door Inga Larson turned to look at Chris Mackinder. 'I've met Amber Coetzer, but I've never met your Epton-Howe woman, can you fix it up for me?'

'No problem ma'am.'

'If anybody can think of any questions we need to ask the good lady, throw them at me. She must know something, just one tiny little snippet to point us in the right direction. Thanks everybody, back to chasing moonbeams if you will.'

31

Rebecca Faraday was sure Keith would have opened his big new Hot Tub depot in the Lake District by now. Since their day together in the simply delightful beach hut in Southwold she'd heard nothing from him, save for a sweet 'thank you' text when she'd got home.

Not completely unexpected and he had warned her how busy he was going to be over the next few weeks what with one thing and another.

She appreciated his position and hadn't expected too much too soon what with all the stress he must be under to launch such a big operation and it being so vital to his whole concept and future. In his own words he'd be working "24/7 and more hours in the day and days in the week if need be."

Rebecca had never set up and launched a new business. Hers was there for her from day one. Flowers by Felicity had been there for more than forty years and then fortunately when Felicity Crutchelow became ill, she kindly offered Rebecca the opportunity to run it on her behalf and then when there was no chance of her taking up the reins again and returning to the helm, the old woman just sort of handed it over.

It was still a trifle worrying how after so many e-mails and texts over such a short period between her and Keith, and bearing in mind how well they had got on together, to then hear nothing at all did cause Rebecca Faraday some concern.

She'd sent him texts but there had been no reply, and the same with calling him it just rang and rang, but if he was up to neck in all the preparations it was understandable.

Not something she could take to anyone about really. Victoria and David would never understand why she needed someone in her life, and the girls who worked for her as nice and kind as they were would probably gossip a bit about a woman of her age going on a dating website.

Rebecca had never been one to just sit around moping; the days of feeling sorry for herself went with Ronnie. Time she decided for some action. Sunday was a completely free day and if she didn't get off her backside what else was there? Going through the books, going through the till print outs for the week.

Southwold as it turned out was nowhere near as warm and sunny as it had been when she was there before with Keith, but regardless it was still a delightful place. Despite the heavily overcast sky it reminded her somehow of a place time somehow had forgotten, as if the world had passed it by in a funny sort of way.

Had been a week or two but Rebecca was still slightly confused about exactly where the beach hut was. Knew it was pale blue, and then discovered of course there was more than one hue of blue amongst the multitude of colours.

She was sure she was walking the way Keith had explained were the most popular for some reason. Not much more than sheds up on the promenade in truth but their position made up for it. Looking down to the sandy beach and out to sea.

There were certainly less people about than during her previous visit save for one or two on the beach walking their dogs. No shirt sleeve order as there had been on her previous visit. Nobody in the gently lapping sea as far as she could see, but hardly surprising.

Had to be in the next batch along. There she decided looking ahead, where she spotted a man sweeping outside his hut.

Now Rebecca had a dilemma. Perhaps he was Russell the owner, could be he was just tidying up before the sale went through.

'Excuse me,' she said as she approached him. 'Apologies for asking, but are you Russell?'

'Sorry madam,' he said and immediately returned to his sweeping. Tall man with greying hair dressed in a navy sweater and jeans wearing those boat shoes or whatever it is they call them.

'Do you know Keith Bradley by any chance?'

'Sorry madam, I'm afraid I don't,' he said as he stopped sweeping and looked up.

'Do you know of any beach huts for sale, or know anybody who has just sold one?'

'Couple have I understand, but I don't know who exactly.' He rested his hands on the top of the broom handle. 'There's an association most of us belong to, you could ask them.'

'It's just, a friend of mine was buying one, and for the life of me I can't remember which one.'

'And he is who?'

'Keith Bradley.'

'Oh I see.'

'And you're sure you're not selling yours.' Rebecca was more and more convinced this was the one, as she shuffled closer. The view was just the very one she remembered.

'No,' he chuckled.

'You didn't have a sale not go through recently by any chance?'

'No,' and he shook his head with a wide grin.

'D'you loan it out to friends at all?' was her next tack.

'As it happens, yes I do.'

'Few weeks ago?'

'Probably.'

'Who to?' she threw at him.

'I'm sorry madam, and I don't wish to be rude, but who I hire my beach hut to or lend it to quite frankly really is none of your business. I don't know this Keith Bradley, I've never heard of a Keith Bradley, so if you wouldn't mind,' and his immediate motion with his broom was as if he was about to sweep her away.

Rebecca had no alternative than to turn and trudge away, walk slowly away completely dispirited. She was sure she was right. It had to be. She stopped to just glance back convinced more than ever as confusion reigned.

Sunshine, happy people, the sound of seagulls cawing in the distance, sights and sounds she had so enjoyed with delightful Keith were not there on such a dull day.

As she walked back Rebecca considered stopping at another beach hut where she could see people and asking them. She didn't, the whole experience had been enough for one day. Not at all how she'd hoped the journey would turn out on her one day off.

Rebecca increased her stride and headed back to the car, away from the beach, away from the damn beach huts and the obnoxious man.

Shouldn't have come, should have stayed at home. What a waste of time and what a nasty man he was. She'd just have to drive all the way back home and wait for dear Keith to contact her. Then when it was all sorted out she'd return and then could stick two fingers up to whoever he was. Sort of self-righteous nobody she had in the shop from time to time.

She was sure Keith would have something to say about him.

32

Since the peculiar incident with Josef Dudek things with Inga Larsson appeared to have settled down as far as Jake Goodwin was concerned and pretty much returned to normal except she just didn't seem to be as hands-on as normal. Almost as if she was taking a back seat. Were there problems at home, was her relationship with Adam in trouble? Jake is not one for poking his nose into people's private affairs and was never going to ask about for inaccurate scurrilous whispers of what might be the problem. Then right out of the blue she threw a question at time.

'Any chance you can spare a couple of hours tonight?'

'Tonight?' He knew of nothing going on to require his services, save for a spot of interesting tele. If he missed *Inside The Foreign Office* he'd watch it on Catch Up.

'Just a couple of hours, tell Sally it's my fault. I'll pick you up say about six thirty from your place.'

'Don't see why not, I'll just check with Sally.'

'We're going for a walk so you'll need a jacket, if you can't make it, give me a bell, ' there was no opportunity to ask what it was all about as she just wandered off and out of the office and he didn't see her for the rest of the afternoon. Right out of the blue they had returned to odd-ball situations and he was concerned.

Jake was stood outside his house wearing a leather jacket and an old cap he sometimes used, having explained to his nurse wife he had no idea where he was going or why. Inga pulled her new blue MG3 up dead on half past and Jake got in, and it then was a journey in which she chatted on endlessly about anything and everything except their reason for the journey. By the time they drove into Washingborough he was very concerned. This must be a Neighbourhood Watch area he surmised; they always have a certain look about them, but he still had no idea why he was there.

Inga weaved her way around the roads of the village and eventually slipped into a parking space just below a few shops huddled together.

'Let's go,' she said, and when before he had moved a muscle Jake went to open his door she put her gloved finger to her mouth. They got out and she led the way as they walked side-by-side up a slope to the shops. A Co-op and Pharmacy, Fish Bar, Chinese Takeaway and a couple more. They walked then up to Oundle Close at the back, turned right and headed up to a junction, took a left turn into Marlborough Avenue and walked on. Jake mentally noted Cambridge Drive as they trudged along in case he was asked questions later and eventually they turned into a cul-de-sac.

'See the house over there,' Inga virtually whispered, 'with the flowers and all that caper. Go and knock on the door, see if anyone's in.'

'Hang on, hang on,' said Jake as he turned and stood in front of her.

'Amuse me, please,' was only just audible.

Jake reluctantly did as he was told, crossed the road, walked thirty yards turned right down the path and up to the door of the bungalow stepping over dead and dying flowers and a huge pile of football scarves, cuddly red devils, bobble hats and memorabilia. He knocked at the door, just as Inga had instructed and looked all around. He felt self-conscious just stood there and the cap didn't help and knew he must look very suspicious. He knocked again and when he looked back down the road to Inga stood across the other side she beckoned him back over to her.

When Jake reached her, she slipped her arm in his and walked them back along the close round the corner and stopped. He was pleased she'd told him to wear a warm jacket.

'Amber Coetzer's house.'

'So I gathered.'

'That was you being Lucas Penney, turning up mid-week like he used to. You knocked on her door and if she was expecting you she'd have opened it and invited you in, or even put the door on the latch. Did you see anybody?'

'No.'

'And from what I could see no curtains twitched, no lights came on.' She looked at him with a self-satisfied grin. 'Nobody knows Lucas Penney has just visited Amber Coetzer.' Jake went to speak, but she beat him to it. 'It's an old Craig Darke trick he told me about I remembered today. He once couldn't understand how somebody had just walked up to a house knocked on the back door and when the woman answered, the bastard stabbed her to death, and nobody heard a thing.'

'Because...'

'It's evening, it's in the dark and everybody's curled up on the sofa indoors with the tele on, playing music with headphones on, using their tablets and all the rest of their gizmos.' She motioned across the road. 'Just look at these properties. They're all detached. Her front door is just down the left hand side of the bungalow, the one next door has theirs on the right, means they're a good distance apart and is where the neighbour lives who reckons she saw somebody visiting.'

'No chance,' said Jake.

'Just look all about. Quiet as a grave.'

Jake was nodding. 'Reason why nobody has ever seen him. And this is why people want to live in a good neighbourhood like this.'

'Exactly,' she said. 'Now back we go,' and she was off again. Back eventually to Marlborough Avenue and they crossed the road together having waited for a car, and Inga slowed. 'The bungalow on the left,' she pointed. 'Is where Coetzer is staying with the nosey friend Myra Gaunt.' They strolled casually back across the road and headed in the direction of the shops. 'See the house there,' she gestured towards the back of a property. 'Where Josef Dudek lives. To see what's going on at Amber's house he'd have to deliberately go that way. Truth is people who live in this road turn right at the end, then right again to come round to the shops or left to eventually reach Main Road and head off out of the village. They don't go left, then left again and then right into a cul-de-sac.'

'How do you know all this?' he wanted to know.

'Spent the afternoon out here. Getting the lie of the land, watched people come and go.' She looked at her watch. 'How long we been here? Twenty minutes max. We've just seen one car, but no people; haven't seen a soul have we?'

'Middle of the week Tuesday Wednesday evening when football's on and Graeme's off to a match, most folk don't move an inch. Not because they're interested in footie if it's on but because they're nothing days.'

'Settle down with some nonsense on Sky or Netflix.'

'Except it was Bonfire Night.'

'When people said they thought Penney was visiting, they had no real sightings. Might be interesting to ask Coetzer's neighbour in the morning if she heard anyone call this evening.'

'Bet she didn't,' said Jake. 'Certainly not on Monday with the noise of fireworks, indoors with the tele turned up to stop the dog being frightened.'

'Usually we've got witness statements we can go through at a time like this.'

'What witnesses?' Jake shot back. 'I don't think anybody actually hand on heart witnessed anything, like I bet nobody has seen us. If anything they'd be in the back garden looking up at the sky.'

'Josef Dudek is never likely to spot Penney in middle of the week once a fortnight or so is he? Worst case scenario for our Penney is if he's parking his car by the shops and Dudek happens to call in for a bread loaf. Bearing in mind he doesn't have a clue who he is anyway.'

'Could be Father Christmas and he wouldn't have a clue.'

'So he could be real. He probably is a real person.'

'Every two or three weeks this time of night he might as well be the invisible man.'

'But, and this is a big but,' said Inga seriously. 'Chances are he'll not appear again so how do we trace him, and the woman in Spalding who bought a non-existent horse will more than likely never see her bloke again either, and the odds are, nor will we.'

'And it could very well be the same person.'

'Something niggling inside says it's still a bit of a long shot, but why not?' and Inga took him by the arm again and together weaved their way back to her car. 'This spot is handy,' she said stood by the car. 'Could easy be where Penney left his car. Makes sense, better than leaving it outside Amber's place.'

'But didn't some kid say what the car was.'

'Bet it wasn't his car at all, could be someone visiting over the road or next door,' as her transponder key activated the car and they both got in. 'Could be this is where he parked his Mazda or whatever, or somewhere similar,' she said as she slipped on her seat belt and Jake pulled off his cap.

'Or Skoda.'

'When I was surveying the place this afternoon you quickly realize it's just a nice village, it's not heaving like Oxford Street.' Inga looked at her sergeant. 'What's your thoughts?'

'You could very well be right.' He wasn't going to ask why they'd had to go through this whole charade. 'What was it you said, bet Craig Darke would have it sorted by now? To a certain extent you can see why, this is a different way to look at things, and it almost puts us at the scene.'

'And Chris is fixing up a meet for me with his woman with the horse.'

'Without her horse.'

'You're right.'

'How long would it take from here to Spalding do you think?'

'Not put it to the test but I reckon an hour or more at the outside, this time of night, this time of year with no holiday traffic clogging up the A17.'

'No tractors and no shed pullers.'

'Give him enough time to stop somewhere to get changed.' Inga smiled at him. 'Home James, it's been a really good night's work.'

'Am I seeing a new you?' Jake dared as Inga started the car. 'The business with Josef Dudek and now all this.' He held his breath.

'I'll be honest now,' she said as she sped off right and drove away. 'Been told to delegate more, be a bit more strategic. Not me, but there you go. I didn't think it was fair just to lumber you with all this and put you under pressure.'

'I thought at times you were skiving,' made them both laugh. 'Or were heading out for pastures new.'

'If I don't find whoever killed Graeme Coetzer I may have to, but it'll be none of my choosing.'

'I think you may well be right, I think maybe it was Lucas Penney alias Edward whatever.'

'McCafferty.'

'He's the one.'

33

Hello people. Jacqueline here again. Right. Where were we?

It was near close of play one day at St Joseph's when I next came across Martin Pearson. Remember him? We were all just having a cup of tea and an apple once all the work was done and I had prepared menus for next day, when he joined us.

To be honest by this time I had become used to not hurrying off home to an empty big house, Radio 2 and nothing very much. I was better off amongst friends, even if I hadn't got round to giving everybody a hug and kissing the air passing their cheeks.

Feeding people who literally have no idea where their next meal is coming from is not something I treat lightly. This is not just a case of sticking my hand in my pocket and coming up with the readies like some would do.

When I'm in a kitchen you'll get none of the pretentious offerings you read about in the media. None of your daikon radish or taster tots. When I first heard that I looked it up as Cordon Bleu never covered such twaddle.

It turned out to be deep fried grated potato. What they mean of course is fry bits which some folk confuse with scrumps or scraps.

Conversation that day whilst we were all working away had gone through the never-ending Brexit nonsense of course, the lack of police resources and then we'd discussed some of the political correctness stupidity.

We all wondered who it is who comes out with all the gumph. Are people actually paid to waste our money on little more than utter claptrap? The sheer madness with things such as not calling women expectant mothers.

At one point we were discussing children being controlled by their peers. Were they called peers when you were at school? Me neither.

These chats we have were often very informative and it soon became obvious from his opinions how Martin had obviously suffered badly in the hands of some bitch as a result of a relationship going wrong.

He was adamant that people should get married. He had obviously not been and had suffered untold life changing horrors, and I assume is how he found himself living the life he did now. He was adamant about living with someone means you have no rights and any who believe they do are just listening to urban myths.

'What about common law wife?' one of the women asked.

'There is no such thing as common law, and being in such a silly arrangement has no status in law. In fact in Quebec for instance living together gives you absolutely no rights whatsoever.'

Then another day he was very vocal about having joint bank accounts in any relationship.

'Why?' I'd wanted to know.

'If he falls under a lorry you have no right to access to his bank account. Have you got enough money in your own account to pay the bills?' he asked Olive and she looked sheepish. Chances are she only had her housekeeping money or is that some outmoded system from years gone by?

In reality it was not relevant to me. I had no husband or partner or even boyfriend or girlfriend and had no need of joint accounts, but it was an interesting thought.

One afternoon I tossed in a question. 'I've got one for you. What is hug therapy all about?' got a few grimaces. 'They tell me people are making money out of it.' I pressed on to complete silence. 'Read a couple of days ago how some describe a cuddle as being more about the actual experience of being able to develop a relationship of trust. I'm just gobsmacked me.'

'You're not the only one.'

'You read some rum magazines!' said Martin. The looks of disinterest amongst the silent others was such it was as if I'd asked a question in Serbo-Croat. 'But then why are vests now called base layers, and why don't youngsters have handkerchiefs?' Martin asked. I didn't know they don't but was not about to show my ignorance again. Mummy always made sure I'd got a hankie.

Time I decided to bring our chat about something and nothing to a halt. 'Right, let's get these cups washed up and we can all get off home.'

34

Detective Inspector Larsson discovered she was fairly early for her appointment down near Spalding with this Jacqueline Epton-Howe woman when she got within spitting distance of Oakdenne House near Spalding, courtesy of her sat nav.

In order to understand the scenario she drove away and tried to view the property from a distance. Single woman in her forties living in such a place, Inga wondered what it was all about. From where she had parked up she spotted this old fella riding around cutting the vast lawns on one of those big mowers she'd always wanted a ride on. The house appeared to be from the Victorian era with two impressive chimney stacks and big windows. She guessed the very pleasant whitewashed cottage was more than likely where DC Mackinder's pal lived.

Spalding and the surrounding area was not somewhere she knew well. Had heard of the Flower Festival and seen it on the local news in the past but had never attended, and living in an apartment as she had at one time had little need for the garden centres and nurseries proliferating everywhere.

The Swede had no plans to take Jake Goodwin with her on this occasion, and as it turned out it was good she was not relying on him. Jake's wife Sally the nurse had gone into labour with their first child. She was in the maternity ward at Lincoln County, the very hospital where she worked as a Senior Sister.

When young Chris had phoned to say his boss wanted to meet me, I had no idea why. When this 'boss' of his arrived at my front door I have to say it was a most pleasant surprise. I don't know why, but it's not the sort of job I normally associate with a very attractive astute woman. There's no reason why not of course, just how in this day and age. Her sort seem to be skipping off to catch the train to

London heading for a role in PR or marketing, technology in one big laptop bag and the mandatory to-go coffee in the other hand. Like a badge of honour these days it seems to me.

One of the criteria by which I always judge people is their timekeeping. Throwback to daddy I'm afraid; all his fault. I lost count of the number of meals spoilt over the years by his attitude. Think in the end he learnt his lesson with me as others have. I will not stand for it. I will not stand around waiting for anybody who does not have the decency to be on time.

Waiting for people more senior than them is a bane of many people's lives, top dogs absurdly exercising their power by keeping people waiting is not clever. It is downright rude and doltish. My dear old dad got both barrels more than once.

This Inga Larsson, this Detective Inspector copper was a couple of minutes early. Good on her.

Did my heart good to see a young woman in authority. I know there are not nearly enough woman MPs, surgeons, heads of major companies and top chefs, but I am concerned how before this can happen, those already in any position of authority need to get the feminist house in order first.

I am aware alcohol dependence thankfully amongst young men is in serious decline, but to our discredit women have taken over the mantle.

I consider we seriously have to put our own house in order before we can push onto equality in its purest form. Bitches, trollops, hags and all the others who live for the next bottle to neck. The Friday night glass or four need seriously sorting.

When I saw this big blonde Detective Inspector stood there on my doorstep I immediately thought perhaps somebody like this copper might be just the person to crack down on the world of cocaine, chilli and cocktails intent on

dragging us women down.

This Inga Larsson was a very pleasant young woman and I liked the cut of her jib. There were no airs and graces or the feeling I was under the microscope. I'd got things organised before she arrived of course and we sat at the table in my kitchen, a mug of good Latte Macchiato each and Lemon Drizzle biscuits she certainly seemed to enjoy. I like a woman who enjoys a good nibble with her coffee.

All the usual introductions over, a quick resume from her, mention of the work Chris had done and we were soon down to business. This Larsson quickly had her tablet in front of her on the table ready to go.

'How about if you just talk about Edward McCafferty. Treat me as an old friend and you're giving me an update on what's been happening in your life, but remember I've never met him.'

'What can I say?' I said before I hesitated for a moment. 'He's about my age, maybe a bit older,' and noticed the policewoman smile. 'I'm loath to repeat what I was told because as far as I can see it's a whole shebang of lies, but he did say in the early days on the lonely hearts thing how he was forty five.' DI Larsson didn't have to ask the next question. 'I'm forty two.'

I then plucked up the courage, hands around my mug of coffee and began talking about making contact with this lonely hearts club, how this Edward McCafferty popped up, how we got chatting on line, met for coffee down in Newmarket, he called over one Saturday afternoon and then we just took it from there.

'How would you describe him?' I was asked. 'No, let me describe him for you,' was puzzling as this Inga Larsson slid pages up on her tablet. 'He's close to six feet tall, well built, has a full head of well-groomed close cropped dark brown hair but if he was bald might look like the actor Ross Kemp who played Grant Mitchell in EastEnders many moons ago.'

'How do you know?' I shot at her with a chuckle. 'That's him. Now I come to think of it, it is who he looks like. Not that I watch the programme these days, but he was a well-known face once upon a time. Married to the former News of the World woman if I'm not mistaken. Am I right?' Larsson nodded.

'At one time I think you'll find.'

'Thing I've thought about since with everything going through my mind, pretty much everything was grey. Suit when he got here and when he set off again was grey. Wore grey trousers, even a light grey shirt and sweat shirt.'

'Non-descript. In cognito.'

'What you're saying is, I gave my money to nobody.'

'Mr Nobody.'

'How do you know all this?' I just had to ask slowly and deliberately. This Larsson woman was wearing a lovely business suit, but it was a brighter royal blue than I imagine I could get away with. Not the sort of elaborate power outfit some would wear to impress. Still very nice all the same.

'How do we know?' the copper repeated with a smile and then answered immediately. 'Don't think you're the first. Same description another victim has given us.' This Larsson lifted her cup. 'This is nice coffee by the way.'

'Another victim?' I repeated. 'Did she buy a racehorse too?'

'No,' was Inga's turn for a chuckle. 'May of course be others we don't know about, who as yet haven't come forward.'

'If it wasn't for young Brandon next door, I doubt whether I would have,' I admitted.

'Any reason?'

'Ashamed. Angry in the way I've let something of this order happen to me. I feel such a damn fool to be honest.'

'It's a bit ago now but I don't suppose by any chance there is anything he left behind or anything he just might have touched,' Inga queried.

'Such as?' This was getting serious.

'Bedding?'

I threw my head back as a reaction, closed my eyes and made a weak moaning sound. 'Moment I realized I'd been taken for a ride I...' I sat back up straight. 'Stripped the bed, threw it all in the washing machine. Came very close to dumping it, I can tell you. How is it the song goes, *gotta wash that man right outta my hair*?' and this Larsson woman was back to smiling.

'Understandable. Nothing he touched maybe you've not used since do you think?'

'Hold on there a minute,' I chided. I could see just where this was heading. 'Can I just clarify one thing? We didn't, how shall I put this?' I had to take a breath. 'Share a bed.'

She shook her head slightly. 'Fine. Not an issue at all but he did stay, so can we think about it?'

'I'll have to give it some thought.'

Inga knew we all have back stories and wondered what this woman's was? Why not a man in her life? Had there been and if not now, why? 'What would you say if I asked if my forensics people could run a rule over the house?'

'Is it really necessary? I asked.

'Looks as though we have a match with your man and this other person of interest, but we still don't know who he is. The bank account he used was there one day and down to one lousy pound the next at a false address, same with his phone and with the other woman there were different issues but they've all gone to nothing. With a bit of luck they'll come up with something to link his presence here to our evidence chain.'

'Why not? Can't do any harm.' I sipped my coffee. 'Can I ask? This other woman, how much did she lose?'

I noticed how my question brought the policewoman up short and I watched as she pretended for a moment to search for something on her tablet. 'Twelve thousand.'

'Not a bad living is it? Going around filching money off people.' I said. 'Got to have a lot of nerve though, is what I keep thinking. He was sat right here at this table many times, actually sat in that chair,' I pointed to the one next to the detective. 'Having a meal and all the time he was living a lie. You've got to be some cool customer to be able to handle such a situation.'

'Don't touch the chair,' said Inga. 'If it's all right with you I'll call up a team get them in here pronto see what we can find. Might be a bit too long, but we'll see. You sure you're fine?' I nodded and sipped more of my coffee. What was the point in protesting as the chances were they'd do it anyway? 'And while you think about him sitting here being cool, have a think about what else there is about him we'd find useful?' Inga Larsson got to her feet. 'Excuse me,' she said as she pulled out her phone and walked off into the hall.

I found it all quite exciting, I had this delightful policewoman who I had quickly guessed was as sharp as they come, noting down everything I said on her tablet and now she was calling in people from goodness knows where.

Appeared from my perspective to be a great role in life, but I guessed she'd be under constant pressure to produce results.

Bit like those CSI people I've watched on television a few times, sort of thing they'll love at the St Joseph's Sanctuary, when I tell all the old lads about what's going on.

Despite all this my mind was still able to produce silliness from somewhere. Sat there listening to this Larsson woman it just occurred to me out of the blue how this Edward was nothing more than a thoroughbred bounder.

Every now and again in life I become envious, and this was one of those rare occasions. Seeing women out with their children sometimes just gets to me and now my emotions were there with this Detective Inspector. I could have been her, I could have joined the police force become a detective, what a great job she must have.

Oh daddy why oh why?

Inga Larsson recognised the old-school respect this educated woman had for the police. Good upbringing would be behind her attitude she guessed. If only the world could take the time to turn back the clock with regard to attitude was something she constantly wished for.

'Be with us in a couple of hours,' said Inga when she reappeared and returned to her seat and I naughtily pushed the plate of Drizzle biscuits in her direction she could not resist. 'The last time this Edward McCafferty came to see you, when did he turn up?' Inga posed, biscuit between her fingers.

'Be Monday, Bonfire night actually…'

'Time?'

'Time,' I sucked in a breath. 'Think he was a bit late if I recall, I say a bit late but later than he had been before, seemed a bit hassled when he got here, guessed he'd had a bad day. Knew from life with my dear old dad, not to ask, just offer a glass of something and let it rest. Probably nine-thirty, ten o'clock I think.' Inga tapped the info into her tablet.

'What did you two talk about?' this Inga posed next.

'World in general, things in the news but steering clear of the Brexit hotchpotch. He always wanted to know about my background, how come I live in a place like this,' I said and raised my hands. 'About daddy, what he was involved in. Probably up to no good if the truth be told,' I said and sniggered, then realized who I was talking to. 'Daddy always had his fingers in many pies, wheeling and dealing, stocks and shares and a lot of property,' I just hoped would suffice.

'Was there anything specific you can think of might give us just a tiny clue to him?'

'I talked about the Commonwealth Games I'd been to earlier in the year.' I just sighed out a big breath, 'When I was talking to your Chris he thought he'd latched onto me because I'd got a new car. Since then I've realized I'd talked about going to the Gold Coast for the Commonwealth.' This Inga Larsson sucked in a breath of caution. 'Probably a bit too much if the truth be known. There was then a discussion about the demise of the Flower Festival I think. To be honest I've been running all these through in my head, wondering what I might have said to upset him.'

'Think the car and Commonwealth Games'd be enough,' she told me. 'Anything controversial?' Inga asked.

'We did discuss equality, I remember.'

'Equality?' was not quite what Inga was looking for. 'How do you mean?'

'Lot of places you go to, 'specially linked to local government they always hand you a comment form to fill in and question number one is your ethnic background. What for?'

'I think the political correct line is to check their marketing is getting to everybody.'

'But I thought in this day and age it is all about equality. Surely if we are all equal what does it matter if you're white, black Caribbean, Chinese or green?'

'Or other white.' I didn't follow what she meant and it must have showed. 'I'm Swedish, and I was once told I need to tick the Other White box,' this Inga chuckled. 'Agree with you to be honest, it's against everything other people are working towards.' She looked down at her tablet.

'I think all this politically correct nonsense has got completely out of hand. Nosey parkers aligned to the do-gooder brigade demanding they can stipulate how I should talk about the obese, people of a different hue, those with a sexual orientation poles apart from mine, given half a chance. They probably even have a special word to describe dopey men with pony tails. Don't get me started on the sisterhood and their rants about sexism, please. I'm quite sure next time I happen to hit my funny bone there'll be one of these batty and obnoxious people telling me how loud I'm allowed to curse.'

'Back to it,' said this policewoman, and I guessed she wasn't allowed to voice an opinion on such matters and any she did have she was forced by such people to keep very much to herself which is another nonsense. 'If you don't mind I'll stay until my team arrive.'

'Fine by me.' How exciting eh?

'When they get here we'll need you to point out things like which room he stayed in. Any problems?'

'Certainly not.'

'Good. When was the last time you spoke to this Edward character?'

'His call from France.'

'Which probably wasn't,' was difficult for me to accept. 'Quite possibly from a phone reserved just for you, one bought for the purpose off a market stall or from some guy in the pub, could well be stolen the day before off some poor soul. Could even have a label on it saying 'Jacqueline' so he never got people muddled up. Sorry to say this, but he could be running more than one person at a time. As it looks as though he's done with you, he's now probably off to pastures new and somebody else I'm sorry to say is going through the process right now.'

'You talking about him in such a manner suddenly makes me feel dirty. I gave myself to a lie, and I've got to tell you it hurts.' Why do things just pop into your brain out of nowhere? A line from a book or film probably, was there in an instant. 'He doesn't do meth for breakfast, so he's not all bad.' This Inga woman looked at me. 'Sorry, just a line from somewhere.'

Have to admit there have been times of late when I've become very emotional but I've done my best not to let it show in public and it was one of them right there and then sat there in front of a smart as heck blonde policewoman.

'All for a horse you'll never see.'

'It's ridiculous really, I've never been very interested in horse racing. Take notice when it's the Derby or Grand National and have never bet on a horse in my life. Had a flutter on the Tote when I've been a couple of times, be about all. Now if I'm perfectly honest I probably bought a horse to please him, to keep on side with him. Almost as if I was buying a horse to stop him dumping me like the others in my life.'

'It's where your case is different. This sort of case normally follows a certain pattern. Once contact has been established and he's pretty sure you're hooked we would normally expect you to have got the sob story. About a sick child, elderly relative or an accident and a request for money. Just to tide him over is the usual twaddle. Certainly something to tear at your heart strings.' Larsson looked at me and smiled slightly. 'A horse. Certainly different.'

'Sat here on my own of an evening I realize how little I knew about the man. Stupid things like he never uses salt and pepper on his food.'

'Nor do I,' she responded. 'Never add salt,' was no real surprise with her being young.

'Even made a gravy with the roast beef juices, but he didn't touch it when a few people still just lather it on and ruin the meal.'

'Back home my mother makes the most delightful vaniljsås - vanilla sauce and another you'll not find around here is liquorice. Absolute delight with venison.' Inga grimaced. 'Must say I'm not a jug of gravy person either.'

Even I had to chuckle. They call this helping the Police with their enquiries!

35

They had no arrival time for Lucas Penney in Washingborough, but the Home Office Pathologist bless her cotton socks had said she estimated time of death at around eight or nine. Sort the house out, clear up and get on the road down to Spalding could all be done quicker than two hours. Would give him time to take a break somewhere, calm his nerves, clean himself up if need be, even change his clothes.

Was it worth tracking his likely route and checking CCTV at anywhere like a Little Chef where he might have stopped even only for a wash and brush up and a cuppa? If only they had his registration number they could have an ANPR search done for the day in question.

'When this McCafferty turned up the last time on the Monday was he wearing the grey suit?' this detective asked me.

'I think so,' I responded with a lack of enthusiasm. 'Yes I'm pretty sure he was.'

'And what did you learn about McCafferty and his background?'

Inga knew he had never murdered Graeme Coetzer in his suit with all the vomit and god knows what. McCafferty or Penney or whoever he was had most probably had need to stop off somewhere to change. Inga was aware how if it was all she gained from this trip it might just all have been really worthwhile.

'Very little,' I had to admit. 'Thinking about it now, he generally brushed over it, wanted to be a jockey, went to work in a stable as next best thing.'

'Family? Background?' Inga asked.

'Sorry.'

'And he came from Worcester you say.'

I raised and lowered my shoulders in a shrug. 'As close as I got I'm afraid.'

'You say you talked about the world in general. Anything in particular?'

'Just what was in the news to be honest,' was my response but I feared she was not being very helpful. 'Wish I could be more use I really do.'

'When he...'

'Football lads murder,' suddenly came to mind. 'Remember now. He was sat here having his breakfast on the Thursday morning before he went off to France, and it was on the radio about that murder.'

'What murder?' Inga Larsson asked.

'The man in Washingborough.' I threw back quickly and watched the copper hastily tap her tablet.

'When he stayed over, what time did he leave?' she asked as she tapped.

'Usually about nine I would say, but last time it was a bit earlier. Remember saying to him about the murder of the Man United lad up in Washingborough being on the radio. Would have been eight o'clock news and he left soon after. Twenty past I should think, half past at the very most, but then he had a boat to catch.'

'Except he didn't'

Utter disappointed shrouded me. 'You sure?'

'We're sure nobody called Edward McCafferty caught a boat or a train to France.'

'So when he phoned me from Dauville...'

'It was probably Worcester or wherever he was heading off to con someone else.'

I just planted three fingers onto my forehead and was looking down at the table, as I realized the full truth had finally dawned. I now had the truth, the whole truth and nothing but. 'And large as life he'd start on someone else, different place, different people, and a different con you say?' I muttered and then looked up.

'More than likely. I think we're talking about a convincing and effective confidence trickster. While we're on the subject of his last visit. Did he always visit mid-week?'

'No certainly not. In fact,' I was trying to recollect as she sipped her coffee. 'It had been Sundays initially, then three weekends and it was the only mid-week visit. Monday night to... Thursday morning.'

'Did he say why?'

'Just he was on his way to...' I just had to sigh.

'France.'

I chuckled. 'Yes France to buy me a horse, because it was when the sales were.' I looked at this Larsson focused on her screen. 'Except they weren't I guess.'

'Oh yes they were, but nobody of his name or description made a purchase or was even registered.'

Every time conversations went like that with Chris, with Brandon and now this Inga Larsson I really felt so embarrassed as if I was repeatedly emphasising my dopiness. Daft is probably a better term, for being so utterly vacuous.

'This what you deal with all the time?' I asked this Inga Larsson.

'Major investigations, often high profile crimes.'

'And you're one of a team are you?'

'I head up a team called MIT....Major Incident Team, we deal with anything including murder. It's the Humpty Dumpty scenario. We pick up the pieces and try to put them back together again.'

'Goodness me. Must be really interesting.'

'Often not at all nice, frequently very sad and I keep asking myself why one human being does such things to another. Knocking on a door and explaining to a wife is not a nice job at all.'

'Guess not.' How I wished I'd been given the opportunity to fulfill my life, reach my potential, make a real difference somehow, somewhere rather than becoming a carer for a very able mother as she was at the time. Guardian angel more like. Not protecting as such, but I guess my role had been to keep an eye on mummy to keep her busy and active and out of the way to ensure she didn't start poking her nose into what daddy was really up to and with whom.

'Are you anything to do with the murder up in Washingborough then?' was something I just had to ask.

'You could say that.'

'Gone a bit quiet,' I cheekily suggested.

'Sometimes they do I'm afraid.'

'Did I hear the mother was involved at one point?' You can't blame me for trying.

'Think she was what the media were pinning their hopes on.'

'Still not got anybody then?' I probed.

'Not so far.'

It was ridiculous really, this Inspector was never going to give me all the gory details was she?

'Can't be easy to take these sort of experiences home,' I suggested.

'Especially not to a man who spends his life playing with women's buttocks,' Larsson chuckled. 'He's a physiotherapist,' she explained instantly to ease my confusion and sighed inwardly at the change of subject.

'I was going to say! He Swedish too?' Being a nosey I wanted to know.

'No,' this Larsson smirked. 'British.'

'Physiotherapist you say? Useful.'

It is out of the blue moments like these which really get to me. Aware I am no longer in the spring of life, have never ever been a great beauty or a willowy gorgeous young thing, but I still think I have so much to offer. If only.

In truth I'd prefer a husband, but to be perfectly honest just a casual sodding date with someone honest and respectable would be a bloody thrill just once in a while.

'What about your friends. Did any of them ever meet him, who just might have noticed…?' Me shaking my head brought that train of thought to an end. 'Is there a problem?' Larsson must have perceived a look about me.

'My life's not… how shall I put this?' I pondered. 'Like the norm. The social system which provides people with the opportunities to make friends has to a certain extent be denied me.'

'In what way?' meant I just had to go on regardless.

'None of my school chums,' and I used the word with an element of emphasis, 'live within a hundred miles of here. They were all from the home counties, places like the Cotswolds or from abroad.'

'After then?'

'Next up is university I suppose, a location for friendship and relationship development has been denied to me.'

'Can I ask why?' she persisted.

'My father wanted me at home to act as a companion to my mother. Fully fit woman at the time, but nevertheless was exactly what he had planned out for me. True mummy had me late in life, but even so when I was twenty she was only just in her late fifties.

As a result not only did I not go to university but I have also never had a work colleague or been part of a group working and thereby socializing together, because I've never worked.'

'Lucky you.'

'No,' I told this Larsson firmly who I noticed was on her third biscuit. 'You have no idea how isolating it can be.'

'And now?'

'The only contact I have nowadays with people are mostly women at St Joseph's Sanctuary where I help out a few times a week and at a drop-in centre for the lonely.' Inga Larsson never said a word but her expression asked the questions. 'They all have established families with their own lives and interests, none of them are still making their way in life, trying to build new relationships and I'm sorry but they don't want some old curmudgeon pushing her nose in to their private affairs. At the end of the day these people all head off to another world I'm not part of, living amongst people I've never met and are never likely to. A world of giant televisions, gaming and those X-box things. Social media, bags of alcohol and take-away food seems to me.'

In my very dark moments my lack of real friendship is something I ponder and worry about a great deal. In amongst those thoughts is of course the realisation of mummy also having no friends. There were people from the church she would talk about if she was in the mood, but looking back now it was obvious how daddy had manoeuvred her away from those she once knew.

They never socialised with anyone from the church, nobody ever called round, popped in for a natter and they certainly never met up with any of them for a meal out somewhere.

Probably the most exciting thing I had ever done with mummy was visiting National Trust houses and old churches. Mummy's idea of an exciting day out, the sort of thing she'd actually look forward to.

'And you and this Edward McCafferty never went out at all?' I just shook my head in response. 'Could have been useful,' said Inga. 'Get somebody else's opinion on him, see him from a different standpoint.'

'Sorry,' I offered sadly, and the policewoman in her must have seen the look on my face.

'You all right?'

'My problem now is who can I trust?' There was no need to tell her about what had happened with Roger.

'Not easy is it?'

'You can say that again.' I slapped my hands down on my thighs, aware depression was creeping up on me. 'More coffee?'

Not something I've ever suffered from, envy. But to be perfectly honest sat there I had become seriously envious of Inga Larsson the copper. What a clever, sharp, decisive and attractive individual she is. Carrying enormous responsibility in such an exciting world and the job fulfilment must be so satisfying.

Me on the other hand I don't think I'm any use to man or beast.

After the police Inspector had gone and I had this team of investigators all over the house, I just sat there in my kitchen thinking how she would do very nicely as a girl-friend for me. One to meet up for a coffee. Might be an opportunity improve my social education by trying a Flat White or a Café Bombón without being ridiculed because of my ignorance. We could lunch together, even go shopping once in a while and really strike up a good relationship. Good bright, intelligent, successful woman like her would suit me down to the ground.

36

Once all the chatter had subsided about Jake becoming a new father with Sally giving birth to Tyler, the Detective Inspector was able to get down to business concerning her trip to Spalding. She'd already made a note to get a card to send to Sally.

'What a lovely lady,' said Inga Larsson to her troops next time they were all together. 'Best bit is, we can call on her any time we need answers to anything. CSI are in there now giving it the once-over.' She looked at Ruth. 'You missed out on scrummy Lemon Drizzle biscuits,' and improving Ruth created a surly pout in fun. 'Anything you want to know, tell me and I'll give her a call, doesn't matter how insignificant you think it is, nothing's too much trouble. Just my kind of woman. Different kettle of fish to the dozy Coetzer female.'

'But gullible,' Raza Latif suggested quietly.

'Tell you what Raz. If she can be easily conned then there's no hope for the rest of us. She's a very astute woman but is vulnerable and the man we're looking out for hit the right spot. Way she was brought up and her acute loneliness have created a blind spot he fed into.'

'What my gran would call hornswoggled.' They all looked at Ruth. 'Word she uses sometimes means being swindled, cheated, hood winked.'

'You even more convinced it's one and the same?' swarthy Raza asked his boss after he'd grimaced at what Ruth had said.

'Yes, and I'll tell you why. The difference in the two women. The amount of stuff this Jacs told me and has already told Chris is heaps more than we've ever got out of Coetzer. She takes a real interest, you can have an adult conversation with the woman, its not just question and answer nonsense and utter drivel with her. You don't have to drag the stuff out.' Inga sighed. 'It's a whole different scenario with her than being with Coetzer and the dopey drippy Gaunt woman sat there poking her nose in. I felt as if I was intruding with her and she couldn't get rid of me fast enough. I could have spent another hour or two with Epton-Howe and no mistake.'

'She's the one where we have a bank account, phone and website data,' said Raza. 'It might all be false nonsense and leading us up the garden path but at least we have something.'

'If we had the same from Coetzer,' said Inga and looked at Ruth. 'Could the eboys really not come up with anything?'

'Nothing. Just chit chat on her phone and you know full well what Graeme's laptop was full of.'

'If we consider this Penney is in reality not who we think he is there are other possibilities. As you know there are loads of cases of identity fraud. Who was he originally, this Penney? Was Lucas Penney maybe a dead child which is often the route these toerags go down?'

'There was a case somewhere, boss,' said Raza. 'Of this scrote committing identify fraud who assumed his dead brother's identity, would you believe. Of course it made life effortless for him as he knew everything, even had his brother's birth certificate, National Insurance Number, the works.'

'As a take-off point,' Inga continued, 'let us assume this Edward McCafferty is real, and he'd stolen the identity of someone called Lucas Penney. Raza,' she said and looked at him. 'Take the lead on this please. Get together all we have on Penney and nip down to have a word with Alex Kemp and his fraud team. They've got a system for finding people in these situations apparently, and if all else fails they're in touch with the National Fraud Authority. If they're too busy at least they'll point you in the right direction, and just see if by chance he had a brother who happens to be dead.'

'Excuse me ma'am,' said Raza in response, before she moved on. 'What if McCafferty's the stolen identity?'

'The man we're looking for could be either of them,' Raza said. 'McCafferty is real and stole Penney or the other way round.'

Inga was pleased with Raza's performance since Jake had taken a few days maternity leave, but knew her second on command would be back shortly with this case a priority.

'McCafferty to my mind does seem the more real. Jacs, the woman I spoke to down in Spalding is nobody's fool might I remind you,' Inga said. 'Remember first time out she met the guy in public for coffee. As far as we know Penney has never been seen out and about by anybody. Just a name, not a real person. So, for now we'll assume for this exercise McCafferty is who he says he is and we try to discover who this Penney actually is or was.' She looked back at Latif. 'No more faffing about, get off down to see Alex and tell him I sent you.'

'Your wish is my command, ma'am,' he said. Inga sighed and shook her head.

'Why do some people allow things to take over their lives like this football, business?' she asked nobody in particular.

'Means then,' Raza said carefully as he stood up. 'This Penney turned up unannounced. Didn't phone in advance, knew Amber would be away.'

'Only thing he was concerned with would be Graeme and it would be easy to work out when he'd not be at home,' said Inga. 'Just hang around to see if any of the neighbours popped in, ensure the coast was clear.'

'And Bob's you uncle.' she looked at Raza by the door as if he was talking in a foreign language. Which in truth he actually could.

'And Amber Coetzer doesn't even know the bank account supposedly in her name,' Chris Mackinder offered.

'No bank because she hands over cash, no website as there's no lonely hearts,' said Ruth. 'Easy one.'

'Except for the Man U fan.'

'Having one in Glasgow, one in Sheffield and another in Derby really isn't as confusing as it first appears, because he doesn't need two or three for every con. All he has to verbally remember for Coetzer is Hull and Grimsby.'

'Here's one for you,' said Chris. 'Why are they both Lincolnshire?' did not produce an immediate reaction.

'Epton-Howe,' said Inga eventually. 'She went on the spurious website by chance which one has to assume he is running and then he read about Amber Coetzer getting her compensation in the papers, realizes he can do a double header.'

'But is this where he's from, is Worcester just another place to add to the list?'

'With Epton-Howe he only needs to remember Worcester.'

'More likely to bump into one of his victims, though.'

'What are the odds on you bumping into somebody you recognize in Skegness or Lincoln if you're Epton-Howe?'

'Aye. When I was at school, during the holidays I was in Wales and I climbed Snowden,' said big Sandy. 'When I got to the top there was a lad from my class in the café having a cup of tea with his parents. What's the odds on that?'

'I can do better,' said Ruth. 'Couple I know were in Beijing, sightseeing in Tiananman Square and this fella asked them to take a photo of him with the famous background. Turned out he was a schoolteacher from Hartsholme. They lived less than three miles apart.'

'Don't think even Ladbrokes would give you odds.'

'What's wrong with a selfie?' got Chris several looks.

'Apart from everything?'

37

Hideous aspects of real life can overwhelm us at times, as I know to my cost. Then almost out of the blue without warning there's this complete change, and life suddenly feels worth living again.

I was still enjoying thoughts of being interviewed by Inga Larsson. Probably all come to nothing in the end, when some bigger case rears its ugly head or she gets more involved with the lad's murder in Washingborough, but it certainly was an interesting experience.

I felt immensely reassured the investigation was in safe hands. A lovely woman, but I bet you'd not want to get on the wrong side of her in an interview room.

Venturing into town reminded me how Christmas was fast approaching with all the shops decked out with festive offerings.

It was just a few days after my interview with the policewoman and I was in Hall Place in town wandering around the twice-weekly market looking to buy fruit and veg when I spotted him, tapped Martin Pearson on the shoulder and when he spun round I surprised even myself.

'Coffee?'

'Thank you. What an absolute delight,' he said and the pleasure was written all over his strong face. Martin simply slipped his arm in mine and without another word we walked off briskly to find coffee.

I know some of the women I associate with would have not been seen dead with Martin in the state he was in. Looking back now, distressed is a nice way to describe his attire. Having said that, these days you can see abominably dressed people walking along every street.

I was pleased I'd made a bit of an effort with the brown trousers I like so much and the tweed jacket over the cream cotton blouse. Yet I did feel rather over dressed with him.

He was as expected, the perfect gentleman and insisted I find a cozy seat at a table in the corner whilst he went to the counter with my request for a cappuccino – and in case you're wondering I didn't confuse him by asking for an extra shot.

Manners maketh man not the shreds they can afford.

Sorry to say I had to do my best to shake myself out from beneath a storm I'd allowed to hover over me. As we walked in together we'd passed an assortment of snack foods, and included was an array of delightful croissants.

Martin in the queue of four and there I am with nothing but my thoughts. My mind had immediately linked croissants to Edward. Nothing to do with France, and his suggestion about being there. It was the fact he often dipped fresh croissants I'd made for him, into his black coffee at the brunch table in my place mid-morning.

It's an action the French call *tremper* (to soak) or dunk most of us would say. Just one of the many things I'd picked up on the Cordon Bleu course daddy sent me on at one time.

Edward thoroughly loved my hand crafted croissants dipped in his coffee. A memory to linger I had to rid myself of before Martin reached our table.

'And to what do I owe this pleasure?' he asked down to me as he placed our cups onto the table and ditched the tray onto the table behind him. It would have been easy to come out with some old baloney, but to be honest I just felt really good.

Thank God he'd not surprised me with fresh croissants!

'I owe you one,' I retorted as he sat down and I relaxed.

'My pleasure. Thoroughly enjoyed it.'

'How are you getting on?' I asked.

'Softly, softly, catchee monkey.'

'Problems?'

He grimaced at my remark as he added a sweetener to what looked like an Americano. 'Not that you'd notice, but I'm working on it.'

For a moment I was about to offer my help when thoughts of the men in my life reared their ugly heads. With my track record, offering help even without any finance involved was asking for trouble. Especially with someone who obviously has personal issues he's trying to solve revolving around what to me sounds like a broken relationship and who is currently sleeping in a refuge for the homeless. Not the finest prospect I've ever come across in life.

'You're not from around here,' I suggested as an alternative.

'On the run,' sounded like a jokey remark, but he was probably serious. Then he smiled. 'Enough of me and my problems,' I had to give him great credit for. He could so easily have spent the next forty five minutes relating all his torrid life story and hung out the begging bowl. He could even have pleaded poverty and wangled things so I paid for the coffees. Not a bit of it and he simply wanted to talk about me and my work with St Joseph's.

What he appeared loath to talk about, was where. I'd mentioned he's not from around the area, but he had avoided the subject like the plague.

In the end we spent close to an hour sat together at the table talking openly and properly as two adults and the more we communicated the more I felt really at ease with him. In the end, when it really was time for me to go, back on the street as we parted I could so easily have hugged him.

I wanted to thank him for not controlling our conversation with stories of how bad his life had become, how he had been deceived and eventually battered into submission.

Steering well clear of Brexit we both chuckled at the idea this was apparently called Black Friday. Ignoring such nonsense, amongst the items of news we discussed that day was the continuing saga of the Novichok business in Salisbury. How that poor Detective Sergeant had become embroiled in it all and although he has fortunately survived, his life is ruined.

He has lost his home, his car, all his clothes and belonging and even his children have lost all their toys because of the possibility of contamination. There are some evil people about aren't there?

I'd been told by one of the 'inmates' at St Joseph's how Martin Pearson had fallen foul of an unfaithful nasty piece of work. Somebody he'd been living with who had no affinity with loyalty and honesty, and assisted by an unscrupulous father and brother had taken poor Martin for every penny he had. What little he had left after paying off huge debts they had run up in his name was spent on lawyers in a desperate attempt to defend his right to a share of what all right minded people would consider to be joint ownership. The reason I then realized why he had been so vociferous during the chat in the kitchen about dangers of co-habiting.

Now I understand he is trying hard to pay off the last of his debts before he can even consider dusting himself down and getting on with the rest of his life. To look at him you'd never know the absolute financial pickle this poor man had found himself in. Another ticked box was him not trying to hide from the world.

Without attempting to delve too deeply into his affairs I understand his problems tended to portray the insidiousness of both financial and emotional abuse.

'From what I can gather,' Daphne had told me one afternoon when only she and I were left in the kitchen at the close of play. 'He was living with his childhood sweetheart. They'd met up again years later after university, apparently.'

'What does he do?'

'Architect.'

'Now living like that?' I threw at her.

'From what I can gather it's been worse than this for him. Told one of the lads he's managed to come through his lowest moment living on the streets.' The thought of which literally made me shiver.

'He?' I did a drinking motion with my hand, and Daphne chuckled.

'No. Far as I know he's sober and clean, just had big money problems. Embarrassed he can't afford things like getting his suit cleaned.'

Not all sweetness and light though. Martin had told me next to nothing at all about himself. Certainly just like Edward he had made no mention of this family. Without doubt something to worry about. My newly acquired sensitive brain noted he had not told me where he is from and harping back to the swine 'from Worcester' was something to bear in mind. Guess that's what I'll do from here on in, allow my new way of thinking to pick up on every little foible.

'If he's an architect, how come he's sleeping somewhere like this?'

'Debts,' was all Daphne said for a moment. 'Choice is they say, he rents a bed sit or pays off his debts and because of his general situation it means he can only do bits and bobs of casual work. Can't do both, unless he turns to crime.' We were on our own but even so

Daphne looked all around just in case. 'Don't take this as gospel, but one story going the rounds is a bit back he fell foul of debt collectors on more than one occasion and all this puts employers off. Debt collectors,' she said as she smacked her fist into the palm of her hand.

'And the woman?'

'According to old Baz he last saw her at a meeting of solicitors. Since then nothing, no word.'

'Family?' I needed to know as much as I could muster.

'She did.'

'How d'you mean?'

'Soon as she cleared off she shacked up with some nasty she'd been seeing on the quiet.'

'And he's never heard a word since you say?'

'Nothing.'

He's the second I've heard about and to be honest I worried for Martin. Jayne who lends a hand at St Joseph's from time to time told me about a man we both knew slightly who had been in a similar position. He'd had huge debts run up in his name by his runaway wife and her erstwhile lover, who then arranged for her father, some sort of Grand Master Mason to have him sacked from three jobs for no reason.

Neither of us have heard anything of him for at least twelve months or more.

As you know I have been going on for some time about being aware of how I needed to grab my life by the scruff of the neck and shake out all the worthless elements and almost start afresh. It's a lot easier said than done I can tell you.

It was almost as if the moment I felt life was set fair young Chris had popped up to refresh my memory and now I'd had the delightful policewoman, as lovely as she was as another stark reminder.

I think I've already told you how I'd had my hair done in a slightly different shorter style with a few highlights but not too much as Lisa said it was not in vogue. I'd also done a bit of shopping during a day out in Peterborough and freshened up my wardrobe a little.

In an odd way my life had changed without my really having made much of an effort. I had deliberately moved myself away from the lonely to a degree as you know. Not having anything against them, but because I felt it was having a negative effect on me personally. I had replaced attendance with them by putting my name down for more shifts at St Joseph's. Even so, over this fairly short period of time my life had seen other changes.

Alas I'm still a bit grumpy.

I'd organised another evening with the lads for their tablet and laptop tuition and just like the first it had gone down very well. Just one person failed to attend the second time who had been with us first time around.

This time it was interesting to see those attending becoming more involved with their questioning. Suzanne Rathbone for example asked allegedly on behalf of her husband, why millions of people watch others play video games.

I had met Martin for coffee by chance of course, and to be honest I seriously cannot remember the last time I had coffee with a man except Edward back at day one.

Hadn't really noticed back then but since Daphne mentioned it I had looked at how he was dressed and I guessed it all came from charity shops so ill-fitting were his trousers in particular.

Even my time at the Sanctuary had changed as I now spend more time once all the work is done, chatting with both volunteers and the inmates. It is no longer three o'clock in the afternoon when I reach home with the remainder of the day stretching out tediously before me being time for the loneliness to develop.

Guess the next step will be to somehow link up with a couple of women to chew over the cud from time to time.

38

It was all men during the week and I was no nearer finding a couple of girl-friends. Martin Pearson one afternoon in town and then when I answered a knock at the door early one evening at home, there stood young Brandon. I invited him in, poured a glass of wine for us each and settled down for a chat.

Had I not been treated abominably by Edward, then I am sure I would never have developed a relationship with Brandon in the way it has. Was it in fact Edward I had to thank for my changing life? Developing relationships at St Joseph's, meeting Martin for coffee, now young Brandon popping round for a glass or two.

As our relationship had slowly developed I was less reluctant than I had been initially to ask questions. I know how the way my life has developed over the years has resulted in me missing out on a great deal.

At one time I'd never have asked Brandon some of the questions I now posed, and Twitter was one I asked him to explain. At times the world is rather like eavesdropping on another planet and when I gently asked him to explain how people claim to get to know things through their Twitterfeed he laughed. Not at me but in an advisory way.

'Inconsequential bilge,' I remember was how he described it before he went on to explain how if it wasn't for him it most certainly would be of no use to me.

'Have you seen anything of Chris?' he asked once we'd moved beyond my silly questions and a resume of what he had been up to.

I shook my head. 'Not him, but the police have called. They sent a woman, his boss so he said. Chris phoned me asked if his boss could pop over and she turned up.' I sipped my Burra Brook Rosé. 'Lovely woman, hard as nails I bet, got to be doing her sort of job I suppose and Swedish apparently.'

'In our police force?' Brandon queried. 'Chris's never mentioned her.'

'She sent in a team later that day, those Scenes of Crime people it was, bit like CSI they were poking their noses into everything, checking the place all out and I was making coffee left, right and centre.'

'Mum said she'd seen a couple of vans. CSI Spalding, has a good ring to it,' Brandon quipped and chuckled.

'All dressed in those white suits and searching for fingerprints and all sorts. Be all the DNA stuff too I suppose.'

'Woman in charge you say?'

'Detective Inspector,' I advised as I got to my feet and walked off into the kitchen. 'Detective Inspector Inga Larsson with a law degree,' I said and wandered back in reading her name from the business card she'd left with me. 'Says she might be back.'

'What seems to be the problem then?' Brandon asked.

'Can't track down Edward.'

'Thought in this day and age they could track down anybody anywhere.'

'Apparently somebody else has been filched by him.'

'You're joking,' he said and chuckled. 'Must make you feel a bit better, knowing you're not the only one. What was it this time? Not another horse was it, do the Jockey Club know what's going on?'

'Apparently not. She didn't actually say. Really cagey when I think about it, had a good long chat with her but in the end I don't know much more.'

'But I bet she does. All in the training apparently getting you to tell them what they want to know but keeping everything close to their chest.'

'You can say that again. Tried to ask her about the murder up in Washingborough she said she was involved in, but got nowhere and I forgot about the other thing. Remember the unexplained death in Lincoln of a woman. Folk at St Joseph's are really mad I didn't find out what it was all about. Another one to have gone quiet.' I sipped my coffee. 'What annoys me is, in nine months' time the case will come to court but by then you won't be able to remember what it was all about in the first place. Or as has happened in the past, you're away when it comes to court and you never find out.'

'Could have done with you asking her why it all takes so long.'

'I know,' I responded. 'Crown Prosecution Service are given six months to put their case together,' obviously surprised Brandon by the look on his good face.

'If they know there's been another victim how come they don't know who Edward is? Doesn't make sense surely.'

'I've no idea.'

'All seems very odd, don't you think?'

'Wouldn't be something else they're keeping close to their chest for some reason best known to themselves would it?'

'You don't think he's high profile or in the government or something and they want it all hushed up?'

'Now you are being silly,' I suggested.

'Why?' I sat there trying to picture Edward McCafferty. 'If he's a top civil servant or a spook or something.'

'Stop it now.'

'I don't understand,' said Brandon. 'Are you saying you don't really know who he was?' I grimaced and shook my head. 'Why didn't you say?'

'I told Chris,' and saw Brandon put down his glass and close his eyes.

'I never knew it was an issue.'

'What difference does it make?' I shrugged.

'I've got his car on disk, they must be able to trace it surely, unless he used false number plates.'

'Say that again!' Brandon just looked at me. 'You know who Edward is?' I almost shouted.

'Not who he is apart from he's Edward whatever, but he triggered my MVV a few times. Must have it on disk. I assumed you knew who he was.' I looked at him open mouthed. 'You agreed I could experiment with one of my miniature sight and sound drones on your drive. Don't you remember?'

'Why would it pick him out?'

'Heat source is just one element,' he said and I just looked at him. 'It won't film a leaf falling off a tree, but it you walk past from whatever direction it films you, same goes with the heat from his car. Heat and sound source and three sixty. The system is like CCTV but without the need for an operator.'

'It what?' I gasped. 'It films through three sixty degrees?' Brandon nodded as if it was obvious.

'All at the same time.'

'We have to tell the police. Always been the big problem, he's disappeared without trace and I don't know who he really is and nor do they.' Brandon just stared at me open mouthed. 'Mr Nothing.'

'I didn't know,' he said as he frowned and Brandon Wishaw downed the rest of his wine in one gulp, was on his feet and gone within seconds. When he returned fifteen minutes later he had his laptop and a disk. I sat there full of anticipation waiting for him to set it all up, then waited while he wizzed through hours and hours of what his tiny camera had recorded half way up my drive.

He moaned a bit at me for not knowing the registration number. Apparently had I known it, his system could bring it up instantly, so good was this MVV thingy.

Then suddenly there right in front of me was Edward's car pulling off the road into my drive, clear as day. Brandon stopped the disk, spun it back and played it again and he scribbled down the registration number of his Skoda. Not only that but you could see the face of Edward McCafferty quite clearly. Made me shudder I can tell you.

We all do it. As soon as Brandon finally departed and I was in the kitchen just washing up the few things we had used I remembered viral.

I was going to ask him what it meant. I really will have to write some of this stuff down if I'm to keep up.

Young Brandon has certainly turned out well, and I guess his parents must be so proud. I know I would be if he were mine.

Time then to catch up with the late news, which meant I was back to the torrid apathy of Brexit again. From what I was able to gather from the outcome during these transition periods Teresa May goes on about, we'll be out of the EU but still obliged to abide by their laws and pay them money without any say.

That's quite handy really as I understand this is exactly what these hyper angry self-opinionated anti-EU oafs claimed was happening, when it absolutely was not. What an utter shambles.

39

'Run it past me again,' said a bemused Detective Superintendent Craig Darke. 'This young chap by sheer chance has captured on disk a suspect who cheated his neighbour out of a small fortune and yet didn't say anything?'

'To be fair sir. He wasn't in on any of the discussions Chris Mackinder had with this Epton-Howe woman. Which means he was always unaware she didn't actually know who her visitor really was.'

He screwed his face up. 'Sorry?'

'This lad didn't know Epton-Howe didn't know who the guy was. He knew she knew his name, but he didn't know she was unaware of where he lived, his phone number and all the rest of it.'

'What may I ask is he doing filming cars in her drive or is it just an idiotic question?'

'His family's drive as well, as it happens. His parents live in a cottage in the ground of this woman's big house.'

'Lucky for some.'

'Not sure I'd swap with her, seems pretty lonely if you ask me. Anyway this Brandon Wishaw is working on a project to create a motion sensor not dependent on the way the camera is pointing. He's trying to capture movement through three hundred and sixty degrees and recording in the round. Like having drone CCTV without an operator, how good is that? Works in IT and this is just something to do with sound linked to motion sensors with a search capability apparently, including in this he also has number plate recognition and all sorts.'

Craig Darke had his eyes closed. 'Motion sensor which might be pointing the wrong way?'

'I know it sounds a bit odd, but the woman told me it's AI infused system with whole 360 degree recording which can be fitted to a drone. CCTV capable of following somebody or something without an operator.' Darke didn't look at all convinced. 'Far more complicated than I'm making it, with heat source, radio waves, sight, sound and three sixty activation. Sounds a rare piece of kit to me. Plus she's the lad's neighbour, or rather his parents are but this Epton-Howe woman is also their landlord.'

'He'll put the family in her goods books,' Darke suggested. 'I just find it baffling as to why he didn't say...' Inga shaking her head stopped him. 'Coffee wouldn't go amiss,' he tried instead.

Inga chuckled at him. 'The price we pay I'm afraid for proper behaviour,' she could see the look on his face. 'This Jacqueline woman explained to me how he didn't want to intrude, just isn't the sort to poke his nose into other people's business.' She managed to catch Julie Rhoades eye and beckoned her in. 'Be a pet and rustle up two coffees please. One white, one black in mugs. No cardboard please.' Julie left the small office and Inga went on. 'When Chris went to interview her at this Brandon's request I might add, he excused himself and went off into another room and watched television.' She hesitated. 'Sort of big house where there are assorted rooms you can wander off into and no mistake.'

'What have we got on this McCafferty so far?'

'Car is registered to an Evelyn Cronin at an address just outside Matlock which fits nicely with references we have to both Derby and Sheffield.' Inga put her hands up to stop Darke. 'That's E-I-B-H-L-E-A-N-N pronounced Evelyn so I'm informed.'

'Irish connection.'

'You tell me,' she said.

'Another useful snippet is her insurance policy has a Maxwell Nigel Emmons listed as a named driver on the policy.'

'Max Emmons?' Darke reacted as if he knew him. 'There was a blues folk singer way back called Max Emmons.'

'Not him surely.' The obscure things Darke knew about the music industry knew no bounds.

'Don't be silly, he'd be in his seventies at least now, just an unusual name.'

'Jake and Sandy are headed that way now,' she looked at her watch. 'Be there by now I should imagine. Gone in their own cars for what we've decided should be a watching brief for now. Derby lads know what we're doing so another box of co-operation has been ticked, and we've set up ANPR to see if the car triggers a location at all. We're also doing ANPR history on it with the team down in Hendon.'

'Could be he's up to some other scam if he's your man.'

'Exactly what we thought.'

'You still think the other guy is one and the same?'

'Lucas Penney? Wouldn't bet my house on it, or apartment should I say, but yes.' She sniggered. 'If we've got this right, it's the one Jake christened Mr Blinking Nobody.'

'Reminds me. Little bird tells me you're putting your place on the market,' Darke suddenly tossed at her. 'Am I right?'

'Not exactly,' she responded unable to instantly understand the link. 'Adam and I are looking for a family home, but there's no rush.'

'No patter of tiny feet I should know about then?'

'No,' was very firm.

'Just wondered.'

'We've been out and about looking at various places,' she went on to change subjects quickly. 'But whatever happens we're going to sell my apartment. Overlooking the Brayford it's got everything going for it, with the university close by, probably suit a lecturer or somebody of that ilk.'

'You're probably right and wise in the present climate.' Darke looked at her. 'Always had you down for setting up home with one of your own.'

'One of my own?'

'A Swede.'

'I don't know any Swedes,' she chuckled. 'Remember I've hardly ever lived there. I go home on holiday these days, but it's not the same. All the people of my age have moved on, grown up, but I didn't know them in the first place. Even children of relatives I saw when we went back in the school holidays are not there. Some of them live abroad. I know more people in Nottingham than Stockholm, it's where I grew up and what happens when your father works for a multi-national and gets promotion.'

'Back to the here and now,' said Darke to bring her back down to earth away from thoughts of her and Adam. 'If this turns out to be both McCafferty and Penney all rolled into one then this lad messing about with some sort of IT experiment may have done his neighbour a big favour, sorted her issues over a horse and solved our murder all at the same time.'

'And people ask why we have all this CCTV,' Inga chuckled 'Where's the coffee?' she asked nobody in particular when her phone rang.

There on her screen from Jake was a photo of a glimpse of part of a house set in woods, she assumed was connected to his location. Then her landline rang and the DI sat there with one phone in one hand and the other to her ear.

'Guv, Jake. Just sent you a photo of what looks to be McCafferty's place in the woods.'

'Looking at it now,' she responded and turned her phone away to show Darke what was pictured.'

'That where he is?' Darke asked.

'Not seen him so far,' said Jake in reply.

'That the road in?' Darke queried as he peered at the screen.

'End of the road is back a bit, then that rough lane up to it. Intel we've got over here says only two people live there, nobody else. Not very good photo I'm afraid but being all overgrown's made him a good hiding place. Daren't risk getting any closer. Managed to creep round the back for a better look see. Big extension on the back and what looks like a granny annexe. Four or five bedrooms by the look of it, looks a tidy big place.'

'Who else you sent it to?' Inga asked.

'Local Derby lads and Notts plus Stevens and his eTeam.'

'Seen anybody at all?' she asked in response to a gesture from the Darke boss.

'No sighting as yet guv,' was Jake on obo on the phone. 'We've moved back a fair bit since the photo to remain out of sight. Fortunately we couldn't do a drive-by as it turns out it's the only house along the track.'

'By the way we've got an Evelyn Cronin and a Max Emmons on the insurance for the Skoda. All fitting together nicely.'

'All registered at this address here, I hope.'

'Have the local lads come up with anything on ANPR?' Inga asked.

'Not so far.'

'You two fine as you are?'

'No problem. Bought grub on the way so we're all tucked up and comfortable, so we're all set up for the long haul if it comes to it.'

'By the way, Nicky's back from her cyber-crime course,' she advised. 'Itching to use her new found talent as you can imagine. Where are you exactly?' Inga asked.

'Two Dales is a little village north east of Matlock, few houses and pub sort of place. The house we can just see through the trees from our location is on the outskirts of the village. We're taking it in turns to have a walk through to a better vantage point in case there's any comings and goings. Took the photo fifteen minutes ago along there.'

'You won't need me then.'

'We're fine as we are,' Jake told her. 'Sandy reckons it might have been a small cottage originally and somebody's built this big house on the end.'

'Good to see McCafferty's not wasting his ill-gotten gains,' she chuckled.

'Can you make a point of only calling my phone? The one we'll keep here in the car, and whichever one of us goes walkies will take Chris's phone so don't try to call on it as we've turned it off and we'll only use it to mute text each other urgently.' Inga so wanted to thank Jake for lumbering her with Darke for goodness knows how long. Great boss Craig, really nice fella but you can have too much of a good thing at times.

'I've got CSI on standby from Derby if it comes to it and the local lads are ready willing and able if you need bodies. Leave you to it then.'

'No probs boss. We're sat here window shopping till we're ready to buy.'

As Inga was about to tell Craig Darke what Jake had said when the coffee was delivered.

'You're a hard task master,' Darke chuckled. 'Bet Jake's not getting much sleep with the baby and you send him out where full concentration is a pre-requisite.'

'I know Jake, he'll be fine and anyway he's absolutely full of it. Becoming a new daddy has given him a real lift.'

'Nicky happy to be back?' he enquired.

'Bubbly as usual, be really useful to us. Thanks.'

Darke just grinned his reaction. 'What's the sitrep?' he asked as he lifted a mug from the tray on the desk.

'Case of sitting and waiting. Somewhere near a small village called Two Dales close to Matlock. Know it?'

'No, but assume you can see two dales,' said Darke with a shake of his head.

'In Darley Dale and once upon a time was known as Toad Hole,' made him grimace. 'Citroen on the drive apparently is registered to a Maxwell Nigel Emmons,' she read from her scribbled note. 'At the address which is interesting.'

'What d'you think of this delegation business now then, with them out there doing all the graft you'd normally be poking your nose into?' Inga grinned her reaction. 'Told you this is the way forward.'

'So you said.'

'Got a CD of Max Emmons I think somewhere in my collection. Appeared on the scene around the time of Bob Dylan.'

The DI knew it would have been better in an urban environment, than some two-bit place in the middle of nowhere. The best way she knew to follow somebody is to be in front of them. Find a place where he or she is bound to go then just get yourself there before them.

Make yourself a regular, say in a pub, become part of the regular furniture, not somebody trying hard to blend in but failing miserably.

They'd not be doing any such thing in the woods, getting to know an oak tree or sharing a beer with a bunch of twigs was never easy.

40

I was on my guard and knew recent times and events would have an effect on me for quite a while, maybe for always and forever. Perhaps the major difference now was I was in the company of somebody who had himself also been unceremoniously dumped and cheated on, but even so I was still wary. Caution had become my new middle name.

It would have been too easy to embarrass Martin had I chosen certain restaurants for our meal together. We've all heard about the nonsense some offer these days. Turbot with truffle risotto say, with mouclade velouté, foie gras butter and potato galette.

You know the kind of poncey place. Those who serve up a plate with half a dozen blobs of sauce and think they can cook. Places charging and arm and a leg, serving up next to nothing and when you leave you're still starving.

This was nowhere all la-di-da and posh with the unnecessary frivolities to go with some pretentious places nowadays. This was a basic good home-cooked food restaurant with an unsophisticated glass or two of red wine. It has to be said the food was very good indeed and if I was the sort would have sent my compliments to the chef. It had already been suggested by my companion for the evening how I could have served up a meal equal to the one we had jointly savoured. I made the drudgery of having to cook yet another meal as the best excuse I could come up with.

Can't be doing with all the pompous nonsense around wine. You know the sort of thing: the "mmm enigmatic spices, mmm coffee, mmm intense tarmacadam."

Now where was I? Oh yes.

I didn't want to say anything which might spoil the evening by suggesting there was a reason why we were not eating at Oakdenne House and were instead eating in full view of the public, something of course I had never done with the one who had called himself Edward.

I had another dilemma, apart that is from reading how some goon somewhere had created Christmas mince pies with chilli in.

What do I do about Martin over the festive period? I assumed he will be at the Christmas Day lunch at the refuge, but what about the rest of the time. What about presents? Do I just ignore him, treat them all as if they are just ordinary days? What about the New Year?

I sat there looking at Martin and listening to him chatter away as we waited for our deserts, or as daddy would always say to annoy mummy – pudding.

I'd used a firm of private detectives to investigate the Wishaw family before I entered into an agreement for them to rent the cottage from me.

Should I do that with Martin Pearson? Get my own private gumshoe onto the case and search out the whys and wherefores of this man. Or would it really not be a nice thing to do when all I really need to do this time, is be aware of the likelihood of hidden dangers. Be less languid in my attitude and keep an eye open for little hints of things maybe not being quite what they seem and keep a tight grip on my purse. Except tonight of course, after all I did offer to buy him a meal. Not quite like buying a horse, unless of course it wasn't really beef we'd just eaten!

'I imagine you'll have to go to court, but that'll surely be months away.'

'Don't remind me,' I reacted.

'They have got the right person I suppose.'

'Oh they've got the right one and no mistake. The Detective Inspector kept me in the loop the moment they thought they'd found him. All down to young Brandon who lives next door.'

'The IT lad?'

'He's the one.' I sipped my red. 'What a world we live in today,' I mused. 'Brandon emailed the film he took of this Max Emmons to the Inspector woman who visited. Then later on when they'd located him,' I put up a hand. 'Don't ask me how,' and Martin leant forward to hear as I suddenly remembered to keep my voice down. 'Anyhow, these Lincoln County Police people were over in Derbyshire somewhere so they told me. Watching his house.' I sighed and shook my head.

'What's up?'

'He told me Worcester. Said he lived in Worcester, but it has to be an essential component of his scheme, apparently.'

'Must take some keeping tabs on.'

'Anyway, apparently the police filmed him without his knowledge and they sent it to me. How amazing eh?' I asked with a giggle. 'Having video sent to me sat at my kitchen table.' I chuckled again at the thought of it all. 'Have to say it was pretty obvious who it was, but they sent the video they'd taken to me just to make sure. It was him, as clear as a pike staff living in this beautiful big converted cottage out in the country, living with a woman apparently who's also up to her neck in it they seem to think.' I just looked to my left and right just in case people were sat there eavesdropping. 'They think it was actually her on the website where I originally hooked up with, pretending to be him. Truth of the matter is he was out and about conning other people while she did all the groundwork, ran the website, pretended to be all these men.'

'Sounds like they were running a business.'

'It is a business,' I insisted. 'And a very profitable one by all accounts. According to Inga the detective woman…'

'Hold on a sec. Inga did you say?'

'She's Swedish.'

'In *our* police?'

'Why not?'

'Sounds like we're going back into Europe not coming out!'

'Anyway, she reckons he was running three other women when they caught up with him. Been doing it for years. She's a bit unwilling to discuss individual cases I suppose, but somebody did mention when I was with them how most scams stem from cold calls. Felt a bit guilty to be honest. She told me how scams thrive on people saying nothing.' I just sat looking at him. 'Exactly what I'd have done if it wasn't for young Brandon, isn't it? Apparently, because people don't report what's happened because they're too damn embarrassed, these scammers see it as good news and just carry on.'

'What sort of things was she talking about?'

'Bogus investments, those I've read about when they send a courier to pick up your bank cards. Just con artists who press people into buying straight away to take advantage of a non-existent special offer or to avoid financial disaster.' A shudder ran through me.

'You all right?' Martin asked.

'Not exactly a flashback, but the thought of him turning up at home on Bonfire Night and me greeting him with a glass of wine and he'd just murdered that poor lad.'

'But you weren't to know.'

'When I think back now things fall into place. I remember young Brandon saying his father had seen Edward as he was then, heading my way by a strange roundabout route along all the back roads. Must have been doing it to avoid the cameras on the main roads.' I took a last drink of the dregs in my glass and sat there chuckling to myself.

'Go on,' Martin gently urged as one of his fingers gently stroked mine.

'On the Thursday morning I'd heard about the murder in Washingborough on *Radio Lincolnshire* while I was making his toast and I said it seemed an odd place, and he just poo-pooed it.' I had to snigger. 'Now we know why.'

'And some fools are always up in arms about cameras intruding into their private lives coming out with a load of old guff about liberty. Bet they won't talk such utter nonsense when something happens to them.'

'This tiny one Brandon has invented has advanced face recognition systems.'

'How big did you say it was?' an intrigued Martin wanted to know.

'The size of a tennis ball,' I told him. 'Listen to this,' dropping my voice to a whisper. 'It already identifies number plates, and the face recognition he says he's nearly perfected could well be loaded with the passport photos of everybody in the land, with visitors added as they arrive in the country. We're talking millions of photos, so we'll all be recognised wherever we are.'

'Round like a ball?'

'Can be any shape, he's made one to look like a lump of coal.'

'And protected from terrorists.'

'Hadn't thought of that.'

'Got to ask. How does he get it all in something as small as a tennis ball?'

'Radio and artificial intelligence I think they call it. Like your phone doesn't have millions of Facebook users actually inside it.'

'He'll set loads of these freedom of the individual moaners going,' he chuckled.

So there you have it. Now you know the…whoops! Sorry about that. Using the word 'so' to start a sentence is a real schoolgirl bloop, but it seems these days such grammatical rules appear to have been withdrawn from the classroom if not society. After all some clowns apparently consider even spelling to be out of date. All down to sending those text messages thumbed on phones they say. Shall I start again?

There you have it. Now you know the true unexpurgated story of what really happened to me when I was ripped off, warts and all. Next time you see a woman who you think has probably got more money than sense, don't be envious until you find out the true story, because I ask: would you really want to swap your life for mine?

What about me, what slippery slope am I heading down now you ask? Still know so very little about the lovely Martin Pearson of course or where he comes from. Basics such as what is his story, what about family, what really happened to him? All are just a few probing questions away.

Biggest worry is Martin having no contact with the woman who did the dirty on him. Most divorced couples I know still communicate in one way or the other, even know of one pairing who still give each other Christmas presents although they are happily in new relationships now.

Why does the woman in Martin's life want nothing to do with her childhood sweetheart?

Serious food for thought.

ACKNOWLEDGEMENTS

My sincere thanks must go to a good friend for over forty years who jokingly planted the seed of an idea in my mind. Thank you A.H.E Jarvis.

I really appreciate the information, time and trouble not to mention the coffee, Nigel and Julia Coulson afforded me in my research.

In addition I have to acknowledge the Southwold Beach Hut Owners Association for information they willingly provided.

Amongst the people I must thank in particular this time are all those who in some cases unwittingly, provided me with their personal likes and dislikes, moans and groans about life in this day and age, together with their personal foibles I used to create Jacqueline.

Plus of course my appreciation has to go to the good people of Spalding and Washingborough; thank you for being so welcoming and accommodating during my research visits.

Any mistakes are all my own work and I'll claim they are made in the interests of the story.

There is no Lincoln County Police nor is there a Lincoln Central. One of the advantages of creating my own police force is that whilst I follow systems as much as possible, I am able to get away with concentrating on the story rather than become bogged down in the minutiae of police procedures.

To everyone, a big thanks for just being you…and I sincerely hope we will meet again next time Inga Larsson and her team have another major incident to deal with…

To find out what is waiting around Inga's next corner, read on...

PREVIEW

We are all of us aware how our entire world can change in the merest twinkling of an eye. In Inga's case it was more of a flicker of recognition than anything else there in her peripheral vision. Something her brain told her in a millisecond was somehow not quite right.

Discovery quite often simply consists of one person seeing and thinking in a way nobody has before and this was such an occasion.

An early morning sunshine laden Lincolnshire day with a splattering of low lying mist, the dawning of a new day, a new world each one fresher than the one before.

When it finally breaks through the cold gloom this is always Inga's favourite sunshine. It has to her mind a peacefulness about it, as the drenching of light expands slowly but surely into the world as we know it. Except it never is the world as we know it. Mellow early sunshine focussing on a new world when it is justly proud to present a brand spanking new day to all of us. Nothing stands still, the breeze is wondrously fresh and new, at that time of year the leaves are more abundant than yesterday, the grasses greener, the berries and fruit more plentiful and certainly riper.

Each virgin day bathed in such delicate light brings with it endless possibilities and any vain attempt to look into the future hides the realities of what indeed does lie ahead.

On days like these she thinks it is such a shame half the world is still asleep and will miss the delights of the early morning air.

Sunday morning where the rhyme about a child born on such a day has a certain piquancy about it, in that it is in effect a day like no other. Not just about being *fair of face* or *full of woe* but the Sunday one for some reason is said to be bonny and blithe and good and this that and the other. Pick one, any one of the other six you like, toss it around in your mind for a moment and it really could be any one of them. Sunday is somehow different as if it encourages calm and that tranquil sunlight the others seem unable to.

Cycling has never been something Inga Larsson has ever done because she has to, felt obliged to, told to, been harassed by health experts or badgered by some government campaign into doing. She cycles and bought all the clobber to go with it because she just thoroughly enjoys it. Anyway as far as she is concerned it is whole lot better than any latest fad diet.

Not for her pedaling some odd one-wheel contraption in a gym with her instep, looking at a blank wall or herself in a mirror in need of a clean surrounded by repulsive body odours and fat men's farts. Too much testosterone and the sagging skin of weight loss regimes. Inga Larsson had of course done aerobics at one time and yoga but had never fully understood what the latter's silliness was all about. Was it even a form of exercise or simply something you were supposed to use as a conversation piece? She had always had the impression it might be on the same wavelength as some sad folk's all-embracing need to display the correct magazine on a coffee table to signify what they consider to be their social standing to other dopes impressed by such po-faced nonsense.

Exercise for bums and tums, one to rid the absolute horror of cellulite the bozo's will fatuously tell you can so easily ruin a woman's life forever, that frantic spinning and even at one time a retro popmobility resurgence had never fully tempted her.

Real bike, real world, real unconstituted non-air-conditioned oxygen, two proper road wheels and all the benefits that will bring including not having money sucked from her bank account every month for what seems a lifetime of nothing very much in return.

There was a greenish blue tinge to the man's head and neck, large blisters were starting to form on his skin from the gases inside, he was starting to bloat with rigor been and gone by then Inga guessed and fluids were just beginning to seep from every orifice she could imagine. And he smelt.

Could have done with her Bergamot oil to take away the stench, but it's hardly the sort of thing you slip in your pocket for a bike ride now is it? *I'll just slip that in my pocket in case I come across a decomposing body in Lincoln High Street propped up outside Marks and Spencer.*

The trickle of blood had moved on from red and was heading for a nice maroon and Inga knew from experience how the colour of blood is such a good visual indicator of the time of death, but she'd never have the temerity to tell the pathologist her job. Certainly not if it was the delightful wife and mother Dr Branagh O'Connell; that is if she was duty dog of course.

Starts with crimson then when blood loses oxygen and becomes listless and dull it tends to take on the look of sangria. O'Connell could no doubt pick a time by the look of the hue. For some silly reason when she spotted sangria it amused Inga. Falun a Swedish red and cinnabar had no such effect, just the thought for some stupid reason of folk drinking blood probably. This of course would be sangria without the fruit.

Inga was of course fully aware her training had told her to assess the scene in progress as soon as she possibly could. She'd done that and more and something told her not enough blood.

Whoever he was hadn't been killed in the last few hours, he'd certainly not been killed in the past twenty-four. Inga's guess as she looked and waited was that he'd been dead at least two days. Could be three possibly.

Inga was well aware how no two bodies decompose in quite the same way or at the same rate. There was so much to take into consideration she had no knowledge of. Was he taking any form of medicine that may have an effect, how fat is he or even just how many flies and other insects were there on the riverbank, all adding to the work for others.

Inga knew the perpetrator would take away something of his victim with him or her and leave behind something of themselves, probably DNA.

Forensic pathologist Dr Branagh she knew would be taking a whole host of samples, scraping fingernails, pulling out hairs, swabbing sex organs and taking fingerprints and sweat pores before she got her hands anywhere near a scalpel or saw.

As she stood looking down at the river, then to her left and right, particularly the latter direction from where she expected reinforcement to arrive, she confirmed her initial thoughts to herself. It had been her height that had determined why she had seen a body others had not. Unless of course it had been moved to there recently; overnight possibly. She checked her watch. 06.34.

Inga walked back carefully a few yards on the grass and when she turned it really did just look like a dirty old discarded green welly sticking out of the grass, nettles and bushes along with other bits and pieces of detritus. On her bike, at her height she'd had a view just over that bush and he was momentarily just visible.

The amateur pathologist in her wanted to turn him over just to check if there were dark redish purple pools across his back, an indication that he may have been moved. Dark pools of lividity. No heart to pump the blood, so it settles by gravity. The doc would soon tell her when he or she arrived.

Inga caught sight of blue lights flashing silently without the need for twos. Was that as a mark of respect for a Sunday morning and the lethargic still wallowing in their steamy pits? Whatever, she now knew for sure help was on its way.

What really peeved the Detective Inspector the most was, she had planned a ride right through to Lincoln and back. Probably turn off Spa Road head across the bridge, tootle past *Lincs FM*...oh god she thought. How long before those nosey parkers get a sniff of all this and come tottering out waving microphones under her nose?

Inga knew a dull murder like this if that's what it was would not last long in the papers or on radio. Some random unknown so-called celebrity of the week would be in town for half an hour and capture all the headlines the target audience never listen to or read, if in effect they can read. It'd be that or a non-story about some fat woman making absurdly ridiculous claims about her overworked doctor and send this poor cadaver into oblivion faster than you can say forgotten.

Her plan had been just to turn round when she got to Broadgate and ride back home at full pelt to where Adam as fresh and appealing as a daisy after his power shower would be waiting with fresh coffee and a couple of bacon sandwiches. Bad enough you'd think missing out on them, but the thought that without her he could very well scoff the lot made her really mad.

She'd texted him just after she'd used her Airwave to call in the incident, so he'd know not to wait on her return before getting stuck in. And what's the betting he'd destroyed them with a lathering of tomato sauce? What is it with the British and that ketchup?

Stood there on the Witham riverbank it was a world of no alternatives, no revolutionary action and thoughts of non-conformity had no place in her plans. Inga so wanted to investigate the body but knew she dare not, was truly desperate to be wearing anything but black clinging lycra and bright red Adidas trainers when the Scenes of Crime techy-geeks turn up but what could she do? Gasping for a coffee as well but what chance was there of that? Two – no chance and a cat in hell's.

Sod's Law told her who would be amongst the first to respond to the call after an interceptor. Leading light within the CSI team was sure to be bad penny Liam Ritter a Chemical Enhancement Officer she'd been out with three times before somebody had the good sense to nod her the wink. Be just her luck if his name was high on the duty rota.

Three dates to a dank pub had left her bored to tears with his insipid insight into examining, developing and recording latent impressions or articles retrieved from horrendous crime scenes.

Then there were tales from him of the court cases he had to attend to present the crucial evidence, before her pal Lizzie had the good sense to advise that Ritter the Rotter was married.

No way José and Inga was soon out of that but eggs are eggs and life being the way it is sometimes he was sure to be the dick turning up that morning with her stood there in all her cycling gear; full of smart remarks and nasty quips. Her situation would no doubt make his day and there was absolutely nothing she could do about it.

That episode had all been a year or two back now and through the course of her work naturally she'd bumped into him a few times, turned up at such a scene as this and there he was. According to the grapevine he was still married and so people insisted on telling her still chasing not exactly anything in a skirt, but pretty much along those lines. Perhaps that Vikki he was shacked up with in matrimonial bliss just didn't care, could be of course she was screwing around as well, as some do. Open marriage is it these people call it?

Detective Inspector Inga Larsson had laid her multi terrain Boardman bike Adam had given her for her birthday deliberately across the pathway to halt anybody approaching from the east and she stood guard a good twenty metres past the boot and the attached body. That would do for now to create as best a sterile barrier as she could. Inga perched her scarlet red helmet on top of her bike.

HOW MANY PEOPLE DO YOU KNOW COULD TURN A SUNDAY BIKE RIDE INTO A MURDER MYSTERY' came back on her phone.

Was this a serious issue Adam had landed on? Was she allowing her in-bred sense of duty to control her life and with it was she forsaking all others? Adam in particular. To her mind the strong work ethic which had forced her to stop her cycle ride, get off, go back and investigate what was then nothing more than half a glance had provided. To Inga Larsson there was no choice. No do I or don't I? Somewhere in her peripheral vision a second or two before her early morning brain interpreted what she had spied in a fleeting half moment. She could never just ignore what she thought she'd seen and bike on, think about her enjoyment, a delicious bacon sarnie or two and leave it to some other poor soul to find.

The inner reaction had made her stop, would cost her a breakfast and might very well in the end cost her a day off went hand in hand with outright honesty and with it fidelity in which she firmly believed. With all such responsibility and values she herself would regard as paramount in her role in life. Her father Stefan was and always had been her role model believing his strong work ethic had a moral benefit and an inherent ability to strengthen one's character.

What if Adam didn't see it her way? What if he was annoyed at her attitude? What if this turned out to be a chink in the armour of their relationship she did not want to even consider?

Had Detective Inspector Inga Larsson just made a rod for her own back, an error of judgment she would live to regret? This after all was worse than usual. No matter how fast she was getting off the mark there was always time between the initial call-out and actually facing the crime scene. This time had been different. Casually cycling along in the early morning quite happily and then slam straight into a case.

Even with all she had to consider on a personal level as well as work wise Inga still had the time to ponder an outcome. She'd as yet not had an unsolved on her caseload, but knew this could very well be the one she would not be able to put to bed, wrap up and pass across gift wrapped to the CPS.

This poor sod whoever he was, could very well end up as a cold case. Ignored most probably when he was alive and received the very same treatment as a cadaver. Poor bugger.

Talking of men. She understood her Adam well enough to know by now he would have scoffed her bacon sarnie breakfast. The rat.

REASONS WHY
NOT

Available in 2020

IN PLAIN SIGHT

Another Cary Smith
Lincolnshire Murder Mystery
from 2018

"Couldn't put it down."

"Wow! Best ever."

"How does he do it every time?"

"One of the best books I've read in ages."

Amazon Top 5 Book
Available right now

Lightning Source UK Ltd.
Milton Keynes UK
UKHW022026160222
398793UK00011B/2360